BEASTS of the CALIBER LODGE

A Novel of Espionage Horror

by

L.J. Dougherty

This book is a work of fiction.

****

Espionage Horror Variant Cover Edition

ISBN: 9798553886776

Cover art by Jonny Wise.
Lodge Image design by Luke Newman.

ISBN: 9798553886776

Praise for
Beasts of the Caliber Lodge

"Barmy, crazy, Crichton-esque."

-Ross Jeffery, Bram Stoker Award Nominated author of '*Tome*'

"Entertaining, thrilling, absolute fun."

-Well Read Beard

"A tantalizing cocktail of thrills and entertainment that is 100 per cent wild and crazy fun."

-John Mountain aka "Books of Blood"

"One killer debut novel! Unbelievable genre mashup!"

-Nichi aka "DarkBetweenPages"

"If Spielberg made a Bigfoot movie, it would be like Beasts of the Caliber Lodge."

-Cameron Roubique, author of '*Kill River*'

For Mom & Dad

Thank you for always encouraging my writing.

Sorry it's so violent.

This book contains scenes of graphic violence, sexuality, and profanity.

CONTENTS

.CALIBER COCKTAILS.

"HAND PICKED FOR OUR GUESTS — WE CATER TO YOUR PASSIONS"

.HEMINGWAY CLASSIC.

Cana Brava White Rum — Pink Grapefruit Juice —
Luxardo Maraschino Liqueur — Fresh Lime Juice

.VERY OLD FASHIONED.

Very Old Fitzgerald Bourbon — Angostura Bitters — Sugar sphere

.PANAMA PREMIER.

Napoleon Premier Brandy 10 Year Old —White Creme de Cacao — Light Cream

.SAN MARTIN.

Tanqueray London Dry Gin — Carpano Antica Sweet Vermouth — Green Chartreuse

.SMOKED MARTINI.

Rare Imported Stolichnaya Vodka — Rinsed with Ardbeg Scotch Whisky

An endless assortment of top shelf spirits are also available for your pleasure.

— The Caliber Lodge — 1965 — Second Expedition Party of the Year

How telling, that the place they hung the severed heads of the animals they killed was referred to so casually as "The Game Room."

Chapter One
THE NAZI HUNTERS

Argentina, 1960.

The wrinkled Austrian with the silver hair sipped Campari from a hand-blown rocks glass as he sat on the patio outside Roja Rey's Cantina. He reached into his vest pocket and pulled out a Swiss Wittnauer Revue pocket watch. Popping it open, he checked the time then dropped it back into his vest without a word. As usual, he was the first to arrive, feeling the need to provide himself with enough time to order a beverage and settle in before his counterpart showed up.

What was unusual about that particularly dreary afternoon, however, was the fact that his counterpart had not yet arrived and the clock had passed the agreed upon hour. His partner was rarely early, but never had the Austrian with the timepiece known him to run late.

He listened to the rhythmic patter of the rain as it pelted the top of the patio covering. It had been overcast and murky for two days and his mostly white wardrobe seemed unfit for the weather. He tipped the cream-colored fedora back on his head as he leaned out to get a better look at the looming sky. This wasn't how he expected South America to be. Though he wasn't there to bask in the sunshine, he had admittedly been looking forward to the warmth.

He looked at the other guests sitting around him on the patio, many of them white, Aryan. Even before the war, the Patagonia region was home to many German immigrants and the families they raised. Nazism was commonplace and remained so for years following the collapse of the Third Reich. The local schools even taught the same curriculum and propaganda, and several villages, including this one, boasted authentic Bavarian cuisine.

The table next to the Austrian was lined with sauerbraten, potato salad and red cabbage, and the men eating it, portly Caucasians with gin blossom cheeks.

He took another swig of his Campari and flagged down the waiter who, from what he could tell, may have been the only true Argentinian in sight.

"¿Menú?" the Austrian asked with his distinctly Austrian accent. He kept his words limited. Any of these men around him were potential war criminals in hiding. The less he said, the better.

The dark-haired waiter nodded and hurried away. One of the portly men with the gin blossom cheeks glanced over at the Austrian, eyeing him up and down. He stared back, noticing a bit of cabbage hanging from the bloated fellow's lower lip.

"Buenas tardes," the Austrian said to him. The fat man turned away, focusing on his lunch.

The waiter returned with a ratty menu. He watched a dehydrated hand point at one of the items as the Austrian said, "Esto, por favor."

The waiter nodded again, making his way into the restaurant to give the order to the cooks. The Austrian immediately regretted not ordering a fresh Campari as his was nearing its end. He wasn't a fast drinker, so the visual of the last drops of the red liquid barely covering the bottom of his glass made him check his watch once more.

Something was wrong.

He and his partner, an American by the name of Jimmy Knotts, had been in the tiny village for just over a week, staying at a bed-and-breakfast near the outskirts. The Austrian had left early that morning to do some reconnaissance and had asked Jimmy to meet him at 2:00pm there at Roja Rey's.

It was now 2:15pm.

If his partner had found himself in a challenging situation, the Austrian would have no way of knowing. They had been splitting up since they arrived in town, covering as much ground as they could to determine whether the rumors were true that their target had been in the area. There wasn't much the Austrian could do now but wait.

Ten minutes later the waiter returned with a plate of wurst and sauerkraut. The Austrian raised his empty glass and gently shook it.

"Campari, por favor." Campari wasn't his drink of choice, but it was popular among the locals and he thought it might help him blend in, if even a little.

The waiter returned with a fresh beverage and the Austrian let it sit there undisturbed as he ate, as if not touching the drink would slow time so he wouldn't have to worry as much as he should. He would have sat there waiting all night if need be, but he hoped his friend would show up soon so he could put his imagination to rest.

The rainfall grew heavier, and the Austrian slid his finished meal to the other side of the table. He checked his watch again, nearly a quarter to three. A Nazi Hunter out alone in the German capital of South America was a dismal scenario.

The screech of tires and the blare of a car horn startled the Austrian. He looked up to see who the oblivious fool was that had nearly been hit by the speeding car. A wave a relief enveloped him as he realized it was Jimmy trudging across the center of the street, his arms wrapped tight around his body as the weather drenched him. Rain cascaded off his bowler hat, flowing down his shoulders as he staggered onto the patio and flopped himself down into the chair across the table from the Austrian.

"My God," the Austrian muttered.

The drenched man didn't even attempt to dry himself off. He just sat there, soaked, his arms crossed and his chin tight to his chest in the cold.

"What happened?"

Short of being overly damp, Jimmy Knotts looked good for a man on the cusp of forty. He was trim, healthy, though surely on the verge of catching a cold in his current state.

"Things went a bit south, but based on where we are it was to be expected," Jimmy replied.

"Where have you been?"

"Investigating."

"You had me worried."

"Not worried enough to keep you from your new favorite beverage, I see."

The Austrian looked at the Campari he'd been milking and slid it to Jimmy. "Have some. You look like you could use it."

"I'm not sure if I should take that as a kind gesture or an insult."

The portly man with the gin-blossom cheeks glanced at Jimmy, who picked up the Campari and made a "cheers" gesture to him. The fat man turned back to his friend and let the two Nazi hunters continue the rest of their meeting without interruption.

The waiter strolled up to the table and, in Spanish, asked Jimmy if there was anything he could bring. Jimmy sniffed the Campari and handed it back to his Austrian partner before answering.

"You have whiskey?" The waiter quickly hurried off to collect the drink.

Jimmy crossed one leg over the other and leaned back in the metal chair. The Austrian stared at him from across the table, reading him, giving his partner time to decompress from what he could only fathom was a terrible morning.

"I'm alive, Levi," Jimmy assured him.

The Austrian, Levi Aarons, leaned forward, extended his hand over the table and patted Jimmy on the cheek with a grin.

"You've got chutzpah, kid."

These two men, the American in the bowler hat and the Austrian with the timepiece, had known each other for over a decade. Their paths had first intersected in 1948, a few years after the war, on a street corner in a small Austrian town.

Jimmy, the then 28-year-old American photographer, was working on a portfolio chronicling the aftermath of the war. He was trying to locate a specific building he had seen in a photo some years earlier to capture its current state for a comparative shot. That's when his concentration was interrupted by a vile spewing of verbal venom being hurled at an elderly Jewish woman by a twenty-something, blond-haired, blue-eyed delinquent.

When Jimmy stepped between the young ruffian and his prey, he uttered not a word. The thug's brow furrowed, confused by the silent American standing before him. He attempted to walk around, but Jimmy took a step to the side, blocking his path.

The young man sneered.

"I think you owe this woman an apology." Jimmy said with stern insistence.

"Woman? All I see is a hunchbacked rat standing behind you."

There was no hesitation. Jimmy delivered an uppercut to the young man's jaw, cracking a few teeth, knocking him flat on his ass upon the street.

He never missed an opportunity to correct those still delusional enough to support the defeated world power that was Nazi Germany. He chastised the young man and sent him off with a mouthful of blood and warning of greater retribution should the punk continue his advances toward the old woman.

Jimmy ensured she was all right before tipping his hat to her and saying his goodbyes. He made his way across the street to a small café and asked the girl behind the register for a cloth to wipe away the blood from the ruffian's mouth that had landed on his lapel.

"A commendable act," a confident voice said from behind.

Jimmy turned to see a middle-aged Austrian (who he would soon come to know as Levi) sitting next to the window.

"A necessary one," Jimmy replied, dabbing his jacket.

"Allow me to offer you a cup of tea for your good deed." Levi motioned to the girl behind the register. Jimmy nodded and took a seat at the table.

"Kind of you."

"My name is Levi Aarons," Levi said, extending a hand.

"James Knotts. Jimmy." They shook.

"You're American."

"I am."

"What brings you to Austria?"

"I'm working on a portfolio." Jimmy raised the camera that hung from a thin leather strap around his neck.

The tea arrived, and the conversation slowly developed into questions about Jimmy's experience as a photographer. He explained that his career began in the corn husking state of Nebraska in 1938. He had been fresh out of high school when he got in with a Private Investigating firm and was tasked with collecting photographic evidence for clients, primarily to prove the existence of presumed affairs.

It was secretive work, but Jimmy didn't mind it. He got paid to use his camera, and that was enough for him. When the war came, Jimmy quit his job with the firm and set out to document the chaos. He captured history in Italy, Africa and London, securing his confidence as a world traveler and a professional photographer simultaneously.

While drinking his tea in Austria, sitting across from Levi for the first time, Jimmy caught himself when he began to elaborate on the atrocities he had seen committed by the axis powers. He could tell this reserved Austrian Jew with the weathered eyes had witnessed his own share of atrocities and didn't require an American photographer's detailing of the situation.

Levi gave the slightest of smiles as Jimmy cut himself off. The Austrian didn't enjoy hearing about the deplorable acts, but he loved seeing the anger they sparked within Jimmy as he recalled his experiences. It was the same raw anger that boiled within the Levi.

That day, while sharing stories over tea, Levi offered Jimmy an opportunity to once again use the skills he had learned at that little investigative firm back in Nebraska.

"I work with a group of brave individuals who would do well to add a professional, such as yourself, to our midst."

"What kind of group?"

"We gather information that allows us to identify escaped Nazis, capture them, and bring them to justice."

"You hunt Nazis."

"Yes. We hunt Nazis."

"And when you say 'bring them to justice,' you mean—"

"I mean bring them in alive so they may stand trial for the war crimes they committed. We are not renegade executioners. Our mission is to bring them in, to be judged by the tribunal."

"Giving Nazis a fair trial?"

"Assassinating them would deprive the victims the opportunity to face the monsters and hold them accountable for the horrors they carried-out."

"And an American photographer would be beneficial to this cause?"

"A skilled man with morals would, yes."

Jimmy shook Levi's hand, knowing that joining this team of Nazi hunters was the path he wanted to be on after all he had seen during the war. That handshake was the beginning of a partnership that would cross numerous countries, and result in the capture, imprisonment and deaths of some of history's most evil men. That handshake eventually brought Jimmy there to Roja Rey's in Argentina.

Levi had heard stories about a secret U-boat that traveled to South America carrying high ranking German officers two weeks after the fall of Berlin. Jimmy in tow, the two men traveled across the ocean to the little German oasis where they now sat.

The rumor mill had even included eyewitnesses, who claimed to have seen Adolf Hitler himself step off of that U-boat. People said that the German dictator's death was faked, and he had been whisked away to Argentina beneath the allies' noses.

When Jimmy asked Levi if he believed what he'd heard, the old man told him, "If someone as recognizable as Adolf Hitler were in South America, there'd be a lot more than rumors to go off of."

Levi was sure to point out that their current target, who they were quite sure had found refuge in Patagonia, was a Nazi officer by the name of Wilhelm Stengl.

Stengl was once a Colonel of the SS. He had become a rather well-known figure due primarily to the paranoia inducing task bestowed upon him by the Führer. His job was to investigate members of the Nazi party to ensure they were not hiding any Jewish heritage; an internal affairs of sorts that reported directly to Hitler. During the war he had sussed out several officers who had falsified documents to conceal their true lineage.

He was loathed almost unanimously by his fellow Nazis. They were fearful of him, knowing that all he had to do to have them sent away was to tell the Führer they had Jew blood pumping through their bestial veins. Some believed he had abused his power and had many true Aryans put to death just to keep himself on top. None of that was ever verified, of course, and Stengl remained in Hitler's favor all throughout the war.

Stengl was a clever man, a master of the politics game. He had detailed files and secret dossiers on most of the high command, along with the various butchers and psychopaths that made up the executioner's blade of the Reich, which was precisely why he was such a savory target for the Levi and Jimmy. If they could capture Stengl, they would be in possession of an invaluable tomb of information.

The only problem?

They weren't one hundred percent sure what Stengl looked like.

All the existing photographs of him were blurry, hard to make out. He had brown hair and sharp features. He was slender. That's all they had to go off of.

Identifying him would be difficult, which was part of the reason Stengl was able to escape from Europe initially. He had done well to stay out of the camera's view throughout the 30s and 40s and word had it he once broken the nose of Heinrich Hoffmann, Hitler's official photographer, for trying to take a photo of him during a gala event. Even then he was mindful of his steps, knowing in the back of his mind that one day he may be on the losing side and would find it necessary to make himself disappear.

There on the patio of Roja Rey's, Levi considered Stengl's elusiveness. He believed the Nazi was there in Argentina, and he knew that Jimmy desperately wanted to believe it as well. The impact they could make by bringing the man in would be incalculable.

The rain beat against the patio covering as the waiter returned with Jimmy's whiskey. After getting a few sips in, Levi attempted to start the conversation back up again with his damp friend.

"Whenever you're ready to enlighten me."

Jimmy set his glass down on the table.

"I met with our contact," he said.

Levi regarded him with anticipation.

"We were interrupted."

Two hours earlier, Jimmy was standing in a disheveled bedroom, his arms crossed, looking inquisitively at the far wall where a framed painting of a cow hung. He cocked his head to the side, wondering if the white heifer with the black spot around her eye had sat well for her portrait, or if she had been an unruly subject, wandering about the open field which made up the backdrop of the artwork. He let the slightest smirk creep over his face, imagining what he may have named her.

Betsy, perhaps. Betsy with the black spot.

He adjusted his designer bowler hat and perfectly tailored, checked jacket. Image said so much. Jimmy knew it could tell the wandering eyes who you were, or who you wanted them to think you were, and in his line of work deception was integral.

An Argentinian man sat on the bed staring at the mustard yellow phone on the nightstand. They were both silent, waiting for it to ring. Jimmy's eyes drifted to the Ballester-Molina Argentine pistol, sitting beside the phone. It could have been considered an antique at that point as they had stopped producing them altogether seven years earlier in 1953. The grip was wooden, the metal barrel tarnished. Jimmy stared at it, his wandering mind beginning to create a backstory for the gun as his boredom set in.

The phone rang and the Argentinian man scooped up the receiver and said, "¿Bueno?"

Jimmy watched as the man listened intently to the voice on the other end of the line.

The man said, "Gracias," and set the receiver back down in the cradle.

"Well?" Jimmy asked.

"She say he's there. She say it's him, the man you are looking for."

"How does she know?"

"She say she's seen the scar, the one on his back. The one made by a knife."

When Levi had first told Jimmy about Stengl, Jimmy had asked how they would know the Nazi when they saw him. Levi replied, "If the job was easy, everyone would do it." After sporting a cocky grin, he elaborated further.

"The man has a unique scar that can identify him if we get close enough. He was stabbed in the back by a fellow officer he had been investigating. The knife pierced him just above his right kidney."

"So our plan is to pull the shirt off every German we come across?" Jimmy remarked.

This had made Levi laugh. He didn't laugh often, but when he did, it was hearty and authentic. It was an infectious laugh, one that made everyone around him smile.

"Others will know him when they see him. Others will recognize him and they will tell their friends, who will tell friends of their own, and soon enough we'll get wind of it," the Austrian had said. "Not all rumors will prove true, but eventually one of them absolutely will."

The sentiment had proven true. Jimmy inquired of the Argentinian man sitting on the bed, "How did she see the scar?"

The man looked down at his feet, ashamed. Jimmy didn't need him to say more. He walked to the door and reached for the handle, but stopped when the man shouted, "Wait!"

Jimmy lowered his hand and turned back toward the man on the bed. The man asked, "She will not get hurt, will she?"

"We don't have any interest in your sister, Mauro. We just want the man with the scar." This seemed to calm Mauro, at least a bit, but the calm quickly faded when he heard footsteps creaking up the old stairway outside the bedroom.

He jumped to his feet and grabbed the pistol from the nightstand. He checked to make sure it was loaded and whispered, "I hope you are armed, señor."

Jimmy pulled a snub nose .357 revolver from a small holster behind his back and moved alongside the closed bedroom door. The two men listened, their ears pressed to the wall. They could hear the footsteps creaking further up toward them and Mauro looked at Jimmy to see if he was as visibly terrified as Mauro was.

Jimmy looked calm and composed, like he always tried to. Inside he was afraid, concealing some degree of fear behind his eyes ever since he partnered up with Levi. He knew the job was dangerous, but there in the tiny bedroom in Argentina, Jimmy felt closer to his own demise than ever before.

"Don't hesitate," Jimmy whispered back. Mauro nodded in agreement. The footsteps stopped when they reached the top floor and Jimmy could hear the floorboards bend beneath the weight of at least two men.

The first knock startled Mauro and he nearly dropped the pistol. Jimmy steadied him with a gentle touch to the shoulder.

The second knock came, followed by a man's voice saying, "Señor, open the door, please." The man on the other side of the door was not fluent in Spanish. His gravely voice bared a German accent and an intensity that Jimmy knew all too well; a solider's intensity. Mauro looked at Jimmy for direction and Jimmy held his index finger to his lips.

The third knock was aggressive and the man on the other side of the door shouted, "Open the fucking door!"

Jimmy pressed the barrel of his snub nose against the door and wrapped his finger around the trigger. When the doorknob twisted, Jimmy squeezed. The revolver barked out three bullets, blasting into the hallway beyond the door. They could hear the German stumble backward and smash against something—the railing, Jimmy imagined. Then half a dozen bullets exploded through the door, sending wood splinters spraying across the bedroom.

The door slammed open and Jimmy had to step out of the way to avoid being hit. As soon as he saw the profile of the second man charge into the room, Jimmy emptied the remaining three shots from his revolver into the side of the intruder's head. Blood sprayed across Mauro's face and he stumbled away, colliding against the wall, knocking the framed painting of the cow from its hook in the process.

Before Jimmy could reload his weapon, a third man wearing a beige suit came through the door, shooting wildly. Mauro fumbled with his pistol before raising it and firing back. He emptied the clip and two of the bullets made contact with the attacker's chest. The attacker crumpled to the floor and as if a dormant killer instinct took hold of his body, Jimmy stomped on the German man's neck, just in case the bullets hadn't done the trick.

Jimmy's ears were ringing from the gunshots.

He reached in his pocket for his extra bullets and began loading them into the chambers of the snub nose.

A series of wet coughs drew his eyes to the other end of the room where the cow paining lay on the floor. Betsy was stained in red. Mauro sat beside her, blood draining from his open mouth.

Jimmy rushed to his side and applied pressure to the gunshot wound in Mauro's chest. "It's all right. It's all right," Jimmy assured the dying man.

He looked over his shoulder, sensing there might be another assassin.

But they were alone now.

It was just them and the dead Germans.

Mauro was still squeezing the trigger of the Ballester-Molina, over and over. Jimmy listened to the click, click, click as Mauro's limp hand continuously tried to fire bullets into the floor. Jimmy gently pulled the gun out of the Argentinian man's hand and said again, "It's all right."

As the clicking stopped, so did the beating of Mauro's heart.

At Roja Rey's, sitting at the patio table beneath the cheap covering being abused by the rainfall, Jimmy finished telling Levi about the death of their contact. It was clear Jimmy was upset, but he wasn't about to open the floodgates of his emotions there at the restaurant.

He took a drink of his whiskey.

"All signs point to it being him. The informant's sister saw the scar. We should go out there tonight, get a few photos before we bring the rest of the team in."

"Go out where?"

Jimmy leaned in close, his clothes sopping wet, rainwater still dripping from his bowler hat, his arms holding himself tight. He made sure that no one else could hear the next words he uttered to Levi.

"They call it the Residencia Inalco."

Chapter Two
RESIDENCIA INALCO

Outside the nearby Villa La Angostura, near the Argentine border with Chile, nestled between a dense forest and a crystal blue lake, sat the Residencia Inalco. It was a lavish complex with numerous buildings that surrounded an enormous square with a glamorous stone fountain. There was a stable with a dozen dapple gray mares, a small hangar that housed a pair of seaplanes, and various units setup to monitor the grounds.

The main house sat centered in front of the square and its immense windows were taking the full brunt of the hammering rainfall. The house, along with the rest of the complex, was only visible from head on, and only if traveling across the Lake Nahuel Huapi that loomed before it.

The Residencia Inalco had over five kilometers of coastline on the lake and from all other sides the thick forest kept it concealed. In fact, the only other way to reach the complex other than the lake was a rocky, mountain trail that weaved dangerously throughout the woods. It wasn't wide enough for a car and would have been fatal should a motorcycle have tried to traverse it.

These were all factors that went into the location scouting for the Inalco which had been secretly built two years before the end of the war.

It bore an eerie similarity to the infamous Berghof, Adolf Hitler's mountain retreat in the Bavarian Alps, which made the Nazi refugees living there feel all the more at home. One such Nazi was

Wilhelm Stengl, who stood inside the main house, staring out one of the overly large windows at the lake outside.

He had not been part of the first group to secretly abscond to Latin America via U-boat after the fall of the Reich, but he had found his way there five years later in 1950. His arrival was not particularly a welcome one. The other escaped Germans knew all too well the job the Führer had tasked him with during the war.

A dozen guards patrolled the outside grounds of the Residencia Inalco, all of them former members of the SS, donned with ponchos to help shield them from the rain. One of them strolled through the square past the fountain and as though he could feel a looming gaze upon him, he turned and looked at Stengl through the window.

The expression was very familiar to Stengl. It was the same one most of Germany had given him daily. Part of it was loathing, the hatred they felt knowing Stengl exposed Bavarian lies of men they called brother. The other part was fear, which during the war when the Führer was still in power and trusted Stengl's word, always felt logical; but here in Argentina, over 12,000 kilometers away from the fallen German capital, Stengl was puzzled by their lingering dread. He wasn't a physically impressive man, average at best, and aside from his stoicism there wasn't much he did that he thought should exude intimidation. Nevertheless, the other men were afraid of him and he rather enjoyed passing the time trying to decipher why. Perhaps they saw him as a Rasputin, he thought, having been stabbed in the back and survived.

Stengl watched as the guard looked away and continued across the square. Behind him in the sizeable living room, another man, a former SS Gruppenführer by the name of Josef Hausser, finished stoking the logs in the fireplace. Stengl turned to him and said in German, "Two days. That rain hasn't let up one bit." Hausser nodded and took a seat in one of the plush chairs. He seemed to be the only man at the complex who didn't let his fear of Stengl show.

But that didn't mean it wasn't there.

Stengl made himself comfortable in one of the other chairs and his eyes settled on the antique crossbow mounted over the mantle. The glow from the fire below illuminated the weapon ominously, casting shadows along the ornate, Nordic rune carvings on the handle. He listened to the crackle from the hearth, the small exploding embers flashing in his pupils.

The fireplace and mantel looked almost identical to the one he remembered seeing at the Berghof. He had visited the oversized chalet in the past, invited by the Führer for a weekend getaway, and Stengl had leapt at the opportunity to see the estate. It had proved to be an experience he would never forget, but not for the reasons he had expected.

His eyes drifted to the life-size bust of Hitler sitting atop a Greek pillar on the far end of the room. The statue was gold and glossy and portrayed the Führer's shoulders much broader than Stengl recalled them being. He picked up his glass of whiskey and raised it to Josef Hausser, who acknowledged him back. "Heil Hitler," Stengl said.

"Sieg heil," Hausser responded as they each took a drink.

Stengl crossed one leg over the other and leaned as far back as he could in the chair. He motioned at the golden bust and asked, "Do you know how much money we could get for that?" Hausser looked over his shoulder at the Hitler statue. "Or any of the other memorabilia from back home?"

"I wouldn't know."

"What we have here in this complex, we could trade for a sustainable fortune. For both of us. We could take the money and start over. Change our names, identities, and go our separate ways. Sever all ties from what's left of the Reich."

Hausser was silent. He looked at Stengl, trying to read him.

He leaned forward and with a disdainful tone asked, "You would leave behind our brothers?"

"There's only so much fortune to go around."

"You're a Colonel of the—"

"Former Colonel. Just as you are a former Gruppenführer. The war is long over. We lost." Stengl stood and walked to the bust. He placed his hand atop Hitler's head and patted it. "This means nothing. Not anymore. But it *can* be something new. It can be our future."

"You want to sell off Nazi treasure?"

"I want to sell off this valuable artwork."

"Sell it to whom?"

"I've already started conversations with some collectors. They're willing to—"

Hausser's deep chuckle cut Stengl off. "Already started conversations? Of course you have. Typical Stengl. Always out for himself."

"What I did during the war, I did for the good of Germany. For the good of the party. I did what was asked of me."

For the first time since arriving in South America, Hausser finally succumbed to his anger and spoke his true feelings to Stengl.

"You forged false heritage documents that put good, true Aryans in the camps."

"There's no proof I forged anything."

Hausser stood and adjusted his jacket. "Then admit it now. It's just you and me in this room. Admit that you sent your fellow officers to their deaths so you could get ahead."

Stengl laughed and finished his drink. "Your paranoia is embarrassing, Hausser. I thought you of all people were smart enough not to believe the rumors."

"All rumors have some basis in fact."

"Do they? I heard rumors about you as well, SS

Gruppenführer Hausser. I heard about a certain young officer that frequented your office and for reasons beyond his military duty."

Hausser threw his glass down, shattering it across the floor in front of the fireplace. Stengl smiled at the emotion he was able to elicit from his German comrade. "Watch your tongue, Stengl!"

Stengl strolled over to the fireplace and put his hand on the mantle as he leaned down and stared into the flames. "Do you think your friends here at the complex would be in favor of your secret behavior?"

"I think they would put a bullet in your head if I asked them to," Hausser snarled.

Stengl straightened up and with his back to Hausser he said, "You're probably right."

As Hausser stared at the back of his head, Stengl looked up at the loaded crossbow hanging over the mantel, then turned to Hausser and asked, "Why haven't you?"

"What?"

"Why haven't you asked them to put a bullet in my head?"

Hausser didn't know how to respond as Stengl continued to glare at him.

"You've had every opportunity to do so. The men here, they would of course do as you ask. They are no strangers to following orders regardless of how deplorable they may be. So why not? Why not ask them to dispatch me? Why live here in fear all these years?"

"I do not live in fear," Hausser growled. Stengl turned back toward the fireplace.

"But you do. You don't only live in it. You're drowning in it. It's a gelatinous ooze that engulfs every ounce of your being. It's so palpable, your fear, that I need only to stick my tongue out from my mouth to get a taste."

"I do not fear you, Stengl."

"Fear is not a weakness, former Gruppenführer Hausser. Fear

is a tool. It is your mind warning you to prepare yourself so you do not end up in a situation where you are caught at a disadvantage. There is nothing wrong with being afraid. Your body knows, senses things, before they make any sense to you. A man who is afraid is most often a logical man. I respect fearful men. I've known them to be highly intelligent in most cases. What I don't respect are foolish men. A coward may survive. A fool will not."

Stengl looked up again at the crossbow, gently touched the taut cord and asked, "So, my proud brother, are you a coward, or are you a fool?"

Short of the warm glow emanating from the windows of the various buildings in the Residencia Inalco, the only other light in the dismal night was the reflection of the moon bouncing off the still lake. Levi and Jimmy had made their way through the woods behind the complex and as they reached the tree line, they crouched down behind a row of hedges.

Jimmy readied his Kodak camera and Levi raised a pair of binoculars to his old eyes. At first glance as he scanned the grounds, it appeared the complex had been deserted.

Then he saw it.

One of the guards lying facedown in the soil beneath a rain-slicked poncho.

"What in God's name?" Levi whispered.

Jimmy motioned to another fallen guard sitting in the dirt, half leaned up against the side of the main house. The guard's gun was strewn aside near his motionless boots.

"Looks like someone beat us to the punch?" Jimmy asked quietly.

"*Someone* killed these bastards. No denying that."

Jimmy reached into his jacket and pulled out the Ballester-Molina pistol that he had taken off of Mauro after the Argentinian informant had been killed. He checked the magazine.

"Where did you get that?" Levi asked in a quiet whisper.

"It belonged to our informant," Jimmy responded. Levi could see the growing emotion in Jimmy's face.

"Mauro was a good man."

"We need to apprehend Stengl, or that good man died in vain." Jimmy considered the words as they came out of his mouth as though someone else had just said them. He thought about Mauro, dead on the floor by the cow painting.

The bullet casings.

The blood.

Levi pulled out his snub nose revolver and motioned for Jimmy to follow him. The two of them crept from the bushes and moved in closer to the back of the house. They stayed low and crouched beneath one of the windows along the exterior wall. Levi raised slowly and peered inside.

"See anything?" Jimmy asked in a whisper.

Levi looked at him and replied in a tone barely audible over the heavy rain, "Just a bunch of dead Nazis. Someone went on a shooting spree."

The two men perked up when they heard a loud, wooden bang from the other side of the house. Levi raised his index finger to his lips, and they listened as another loud bang, like a heavy wooden drawbridge crashing against the ground, cut through the rain.

"The hell is that?"

"Sounded like barn doors."

They snuck around to the square where another two guards lied dead near the fountain. The confusion in Jimmy's eyes was heavier than the assaulting rain.

The front door of the house flung open and in unison Levi

and Jimmy spun and aimed their guns.

Hausser stumbled outside and collapsed to his knees, his hands fumbling weakly at the arrow protruding from his chest. The Nazi's eyes fluttered as he saw the two hunters in his peripherals.

"Stengl," he murmured, blood leaking from his slack jaw. Then he fell to his side and his eyes glazed over.

"Levi?" Jimmy whispered.

Levi crept in close to the dead Nazi's body. He touched Hausser's face, gripping it by the jaw, turning it from side to side, examining.

"This is Josef Hausser. He was a Gruppenführer with the SS. I know this man."

"He said—"

"Stengl," Levi interrupted.

The whir of a prop engine echoed through the air and Jimmy and Levi saw the two heavy doors of the hanger along the coastline were wide open.

"Quickly!" Levi sprinted toward the hangar with Jimmy in tow. They bolted across the square, passing over the murdered guards. Jimmy, being younger and more spry, overtook Levi for the lead.

As they reached the wooden hangar doors, Levi grabbed Jimmy's collar and yanked him back just in time to save him from being hit by the wing of the seaplane as it pulled out into the rain. The two men landed on their backs in the soil and shielded their faces as the propellers from the seaplane stirred up a cloud of debris.

Jimmy tried his best to get a clear look at the pilot, but the heavy rainfall on the windshield obscured his view. The seaplane slid out into the lake and Levi rolled into a prone position and fired his revolver. He emptied the cylinder, but the seaplane only took minimal cosmetic damage.

Jimmy got to his feet, took aim with his Ballester-Molina and opened fire. The seaplane was too far out into the lake for him to get a good shot, and a moment later it had picked up enough speed to lift into the sky.

"Damn!"

Jimmy helped Levi to his feet and the two Nazi hunters stood on the bank in silence as they watched their prey escape into the night. When the seaplane was no longer visible, he looked down at the empty gun in his hand.

The gun had failed Jimmy, or maybe he had failed it. He had never been one for firearms in the past, but as he stared at the Argentinian pistol, he felt a powerful urge to provide the inanimate object with a second chance at victory. He felt tied to the gun as though the soul of Mauro was engrained within it. They had failure in common now, and Jimmy felt an oddly romantic poetry connecting his own success with that of the Ballester-Molina's.

"That gun deserves to avenge its original owner. It deserves to take that bastard down," Levi said when he noticed Jimmy's gaze.

Behind them, past the square, beyond the corpse of SS Gruppenführer Hausser in the doorway, inside the front room of the Residencia Inalco, the greek pillar sat bare.

The golden bust of Adolf Hitler was gone.

Chapter Three
ANISEED & LEADS

London, 1965. Five Years Later.

Jimmy Knotts pulled on the rewind knob and popped open the back of his Kodak Retina 35mm camera. He threaded a roll of film onto the spool and pressed the knob back down to hold the roll in place before pulling the leader and closing the back. He removed the lens cap and checked for clarity as the smoke from the cigarette burning in the ashtray fogged up the cargo area of the van.

Jimmy took a test shot of the cherry and the snap of the shutter caused the owner of the cigarette sitting across from him to look up. He was a mustachioed Englishman in slim-fit trousers and a floral-patterned sport coat.

Jimmy cranked the film advance lever and said, "You're aware that's not incense, right?"

"It is for me," the mustachioed man answered as he tossed a handful of salted cashews into his mouth. He chewed the way a cow gnaws on grass., his jaw extending out in an almost perpendicular fashion before snapping back and pulverizing the nuts, bits of which flew out onto his lap with every bite.

His name was Walter, but he preferred to be called Walt for short. In a passive aggressive display of subtle antagonism, Jimmy refused to call him that, and instead stuck to using the full name.

"You keep eating like that and you'll get lockjaw, Walter," Jimmy quipped as he adjusted the ISO on the Kodak.

Walt's lip curled at the sound of his own name and he asked, "Eating like what, then?"

"Like a goddamned wildebeest."

"Sod off." He threw another dozen cashews on his tongue and chomped down. "The fuck's a wildebeest, anyway?"

As Jimmy stood up he had to hunch over as not to hit his head on the roof of the van. He shuffled up between the driver's and passenger's seats and reached into the glove-box.

"Don't touch my fuckin' aniseed twists," Walt mumbled. Jimmy looked over his shoulder.

"Your what?"

"My aniseed twists," Walt said after swallowing the gob of mushed cashews.

"What the hell is an aniseed twist?"

"They're in the glove-box there, ain't they?"

Jimmy pulled out the Sears Trans-Talk 600 Walkie Talkie that he was initially reaching for and saw a clear plastic baggie filled with red gummy candy.

"These?" Jimmy asked as his he scooped them up and dangled them at Walt.

"I said don't touch 'em, didn't I?"

"Aniseed," Jimmy grumbled, shaking his head. He tossed the bag at Walt and sat back down across from him with the Walkie Talkie. He checked his ZentRa watch, then spun the volume control knob to turn on the Walkie Talkie before setting it beside him on the bench.

"Aniseeds are full of minerals, you know? Iron, magnesium, calcium," Walt rambled as he looked at the red candies in the bag. "Probably a bit o' zinc." Jimmy went back to fiddling with his camera as Walt continued. "They used to be a highly prized commodity in ancient Rome."

"So was salt. That why you bought the cashews?"

"Nope. Bought them because they lower the risk of gallstones."

"Gallstones high on your list of worries?"

Walt shrugged and took a drink from his thermos to rinse the particles from his teeth.

"You know, wine's got some good properties too," Jimmy said. "Maybe we should have brought some of that along."

"You like wine, Knotts? I've got a good wine story for you, you know?"

"Yeah?"

"You were in the war, right?"

"I was a photographer."

"Doesn't matter, you'll still get a kick outta this. My aunt, she's Irish, Mary's her name. She married an American, like you. Well, not too much like you. This bloke isn't so hard on the eyes. That's what my aunt says about him, anyway."

Walt dug into his bag of aniseed twists and popped one into his mouth. "They called him Doc back then."

"Because he was a medic?" Jimmy inquired.

"What? No, he wasn't a medic. Because his last name's Murdock. Just listen. Right? He was stationed in France, holed up in a bombed out building with part of his platoon. Things had been quiet for hours but they knew there was this one fuckin' Kraut sniper out there, just waiting for one of those boys to poke their heads out. This invisible, patient fuckin' bastard.

"Now, across the alleyway, in the next building over, was a wine store. After hours of just sittin' there, waiting for their next instructions via radio from their commanding officer, one of the other soldiers suggested they get a few bottles of wine to pass the time. Of course, none of them were overly eager to play gofer due to the ominous threat of the hidden sniper, so what do they do? They end up drawing straws. You fuckin' Americans love drawing straws."

Jimmy's brow furrowed at the allegation. Walt continued.

"Well, as luck would have it, Doc pulled the stubby stick and was given the honor of risking his life for a few bottles of entertainment."

The Walkie Talkie warbled, and Jimmy picked it up. Both men were silent as they listened in anticipation. After a moment of waiting for a voice that didn't come, Jimmy set the Walkie Talkie back down.

Walt pulled out another aniseed twist and offered it to Jimmy, who politely declined. He stuffed it in his mouth and mumbled, "So Doc, fueled by adrenaline, sprinted across the alleyway and into the shop. No shots were fired. He was safe.

"Most of the bottles were smashed on the floor, but there were a handful still intact on the shelves. This fella, he filled his pack with all he could carry before heading back to the hole in the wall.

"Before stepping out, his eye caught a single bottle with the image of a stethoscope on the label. A fuckin' stethoscope, like what a doctor uses, right? It was sitting in the corner, pushed all the way back on the shelf beyond all the brick and concrete rubble. He went to it, brushed the mess away and pulled it down. He said he felt like the label was a sign, and he'd have been a fool to leave it behind. Stethoscope, Doc, you get it."

Jimmy nodded, half listening, half inspecting his camera. Walt didn't halt his tale.

"Stethoscope bottle in hand, Doc walked back to the hole in the wall. He looked across the alleyway where he could see his brothers in arms waiting for him. He took a deep breath and launched himself out into the open.

"He ran as fast as his legs would carry him, but when he made it halfway across the alley—" Walt stopped as the Walkie Talkie squawked with a familiar voice.

"You two ready?" Levi's garbled voice sounded from the radio.

Jimmy picked up the Walkie Talkie and replied, "Present and ready."

"Right about that time," Levi said.

Jimmy stood back up to hunching height and sat down in the front passenger's seat. He raised the camera to his face and adjusted the lens as he peered out the passenger's side window.

Walt crept up behind him and leaned in close.

"He heard the crack of a gunshot and felt the spray of shrapnel shredding his uniform, piercing his skin. His whole torso felt like it was on fire. It wasn't just a single pain point. He felt it everywhere, as if a grenade had gone off, sending murderous shards flying in all directions."

Jimmy lowered the camera, looked over his shoulder at Walt and said, "This is a bit distracting."

Walt kept going.

"Doc didn't stop running, even through the pain, he managed to make it the rest of the way across the alley and into the arms of his fellow soldiers.

"They ripped his jacket and shirt off and the medic began to treat his wounds. Even though he had felt shrapnel, he was sure he didn't hear a grenade go off. He had heard a gunshot—from the hidden kraut sniper most likely—but was almost certain it wasn't a bullet that hit him. Then he heard one of the men say, 'You gotta get that fucking glass outta him,' and it suddenly made sense. There was no grenade. The shrapnel he felt was from the exploding wine bottle that shattered when the sniper's bullet hit it."

Jimmy raised the camera back up to his eye and stared through the viewfinder, focusing on the ten story building with the ruby red awning across the street.

"That's what they gave him the purple heart for; stealing wine from a bombed out wine store in Nazi-occupied France, so that his platoon could get drunk. Needless to say, Doc doesn't enjoy telling that story. It embarrasses him." Walt helped himself to another twist. "I, on the other hand, always loved that story."

Jimmy kept his eye and the camera on the building. A moment later the front door opened and a white-haired man in a gray continental style suit and skinny tie walked out beneath the awning.

"That's him," Jimmy said calmly as he watched the man through his camera.

SNAP! He took his photo.

Walt picked up the Walkie-Talkie, pressed the call button and held it to his face. "He just walked out."

SNAP! Jimmy took another photo.

"Play it smart," Levi's voice responded on the other end of the radio.

The man in the suit lit a cigarette, observed his surroundings, then began to stroll down the sidewalk.

"Don't tail us too close," Jimmy said to Walt as he popped open the door and hopped out of the van.

"Don't tail us too close," Walt said, impersonating Jimmy as he sat down behind the wheel. "Am I a fuckin' surveillance virgin?"

Outside, Jimmy shuffled casually along the sidewalk, staying almost parallel with the businessman on the other side of the street. He had to swerve around a few people headed the opposite direction, but his eyes never withdrew.

The man in the gray suit, Deiter Fuchs, was a morning radio host of a semi-popular station in the heart of London. He had come to the attention of Levi, Jimmy, and the other two members of their Nazi hunting team when their affiliate in the Metropolitan Police, a man by the name of George Shaw, had reached out.

George told them about the disc jockey who had been rumored to pass messages back and forth for German's whose families had been separated by the construction of the wall, putting his own life on the line to do so. He said that people referred to

Fuchs as "the selfless German."

George shared that Fuchs was a man worth looking into, and felt it likely he may lead them to a bigger basket of fish and chips, perhaps war criminals who weren't lucky enough to travel the ratlines to South America.

With that, Levi assembled the usual members of his crew. He utilized Jimmy as the scout, whose job was to confirm the authenticity of any leads they received using his skills as a photographer and in most cases acting as point man.

Walt Corbyn, the mustachioed Englishman, was the muscle, the heavy, the "bag-n-tagger" as he liked to call himself. He was more often than not the man who wrapped the black cloth bag over the targets' heads before throwing them into the back of his Volkswagen van.

Zsolt Baranyai, a Hungarian interrogator with a knack for retrieving information from even the most stubborn of individuals, was the truth-finder. Jimmy had heard that he once got a Soviet General to reveal his secret life as a cross-dresser with nothing more than a bottle of Rhein Riesling and a stiletto blade.

While the team's record was not perfect, they prided themselves on the individuals they had brought to justice, and made a point of conducting themselves according to a moral code.

With the Nuremberg trials long passed, and selfish "patriotic" projects protecting an abundance of Nazis who were worth something to the world's cold-warring nations, men like the fearless Simon Wiesenthal, and the Austrian with the ever ticking timepiece, Levi Aarons, did what they could to play their part in righting the wrongs.

It was not about revenge.

It was about justice.

True justice, brining in the evil responsible for the world's atrocities to pay for their actions.

The next step in that mission was afoot there in England as Jimmy trailed Deiter Fuchs. He thought about Walt's dubya-dubya-two story. That crazy American soldier, risking his life for a few bottles of Grenache, seemed even more brazen than trailing a suspected Nazi down the road in broad daylight.

Jimmy was nervous, as he always was, but he did his best to put things into perspective. Things could go wrong. Of course they could. They could go horribly wrong. Hell, a double-decker bus could jump the curb and flatten him into nothing more than a pulpy mess of bone marrow. A window-cleaner could drop his water bucket down from thirty stories and cave in his head. Anything could happen, and also, nothing could happen. Everything could go as planned. The odds were the same. As much as he could anticipate the worst, he could also hope for the best, and that belief gave Jimmy enough confidence to continue to follow Deiter around the corner into the alleyway.

The German DJ tripped on the curb and looked over his shoulder just to be sure no one witnessed the embarrassing moment. It was then that he noticed Jimmy.

The two men locked eyes for a split second before Jimmy could divert his gaze. Deiter turned back around and continued on his way, albeit more than a bit suspicious.

The German came out of the alleyway onto the next street and meandered along toward a pastry shop with a sign overhead that read, "Davies Delights." He pulled the door open, jingling the bell, and walked inside.

Jimmy came out of the alley and caught a glimpse of him just as he entered. He hurried, in as casual a manner as he could muster, down the sidewalk towards the shop. The bell chimed again as Jimmy entered.

"Let me know when you're ready," the cashier mumbled as he read from a crisp print of Ian Fleming's "On Her Majesty's Secret

Service."

Jimmy surveyed the room. Deiter was sitting in the corner, a steaming cup of earl gray in hand.

"Just a scone," Jimmy told the cashier in his noticeably American accent. The cashier scooped up an almond scone, wrapped it in a thin napkin and handed it to Jimmy.

"Cheers," Jimmy said as he took a bite of the pastry. He sauntered over to a table, two down from where Deiter sat.

Deiter looked up at him as he blew on his black tea to cool it down. "You're American," he said.

"Guilty," Jimmy responded with hunched shoulders.

"I won't hold it against you. We're both foreigners in a foreign land."

"I'd cheers to that if I had a beverage," Jimmy said.

"You can cheers with the pasty, my friend."

Jimmy raised his scone, and Deiter raised his tea. The two men chuckled at their whimsical correspondence.

Jimmy, in an intentionally noticeable fashion, looked around the store. Other than the cashier, he and Dieter were the only people present.

"Say, you don't mind if I join you, do you?"

"By all means. I could use some fresh conversation," Deiter answered.

Jimmy stood and walked over to take a seat at Deiter's table.

"You're German."

"Ja," Deiter said with an overly thick German accent. The two men laughed. "How could you tell?" Deiter joked.

"Sneaking suspicion," Jimmy remarked with a wide smile.

"And why do you find yourself in London, Cowboy?" Deiter asked.

"Cowboy, eh?"

"No offense intended, that's certain."

Jimmy took another bite of his scone and as he chewed he said, "You're the first non-Brit I've crossed paths with since I've been here."

"Well, feel honored to be in my presence then," Deiter commented. They both laughed brazenly at his response. The faux laughter eventually faded.

"I've a knack for singling out Germans," Jimmy said. "You could say it's a gift."

"The gift of finding Germans?" Deiter asked with a smile.

"Could be a gift, yeah." Jimmy took an overly large bite of his scone, leaving only a small morsel left between his fingers. Deiter watched curiously as Jimmy chewed the pastry obnoxiously, the way Walt had done with the cashews.

"Would you like a bite?" Jimmy asked, extending what was left of the almond scone toward Deiter's face.

"No, thank you. I had a proper English breakfast this morning."

"You know, Brits are always quick to call out the hamburger, but I'll tell you right now, the quote unquote English breakfast is the greasiest, foulest plate of mismatched animal intestines I've ever come across."

Deiter let out a loud, genuine chortle. "Well, call it as you see it, Mr. America."

"It's what I do, Mr. Deutschland," Jimmy said. Deiter smirked and took another sip of his tea. "You know, speaking of calling things the way I see them…" Jimmy paused. The entry door chimed as another guest walked into the pasty shop.

Deiter cocked his head like a hawk. "Yes?" Deiter inquired.

"Well, I have to admit something."

"Oh? And what's that?"

"Oktoberfest."

"What about it?" Deiter asked.

"I've learned since I've been here in Europe, that it doesn't actually occur in October."

"Somewhat true, sir. It starts in September, though the ending date is most assuredly in the month of October."

"But you'd agree it's a bit misleading?"

"I—I could agree with that, yes," Deiter said almost begrudgingly.

"Don't feel as though you betrayed the fatherland by saying so," Jimmy remarked with a jovial expression.

"Fuck you," Deiter guffawed.

"Fuck me?" Jimmy asked pressing both index fingers against his own chest.

"Yes," Deiter started. "Ja! Fuck you," he said with a laugh. The two men chuckled together, amused by the openness of conversation. The cashier watched them as they conversed.

"You're a brave man, aren't you Deiter?" Jimmy asked. Deiter continued to laugh until he noticed that Jimmy had called him by his first name.

"Are you—are you a fan of the show?" Deiter asked.

"A fan of the show?" Jimmy inquired.

"You called me Deiter."

"And?"

"You must know the show if you know my name," Deiter explained. Jimmy looked at him with condescending expression.

"I don't listen to your trash show, Deiter." The German's amiable nature faded instantly. "Your life as a radio host is of little interest to me. The atrocities you committed during the war, however, well those are of great concern."

Deiter jumped up, rigid and ready to storm out when Jimmy said, "I wouldn't run off if I were you."

Deiter looked down at him and said, "You're working with the Jew rats. Crucifying every Aryan they can track down?"

"Just the ones who deserve it."

Deiter headed for the door. As he passed by the cashier the newly arrived guest turned from the counter and cracked Deiter in the shin with a crowbar.

Deiter howled out in pain as he collapsed to the wood floor. Walt stood over him, gripping the crowbar in one hand, a black cloth bag in his other.

"Gute nacht, Herr Fuchs," Walt said before bringing the crowbar down atop the German's skull.

Jimmy popped the last bite of scone into his mouth as Walt pulled the bag over Deiter's unconscious head. Jimmy grabbed his feet while Walt lifted him under the arms. The cashier stood in complete astonishment as they hauled the German out the door and tossed him into the back of the van before peeling away down the street.

The skyline was its normal dreary gray and the London streets were the standard level of bustling. Jimmy, lost in his own mind, ignored it all as he weaved in and out of the curbside pedestrians. He turned the corner and entered the grand arcade and passed through to the galleria, a series of shops, most of them empty or bragging only a handful of customers. He strolled up to the café unhurriedly and took a seat at one of the patio tables across from his less than dour partner, Levi Aarons, who gestured to the barista inside behind the counter.

"I'd say that I can't recall the last time you were late for a meeting, but it just wouldn't be the truth."

Jimmy replied with a confident, "Check your watch, Levi."

He signaled the waiter with a flick of his index finger and the properly groomed gent hurried over to the service counter to alert the barista who had somehow missed Levi's initial gesture.

Levi sipped his mint tea, staring at Jimmy who casually glanced around at the other shops. The waiter returned with a fresh cup and poured Jimmy some tea of his own from the ceramic kettle with the café's logo on it—a stiff-eared hare jumping over a tortoise.

Jimmy waited for the waiter to walk away before trying a sip. His face gave the slightest hint of unhappiness and he reached for the sugar.

"How did the interrogation go?" Jimmy added the sugar to his tea, mixed it with the small spoon, then tried it again. His eyes smiled at the taste of the improved drink.

"Deiter Fuchs—the 'selfless German'—sang like a canary."

"And how viable were the tunes he sang?"

"He had a few names—a couple low ranking Nazi officers floating around Europe."

"Where am I headed? France? Italy?"

"The States."

"Your geography is getting poor, Levi."

"Well, he did have one name residing across the pond."

"Who's the target?" Jimmy asked casually.

Levi stared at Jimmy, his expression revealing the answer. Jimmy pushed his tea aside and leaned in.

"We've been without a lead for the past—"

"Five years," Levi breathed.

"Five years," Jimmy echoed.

"That's right."

"How can we trust Deiter isn't lying?"

"The name he gave me—Kristian Beckett—he claimed this is the alias our old nemesis has been using. I did some digging, made a few phone calls to our friends in New York, who made a few phone calls of their own." Levi took a sip of his tea and said, "I think we have something."

"Who's the intel coming from?" Jimmy asked.

"A survivor. Someone who recalls his face from the war. Spotted him when he stopped into the travel agency they work at in New York."

"A travel agency?"

"Kristian Beckett was planning a trip to Alaska."

"Any info on the reason?"

"Apparently he's going to be visiting a big game hunting lodge for the wealthy elite."

"How very appropriate. A Nazi with plans to kill something."

The practice of big game hunting had always disgusted Jimmy. The killing of animals for sport—he could find nothing pleasurable in the thought of it, and nothing admirable in those who did.

Levi pulled a leather folder from his cloth briefcase.

"And you trust the contact?" Jimmy asked.

"No. Not implicitly. She's old—older than me—and the mind starts to go, but it's still possible that what she's claiming is accurate." Levi flipped the folder open and spun it for Jimmy to see.

"The Caliber Lodge," Jimmy read.

Levi slid the folder across the table to his partner, who shuffled through the pages. He looked up at Levi with a more than confused expression.

"Non-disclosure agreements?"

"Apparently secrecy is of the utmost importance to their business plan," Levi elaborated.

"This seems excessive," Jimmy muttered as he read through the files. "These are witness protection level confidentiality documents. What could a big game hunting company possibly be doing to warrant this amount of paperwork?"

"I suppose you'll be able to find that out firsthand," Levi answered as Jimmy continued to go through the file. "I want to send you to this Caliber Lodge so you can determine whether or not our travel agent friend's old eyes are working correctly. You'll go under the guise of an oil tycoon heir. We'll pay your entry fee, have your false credentials, financials, and background fabricated."

Jimmy added another cube of sugar to his tea as Levi continued. "The owners of this hunting company are serious people. They do extensive checks on all the guests. Your acting skills will need to be on par."

Jimmy closed the file and slid it back to Levi who looked into Jimmy's eyes and said, "This could be our moment, my friend. This could be where we finally catch him."

"And the infamous Wilhelm Stengl notebook, the one that supposedly includes secret dossiers on all the members of the high command and their subordinates—you think he still has it?"

"It wasn't at the Inalco," Levi said as he hunched his shoulders. "So he *must*."

"If it's not him—"

Levi cut him off immediately. "Then we keep searching. We search until we find him. One lead or one thousand leads. It makes no difference. The outcome will be the same. We will capture Wilhelm Stengl."

Jimmy nodded his head. He wanted to believe Levi. He wanted to stay optimistic.

"Accurately identify him, report back to me, escort him—and hopefully the notebook—to the rendezvous point. Then it's over," Levi outlined.

"You make it sound so simple."

"Well, it is—very simple, in fact—but simple and easy are two different things." Levi watched as Jimmy's mind drifted, his eyes settling on the spinning tea in the white ceramic cup. "You still have enough chutzpah?"

Jimmy looked up at his partner. "Are you beginning to lose

faith in me, Levi?"

Levi smiled and the maze of wrinkles around his eyes squeezed together as he replied genuinely, "Not even an ounce."

He raised his cup of tea and waited for Jimmy to do the same so he could cheers him.

"Do you still carry it?" Levi asked.

"Every day."

"I pray you won't need it, but should you have the requirement, there would be no more fitting a weapon."

Jimmy was no stranger to using firearms, but he preferred not to do so. They made him nervous, uncomfortable, especially since the incident with the informant Mauro. He was a man of words and had never considered action to be one of his strong suits, despite the desperate moments in which he'd been forced to use them to survive.

Regardless of all that, Levi trusted him and had more belief in Jimmy's skills than Jimmy ever had in his own.

Levi leaned forward and asked him, "When was the last time you went mountain climbing?"

Chapter Four
THE GUESTS

The snowfall had already covered the last set of tire tracks by the time the oil black Bentley Continental came around the curve. A vehicle not made for mountain travel, any later into the season and the driver would not have been able to navigate the pine tree bordered road. This time of year, however, the driver was in luck.

Jimmy sat in the back, a long winter coat over the new expensive suit that Levi had bought him to fit the role, watching the reflection of the driver in the rearview mirror. He turned to look out the window at the snow-covered pine trees whipping by in a blur. They were all he had seen since they began their trip up the mountain.

The pines stretched so high that he had no way of gauging how far up they had traveled. The massive peak that he saw from the base was no longer visible. He couldn't even see the moon in the night sky, though its light managed to periodically pierce through gaps in the foliage.

It had been a week since his meeting with Levi in London, and now, after a few plane rides and a rough boat trip that resulted in a nauseating bout of seasickness, Jimmy was finally in the great Alaskan frontier.

After what seemed like another hour, the driver gave an "ahem" to get Jimmy's attention. A clearing appeared up ahead, and the Bentley emerged from the border of trees into the opening. A handsome, three-story lodge sat nestled on a plateau beneath the continuing kingdom of mountains.

It was a luxury manor, albeit one styled in a rustic mountain theme as though its owner were a frontiersman who had won the lottery. It had a pyramidal center accompanied by two opposing wings stretching out to the east and west. The wood looked polished —lacquered to pretentious degree—and every corner, edge and frame seemed to be intricately hand-carved with a sort of European filigree design.

Warm light glowed from the windows, some of which ran floor to ceiling for substantial lengths of the wings, illuminating the snowflakes as they fell upon the circular driveway where the Bentley slowed to a halt.

The driver exited the Bentley and hurried through the frigid air, around the front of the vehicle, to open the back passenger door for Jimmy, who stepped out and immediately shuddered in the breeze.

As he cinched the expensive scarf around his neck, he considered the way the immoderate material felt against his skin, something he was unaccustomed to. He was a working man, and he saw himself as such. These clothes said the opposite. These clothes said he paid others to do the work he considered himself to be above. In all physicality, the wardrobe of the fictional oil tycoon heir fit him perfectly, and Jimmy knew that this uniform was necessary to pull off the intended guise, but regardless of the soothing touch, he always felt more comfortable with a bit of dirt and dust on his clothes.

He grinned as he thought about Levi's meticulous nature, having strained over every detail from the hem of Jimmy's jackets to the origin of his suitcase. The Austrian was a stickler for details, a talent Jimmy envied not only because of the patience required to execute, but because it helped keep Jimmy alive in situations such as the one he was about to walk into.

The double front doors of the lodge opened gently and Jimmy and his driver turned to see the raven-haired woman in the gray conservative dress step out into the frigid air. She smiled with closed lips, her hands crossed in front of her.

"Welcome to the Caliber Lodge, Mr. Knotts."

Jimmy strolled up the front steps and extended a hand.

"Mrs. Everly. Thank you for having me."

Mrs. Everly shook his hand. For a woman in her early 60s, she still carried herself like one in her prime. Her raven hair was pulled back tightly in a bun, every strand perfectly in place. Her collar was high, her sleeves long. On her left hand, Jimmy noticed a wedding ring, unpolished, tarnished. From what Levi had told Jimmy about Mrs. Everly prior to his arrival, he distinctly recalled the fact that she was a widow, and had been for several years now.

"How was your travel?" she asked him. He gave her the details including his lack of enthusiasm for boat rides but assured her of his excitement to finally be at the Caliber Lodge.

The driver unloaded the suitcase from the trunk of the Bentley and hurriedly shuffled over to Mrs. Everly and Jimmy as they conversed. "Please. Come inside," Everly insisted, and ushered Jimmy into the warmth of the lodge interior.

The driver's gaze drifted to a rack of glossy caribou antlers above the front door. Mrs. Everly snapped sharply at him and motioned to follow with a flick of her wrist. He jumped to it.

The inside of the Caliber Lodge looked like a billionaire's idea of what it meant to be "rustic". The lustrous wooden foyer stretched upward and came to a point in the center, with massive wooden chandeliers, adorned with antlers, hanging down in a tiered fashion. It looked like the great hall of a nobleman's palace—one obsessed with the wilds of America.

An oil painting of the lodge itself hung on the wall to their left, mounted within a sculpted frame that Jimmy imagined was, at the very least, coated in a layer of solid gold. Beneath the painting, a series of vases with what looked like Inuit cave drawings sat on smooth tree stump pillars, spaced five feet apart down the length of the wall.

Around the foyer were a series of rooms, each with their own set of double doors. A few were closed, the rest open and inviting. Jimmy looked past Mrs. Everly and through one of the doorways he could see a lounge area with leather chairs and an antler rimmed coffee table supporting a record player spinning its flat vinyl disc. It crooned out a jazzy tune.

On the opposite end of the foyer from the front door was an ornate, bronze elevator with a frame made of an intricate weave of glistening metal. The elevator led to the visible second and third levels of the lodge where the guest rooms were located. A shiny wooden railing ran along each of those floors, allowing visiting guests the ability to look over and get an unobstructed view of the magnificent foyer below.

"This way, please."

Mrs. Everly led them over to the elevator, and the three of them stepped aboard. The driver pulled the gate closed.

"Third floor," Everly said. The two men looked at one another. The driver looked to Mrs. Everly, who was already staring back at him, waiting. "Third flood," she repeated.

The driver glanced at Jimmy, who nodded at him. He sighed and yanked the lever to begin the ascent. The looseness of the metal weave allowed Jimmy to see out as they rose higher.

"How large is your staff, Mrs. Everly?" Jimmy inquired.

"We are fully prepared to handle any of your needs, Mr. Knotts. This is a luxury lodge and you will receive the highest level of satisfaction during your stay here."

"I'm not used to the owner of such an establishment being the one to take me to my room."

"I do recognize that we are a tad unorthodox here at the Caliber but I assure you we are no less suited to meet your needs. I greet every guest at the door. I feel like an introduction to the owner right off the bat lets our guests know that they are my number one priority here."

When they reached the third floor, the driver pulled the gate open and Mrs. Everly led the way down the hall. As Jimmy followed he looked down over the railing and questioned whether or not at this height he'd still be able to see his reflection in the glassy floor below.

He could.

After passing two closed guest room doors, Mrs. Everly stopped in front of a third at the end of the hall. She pulled a key she had kept tucked neatly behind the fabric belt around her waist and unlocked the handle. She softly swung the door open and said, "This is you. Take your time settling in and come down when you're ready. We are still waiting on two more guests before we begin the evening's activities."

With that, she handed Jimmy the key and looked to the suitcase in the driver's hand. "You may set that there."

Everly turned and headed back down the hallway toward the elevator. The driver waited for permission from Jimmy, which came in the form of another nod. Jimmy watched from the railing as Mrs. Everly led the driver down the elevator and back out the front door.

Inside the room, Jimmy shrugged off his long winter coat and hung it on the antler coatrack behind the door. He pulled the sheer curtain back to look out the window. His room had a view of the driveway below, through which he watched the driver get back into the Bentley and cruise away from the lodge.

He was on his own now, but that's what Jimmy had always preferred. Larger numbers drew too much attention, and in Jimmy's field of investigation it was a benefit to go unnoticed and unquestioned.

He pulled off his tie and unbuttoned his dress shirt, then flopped his suitcase atop the end of the bed. Popping it open, he lifted a stack of neatly folded shirts out to reveal the Argentine Ballester-Molina service pistol he had acquired from Mauro. He regarded it for a moment, its wooden grip and tarnished metal barrel, then quickly covered it back up with a pair of dress slacks.

He walked into the bathroom and spun the brass knobs to turn on the shower, and as steam filled the room, he caught only a glimpse of himself in the mirror before the image was washed away.

Smoke billowed from the exhaust pipe on the ruby red Chevy Bel Air as it cruised up the road toward the lodge. Behind the wheel, the elderly chauffeur tried to focus on the treacherous road as the sounds from the backseat fluttered in his ears.

A young couple in their mid-twenties were in the midst of a passionate embrace behind him. The woman, Betty Blackwell, was blonde and spindly, her hair done up in waves and curls. She wore a cream-colored evening gown and a gleaming wedding ring on her finger with a diamond the size of an almond.

Her husband of less than twenty-four hours, David Blackwell, was dressed in a sharp suit and tie. A shiny gold ring adorned his own finger. He lifted Betty, and she straddled herself over his lap.

The chauffeur cleared his throat. "We are almost—"

Betty giggled as David nuzzled her neck. The chauffeur, through his extreme discomfort, attempted to get their attention again.

"It's not much further to—"

More giggles from Betty cut through his words.

"Not much further to the lodge, folks."

Betty and David continued to ignore the old man. His eyes watched them in the rearview mirror.

He contemplated the choices he'd made in life to get him to this point—driving around the children of the snobbish elite. He wondered if he had ever been so brazen in his younger years. Sure, he'd run over a few krauts in the war with his tank and he'd run his bayonet through a couple bundles of guts—but that was over twenty years ago, and even at that time he was past his youth.

He was never a ladies' man before the old dubya-dubya-two, and after his experiences there he never fully recovered mentally enough to become one after the fact. Those memories were always keeping him from having an agreeable time. He'd often lose himself in his thoughts—just drift away into the back of his head, like floating through a hazy cloud of bloody images. He'd get stuck there for a bit until something jerked him back into reality.

The chauffeur's eyes snapped away from the rearview mirror just in time to see the creature standing ahead of them on the road. He slammed his foot down on the brake pedal and the tires of the Chevy Bel Air locked in place. The vehicle slid a few yards further, the treads barely catching in the snow. Betty and David flew forward, banging against the front seats.

"Christ!" David shouted. He pulled his bride up off the floor of the car and helped her back into her seat. "What the hell are you doing?"

The chauffeur's sights narrowed on an arctic fox standing fearlessly in the road. The small white critter stared back at the old man with its smooth, black eyes. Its small tongue flicked across its furry nose, knocking off some of the snowflakes that had accumulated. When the chauffeur failed to answer the question, David and Betty looked out through the windshield and noted the fox.

"You nearly killed us. For that thing? Run the beast over and let's get moving," David groaned.

Betty chimed in, "I've never seen a white fox."

"If my rifle was readily available, I'd make you a nice stole." He kissed her deeply. They both closed their eyes during the embrace and David swatted at the back of the chauffeur's head.

The old man slowly applied pressure to the gas pedal and the car crunched forward through the snow toward the fox. The animal still did not move, even as the Chevy chugged toward it. Its eyes remained a steely calm, and the chauffeur was forced to slowly steer the vehicle around the fox as it remained in place on the road.

As the Bel Air churned back to its previous speed, the chauffeur once again looked in the rearview mirror, this time at the fuzzy white predator behind them. The fox's head turned slowly, and it watched the car until it disappeared around the bend.

Jimmy, dressed in a fancy evening suit, had just stepped out of his room when Mrs. Everly invited David and Betty Blackwell into the foyer. He heard the raven-haired owner deliver her lines, just as she had done for Jimmy when he arrived.

"Oh my God! David, it's amazing!" Betty shouted as she strolled into the lodge.

"It is, isn't it? Very rustic, yet somehow glamorous at the same time," David replied as he took in the beauty of the open hall. The chauffeur stumbled in behind them, struggling greatly while carrying half a dozen matching suitcases in his arms.

"If you'd like to follow me this way, I can show you to your room," Everly offered.

"Our room? I want to see the rest of this place. Not our room," Betty exclaimed with excitement.

"Of course. Feel free to venture around in that case. I'll escort your chauffeur so that your bags will be waiting for you when you need them."

Betty pulled her husband by the hand and skipped away deeper into the lodge out of Jimmy's sight.

Mrs. Everly sharply gestured for the elderly chauffeur to follow her. Jimmy watched sympathetically as the old man strained to open the elevator gate while still juggling the luggage. He hustled down the hallway to meet them as the elevator reached the third floor and pulled open the gate. The chauffeur nodded at Jimmy and smiled, all the while wincing under the weight of the bags.

"How is your room, Mr. Knotts?" Mrs. Everly asked.

"Just fine, thank you."

Mrs. Everly headed down the other side of the third floor to the open hallway opposite Jimmy's room.

"Come along," she scolded the old man as he dropped one of the bags.

"Oh, dear," the chauffeur moaned.

"Let me help you with those." Jimmy picked up the bag and took two more out of the old man's arms. Mrs. Everly watched the scene unfold with a surprised expression.

"I'm sure he can manage, Mr. Knotts."

"It's no bother." Jimmy helped the chauffeur down the hallway to the Blackwells' room.

"Thank you, Mr. Knotts. We've got it from here," Everly assured him.

"Really. It's fine."

"Go enjoy yourself downstairs. I insist."

Jimmy hesitated for a moment and reminded himself that was here to play a role. His true personality was seeping through, and it was far too early to take any sort of risk that may expose him.

"Take it easy, old-timer," Jimmy said as he patted the

chauffeur on the back, then strolled back down the hall. Through the woven metal of the elevator gate, Jimmy saw the chauffeur smile at him once more, as Everly instructed the old man to pick up his pace.

Jimmy stepped out of the elevator into the foyer and spied what appeared to be a bar top through one of the open sets of double doors. He grinned and headed toward it. He was nearly there when a voice from behind caused him to stop.

"Excuse me, sir."

Jimmy spun around to see a man in his 60s wearing a penguin suit with coattails. His hair was white and slicked back with grease. A convincing smile was plastered across his face as he said, "I wanted to introduce myself. I'm Gregory. The butler."

Jimmy extended his hand and replied, "Jimmy Knotts."

Gregory hesitated before shaking, not used to the crude gesture. "Nice to meet you, sir."

"Likewise."

"Were you headed to the bar, Mr. Knotts?"

"I was indeed."

"Could I prepare a cocktail for you?"

"Gregory, that sounds lovely."

From behind the bar top, Gregory handed Jimmy a cocktail menu. "I've hand selected an assortment of cocktail choices for yourself and the other guests, but should you prefer something off menu you are, of course, welcome to whatever you're craving."

"What would you suggest, Gregory?" Jimmy asked as he pursued the menu.

"The *Very* Old Fashioned, sir. A fun twist on the popular cocktail, made with Very Old Fitzgerald bourbon, a particular favorite of mine."

"I'll go with your recommendation then."

Gregory mixed up the drink in a hand-blown glass and gently slid it across the polished wood to Jimmy, who nodded a thank you and took a sip. He closed his eyes, savoring it.

"I'd like to thank the man who taught you to mix a drink."

"An acquired skill, sir. Over many years."

Jimmy took another sip. It was just as tasty as the first.

"How long have you been with the Caliber Lodge, Gregory?"

"Ten years next month, sir."

Gregory had first met Mrs. Everly and her late husband, Charles, twenty years ago, and it was ten years after that when they'd offered him the position at the Caliber when the establishment had first opened.

Initially, Mr. and Mrs. Everly had met Gregory while he was working as a bar manager in an upper-crust, posh steakhouse in Billings, Montana. Gregory had come out from England to help his cousin, who owned the restaurant, after his cousin was forced to fire his original bar manager when it came to light that a series of incidents involving disappearing cases of whiskey ended up leading to an inside job. Gregory stepped in and got things back on track. He ran a tight ship and handled both the financial and guest service sides of the bar for his overwhelmed cousin.

One evening in 1945, the Everlys stopped into the steakhouse after an enthralling day of big game hunting in the Montana wilderness. They were still running off the fumes of adrenaline after gunning down a ten-point buck—the "thrill of the kill" as Charles Everly liked to call it.

They shared the tale of the hunt with Gregory as they sat at his bar sipping on what they would later recall to be the best gin martinis they had ever set lips on.

It was Mrs. Everly's lips, however, that Gregory struggled to keep his eyes off of. Her beauty was intoxicating to the point that

Gregory had nearly forgotten all about his other guests. She had just crossed into her 40s but didn't look a day over 30. Her jet black hair spilled over her shoulders, strands cascading across her pronounced collar bone. Gregory caught himself staring and hoped that Mr. Everly hadn't noticed.

Charles Everly was pushing his mid-40s. He had a strong jaw covered in a two-day beard. He'd showered after the hunt, of course, but didn't bother shaving. He rarely shaved. It was his way of staying connected to his rugged side while dressed to the nines. His collar hung open, a deep red ascot around his neck. His cufflinks—golden owls—clicked on the bar top as he reached for his martini. He touched his wife's leg sensually as they all conversed.

Gregory's job was to make people feel welcome, make them feel like honored guests, albeit ones that had to pay for that honor. The Everlys had money to throw around, and they had grown accustomed to paying for attention. And affection.

Gregory's hair had just begun to salt and pepper around the temples on the evening he met the Everlys at the steakhouse. He had always been fit. Running around his place of employ, constantly on his feet, hustle had always been the name of the game in Gregory's world. He completed marathons daily, but one would never see a bead of sweat upon his brow because of it.

The Everlys spent the remainder of the evening at Gregory's bar, laughing and joking. At closing time Mrs. Everly casually placed her hand over Gregory's on the bar top. Gregory flinched at first, his eyes darting over to Mr. Everly, but when he saw that Charles was all too comfortable with the situation, he let his hand stay beneath Mrs. Everly's palm.

The three of them ended the night in the Everlys' hotel room down the road, and as Charles sat and watched, he saw not just one but many beads of sweat on Gregory's brow.

Of course, Gregory didn't share any of that with his recent

acquaintance Jimmy Knotts. He left it with the simple explanation that he'd worked at the Caliber Lodge since day one.

Jimmy glanced around the room. The decor was the same in every part of the lodge: wood, antlers, animal hide. Jimmy motioned to the fireplace on the other side of the room.

"Nice touch."

"There are six in the whole lodge, sir."

"Easy to keep this place warm then."

Gregory came around from behind the bar. "Have you met the other guests yet, Mr. Knotts?"

"I haven't had the pleasure."

"Would you like me to introduce you?"

The record player in the lounge was now playing a smooth classic symphony. The logs in the fireplace popped and crackled as the end of an iron poker stabbed into their flesh. Kristian Beckett, the man for whom Jimmy had traveled so far to investigate, stood hunched over the hearth, prodding and twisting the poker into the softening wood. He was a slender man in his early 50s, his face weathered far beyond his age. When he straightened back up, he sensed Gregory standing in the doorway behind him.

"Mr. Kristian Beckett. May I introduce you to Mr. James Knotts?" Gregory said as he guided Jimmy into the lounge.

Jimmy stepped through the doorway beside Gregory just as Kristian turned to them.

That name—Kristian Beckett—was the name Jimmy had been waiting to hear since he arrived at the Caliber Lodge. He searched Kristian's face and waited to hear his voice, hoping for a German accent.

Kristian nodded at Gregory, who gave a slight bow and

backed away out of the room. Jimmy casually strolled further into the lounge and said, "Jimmy's fine, actually." He extended his hand to shake, but Kristian brushed past him on his way to the record player. "People don't like to shake around here,."

"Have you a need to touch me?" The accent sounded American, specifically Midwest, just like Jimmy's. There was no trace of a Bavarian brogue in Kristian's voice at all.

"Just being—"

"Being what?" Kristian interrupted.

Jimmy focused harder, listening. He raised his glass and took a sip of his cocktail. He had never seen a clear photo of Wilhelm Stengl. There wasn't one. Only blurred images that showed little more than a hazy figure in a German uniform. Word of mouth and low quality images were all Levi and his team had to work with in the ongoing hunt for the Nazi war criminal. Levi's words echoed in Jimmy's mind.

Accurately identify him, report back to me, escort him to the rendezvous point and it's over.

Kristian switched the record out and a more lively tune, Elvis Presley's "Return to Sender" popped on.

Kristian looked over his shoulder at Jimmy. "What are you drinking?"

"Very Old Fashioned. Can I get you one?"

Kristian gave a lazy wave.

"You sound like you're from the Midwest," Kristian said as he leaned over the high back of one of the chairs.

"You have a keen ear, Mr. Beckett. I grew up in Nebraska."

"A farm boy?"

"My father owns an oil company, actually. His father before him."

"Oil. You developed a taste for hunting out of boredom then? I imagine you haven't needed to work a day in your life with your father's funds."

"That's a big assumption, Mr. Beckett. And what about yourself? From where do you hail?"

A high-pitched giggle echoed from the foyer and Kristian and Jimmy turned to see Betty and David enter the room arm in arm.

"Oh! You must be the other guests!" Betty exclaimed at the sight of them.

"Jimmy, ma'am."

"We're the Blackwells. I'm Betty. This is my husband David."

Jimmy shook David's hand. "Nice to meet you both." Jimmy gestured to Kristian. "This fellow beside me is Mr. Beckett." Kristian shot Jimmy an annoyed look for the introduction.

"Kristian," he corrected.

"And how long have each of you been here?" David asked.

"I arrived shortly before the two of you."

"Just lovely!" Betty's excitement was still at its peak. The grandeur of the lodge and the situation itself had not faded an ounce in her eyes. She looked to Kristian for a response.

"About four hours, I suppose," he said as if straining to push out the words and engage.

Betty placed her hand on David's chest. "We're on our honeymoon! David's uncle paid our entry fee as a wedding gift!"

"Newlyweds! Congratulations!" Jimmy raised his glass.

Mrs. Everly's voice sliced through the conversation.

"Wonderful. I see you've all been acquainted." She walked up between David and Betty, her hand gently wrapping around their waists. "And I imagine after your journey none of you would dare turn down tonight's dinner."

The walls and floor of the dining room were lined with a much darker wood than the rest of the lodge, and the way the overly long dining table in the center of room blended in, it seemed to be made of the same type.

"African Blackwood," Gregory had explained when he served them their apéritif. "Mrs. Everly's favorite."

Betty and David sat across the table from one another, neither able to keep from smiling. The newlywed bliss was seeping from their pores as they ate the meticulously prepared moose steaks in front of them.

Kristian sat beside David, slicing through the grilled asparagus on his plate. He inspected each piece before sliding it into his mouth. Jimmy tried to act casual as he focused on every move Kristian made, looking for any indication to sway him one way or the other. He was sitting beside Betty, and he could smell her undoubtedly expensive perfume with every breath he took.

Jimmy asked her, "Your uncle, the one who paid for your visit here, what's he do?"

"David's uncle. Well, I guess technically he is my uncle now too." She looked at David. "Right, hun?" They smiled brightly at one another. "He's in the coal business."

"Owns a mining company," David elaborated.

"He came here a few years ago. Said it was the best weekend of his life." Betty took a bite of the steak.

Kristian finished chewing. "What else did he say about it?"

David cut off another piece of moose and answered. "Not much. The non-disclosure agreement saw to that. But he was adamant that we experience it for ourselves. The big game hunting experience of a lifetime, he called it."

Betty turned to Jimmy. "How did you hear about the lodge, Jimmy?"

"A friend of my father's from the oil world."

"Your father is in the oil business?" David asked.

"Whole family is. Myself included."

"Good business to be in."

"Indeed."

"And what about your father's friend's suggestion to visit this place intrigued you the most?" Betty inquired.

"I think we're all looking for something. We're all hunting for excitement. He told me I'd find it here and fronted the tab as an early birthday gift."

"Expensive gift," David remarked.

"He's a generous guy," Jimmy spouted as he moved the moose meat around his plate, unwilling to take a bite. He sliced up his asparagus and stuck with his vegetarian diet despite the role he was playing.

"Generous and wealthy," David corrected.

Jimmy wiped his mouth with the fine linen in his lap. "That would be an accurate description. I assume my father's friend and your uncle would be a dangerous combination."

"An oil man and a coal king. Seems appropriate," David chuckled. "What's your father's friend's name. Maybe I know him."

Kristian piped up with a condescending, "You know all wealthy men, Blackwell?"

"Well no, obviously not."

"But you think you may know this friend of his?"

"I'm just making conversation, Mr. Beckett."

Kristian scoffed.

Betty spoke up defensively. "And what is it you do, Mr. Beckett?"

Jimmy's expression did not betray him as he eagerly awaited Kristian's response.

"I'm a banker." The vagueness in all of Kristian's responses was a good sign. The unwillingness to give a straight answer is exactly what Jimmy would expect from a man in hiding.

"A banker?" Betty asked.

"That's right."

"With what bank?"

"I handle a lot of very important peoples' very important accounts. Let's leave it at that."

"The ominousness of it all is so intriguing, is it not, my love?" David joked.

Kristian let his fork and knife drop on the table and asked David, "Are you finished?"

"I'm only trying to inject a bit of levity into the evening, Mr. Beckett. No offense intended." David raised his glass to Kristian.

"Let me ask you all something," Kristian said, ignoring the half-hearted apology. "What is it about this expedition that could possibly warrant the cost? And the secrecy?"

David went back to chopping at his food. "It's gotta be a bear hunt. Polar bears or Kodiak. Biggest game in North America."

Kristian inquired, "And the non-disclosures?"

"A marketing tactic. Drums up the excitement. If something is exclusive, it's gotta be better, right?" Jimmy engaged.

Kristian flicked a bit of fat off his plate and Jimmy had to lean to the side to avoid the flying niblet. Kristian started, "If I paid what I paid just to hunt a damn bear—"

David interjected, "What else would it be? Caribou? That's certainly not worth the price."

The double doors swung open, and Mrs. Everly entered the room. "Does everyone have what they need?" she asked as her hands gently perched upon the back of the empty chair at the head of the table.

David took a sip of his wine. "Just perfect."

Betty adjusted in her seat. "Maybe Mrs. Everly can enlighten us."

"In what respect, Mrs. Blackwell?"

"Is it polar bear? That we'll be hunting, I mean."

Mrs. Everly grinned and took a seat at the head of the dark table. "That's a wonderful inquiry, my dear. And one I intend to answer, but before we proceed with the increasingly enjoyable parts of the evening I'd like to go through the agreement with you all once more."

Gregory swiftly swooped into the room and set an empty wineglass on the table in front of Mrs. Everly and promptly filled it from the swan-like decanter in the center of the table. Without a single word, he disappeared back through the door.

Mrs. Everly raised her glass and toasted the group. "Now. You've all filled out the legal agreements with our lawyers prior to arriving. This is simply a recap if you will. Part of being accepted to partake in this weekend was the understanding and legally binding acceptance that none of you are allowed to discuss, whether verbally or in writing, what goes on here. Should you break that agreement and disclose any information to the outside world about your experience, other than to say you enjoyed yourself, you and those who covered your payment will be held liable for such a drastic amount of money, that even your families fortunes combined could not front the bill.

"Now, this is not a threat. This is just me stating the need for secrecy. The mystery around this lodge allows us to stay in business. So please, do nothing to endanger our livelihood."

Everly made eye contact with each of the guests at the table and asked, "Is everyone in agreement to stick to the terms?"

Jimmy watched the expressions on the other guests' faces as they one by one nodded in compliance. Jimmy nodded as well.

"Good," Everly said. "You all come from wealth and because of that you've been able to afford the steep price tag that I've placed on this luxurious getaway, but believe me when I assure you, it will be well worth your money."

With that, Everly stood up and pushed her chair back in. She took a moment to look at each of them, Betty and David, Kristian and Jimmy. "When you've all finished with dinner I'd like to invite you to to meet the most integral member of the staff."

Kristian immediately pushed his plate aside and stood with Everly. Betty and David did the same. Their excitement far outweighed whatever room they had left in their stomachs.

Jimmy quickly finished his greens and grabbed a dinner roll from the wooden bowl in the center of the table. He took a bite before standing up with the others, knowing that he'd need every ounce to try to soak up the Very Old Fashioned that he was still milking.

Gregory pulled the double doors of the dining room open and gestured professionally for them to once again step out into the foyer.

"If you'd all be kind enough to follow me to the game room."

Chapter Five
THE CRIMSON BOX

Taxidermy lined the pink ivory wood panel walls of the game room. The lifeless, doll-like eyes of the dead animals seemed to stare at each of the guests as they entered the warmth of the claustrophobic area. Mrs. Everly led the way, sweeping her arm out in a grandiose introductory gesture as she introduced the man of the hour.

"I'd like to introduce you all to Mr. Jonathan Turk."

Leaning over a gaudy pool table lined in burgundy felt, about to knock the seven ball into a corner pocket, was Jonathan Turk. He wore a full khaki outfit like one would don for an African safari. His sleeves were rolled up to his meaty biceps, exposing his tan, vascular arms. The bottoms of his pant legs were stuffed into heavy brown boots, each with a tread like a tank. He had a chin like a shovel, and a movie star smile reminiscent of Cary Grant.

He straightened up, laid the cue across the table and said, "Welcome to the game room." His charismatic voice rumbled low and confident like a rolling thunder.

Betty's lack of a poker face was immediately apparent. This embodiment of masculinity before them left her without words. David noticed, though he pretended not to, and was the first to respond.

"I'm Mr. Blackwell," he puffed his chest. "Nice to meet you."

"David Blackwell. Yes. And this lovely flower could be none other than your wife of only a few hours, Betty."

Betty seemed taken aback. "How did you—"

Turk jumped in before she could finish. "I'm fully aware of who you all are. Mrs. Everly provides me with detailed backgrounds on all of our guests. It's part of my job to know you inside and out." Betty blushed at the thought.

Turk walked around to their side of the pool table and patted Kristian on the shoulder with one of his bear paw sized palms.

"Kristian Beckett. Banker of the opulent." Turk smiled from ear to ear. Kristian tried to read past his charming facade as he moved onto Jimmy.

Jimmy extended a hand to shake. Turk's hand swallowed Jimmy's, and shook it enthusiastically. "Jimmy Knotts. Mr. Oil himself."

David, on the defense, tried to act casual by looking around the room at the various dead animal busts. The walls were covered from waist height to the ceiling in moose, deer, caribou and antelope. Mounted above the stone fireplace was the head of a hippopotamus, its mouth hanging open, displaying its massive incisors that were nearly two feet long.

In the corner closest to the doorway, was a faux rock formation with deceased predators. A lion stood at the top, its mane a billowing, dense perimeter around its snarling head. Below the lion was a bengal tiger and an arctic fox identical to the one that David's chauffeur had nearly run over on the way up to the lodge. Beside the tiger, standing on its hind legs, was a grizzly bear, its claws raised in an aggressive stance, its mouth open as though it died while bellowing out a mighty roar.

Mrs. Everly spoke up, "Mr. Turk will be your expedition leader during your stay."

Turk had picked up on David's discomfort and said, "How are you enjoying your honeymoon? Good, so far?"

"We're having a marvelous time," Betty chirped. David

nodded.

"Very good. We'd be doing a poor job here if you weren't enjoying yourselves." Turk walked over to a globe-shaped minibar and popped open the top to reveal a brandy decanter and six glasses.

"Gentlemen, and lady, as I said before, this is the game room, or trophy room as some like to call it. Now, I know that some of you have experience in hunting and some of you don't, but regardless of your level of experience, trust me when I tell you that after this weekend, you'll have done something ninety-nine point ninety-nine percent of all other hunters on this beautiful Earth have not."

"Which is what exactly?" Kristian asked. "Your company has promised the hunting expedition of a lifetime. Just how do you intend to deliver on that?"

Turk picked up the decanter and filled each of the glasses with the rosy, caramel colored liquor. He motioned at the Very Old Fashioned in Jimmy's hand. "Better finish that up, cowboy. Gonna be ready for this brandy in a second."

Jimmy cooly finished his cocktail.

"How we intend to deliver on that promise, Mr. Beckett, is I'll take you up, deep into the mountains, and you'll hunt something no one else on Earth gets to hunt."

David used his index finger to roll one of the pool balls across the table. "And that is?"

Turk passed out the glasses of brandy. Everyone took theirs with the exception of Mrs. Everly, who politely refused. Turk poured the contents of hers into his own.

"Nations across the world have called them by many names. Here in the great white North they're known as Sasquatch."

Silence fell over the room. The guests waited for Turk to elaborate on the preposterous notion. Then Betty chortled, "Sasquatch?"

"That's right. You're going to hunt Sasquatch."

The patience drained from David as he sounded off with, "Is this a fucking joke? My uncle paid good money for—"

"And you'll get his worth out of it," Turk assured confidently.

Kristian leaned over the table toward Turk. "And when you say Sasquatch…"

"I'm of course referring to the large, hairy, ape-like, human-esque creature that is floating around all of your minds right now. Bigfoot." Turk swirled the brandy in his glass. "Stories of wild men are quite common throughout history, yet no proven evidence has been found—save for the truth we've uncovered on this mountain."

Jimmy set his glass on the edge of the pool table. The notion sounded ridiculous to him. He had heard the term before—Sasquatch—and he knew they were nothing but myth. If they existed, there would have been evidence, either photographic or physical, to prove it. Turk had to be pulling their leg. He expected that any minute the man in the Safari getup and the woman with the raven hair would start laughing and reveal the entire thing to be nothing but a joke.

"Surely you can't be serious," Betty said.

In a bout of unrestrained rage, David hurled his full glass of brandy against the wall. It shattered, sending shards of razor sharp fragments and a shower of liquor through the air.

"I will not stand here and listen to your bullshit about some mythic creature in the mountains! Now either tell us what we're really doing on this expedition or give me my uncle's money back!" His chest heaved, adrenaline coated in anger coursing through his body. "We came here to hunt, not to be told amusing anecdotes."

"Mr. Blackwell!" The volume of her own voice immediately caused Mrs. Everly to take a moment to collect herself. She gently touched her chest as though she were physically suppressing her tone as she continued. "David. I know how this sounds. I know. But Mr. Turk is telling you the whole-hearted truth. I've seen them. Many times. Your uncle saw them when he was here. It's the reason he insisted you come."

Betty had moved in closer to Turk when David smashed his glass against the wood paneling. She asked, "If there was such a thing as a Bigfoot, wouldn't other people know about it?"

It became clear to Jimmy seconds before Mrs. Everly explained, "The harsh non-disclosure agreement—the one that you all signed with your lawyers prior to arriving—that's why we've been able to keep their existence hidden from the outside world. Everyone who's come to the Caliber Lodge, embarked on an expedition with Mr. Turk and hunted one of them, has remained silent afterward."

Turk strolled over toward the fireplace and the looming hippopotamus above it. "The creatures live on this mountain. They have for as long as we can tell. And Mrs. Everly owns the mountain."

"Why would they stay if they're being hunted by the people who come to this place? Why not leave the mountain?" Betty asked.

"They must realize it's still safer than anywhere else. We don't over hunt. We make sure to only kill a few each year. That way their population won't dwindle."

Jimmy asked, "How many of these things are you saying there are?"

David muttered under his breath, "There aren't any. This is nonsense."

Jimmy noticed that Kristian was unusually quiet considering the story they had all just been told. He seemed to be content, maybe relieved even, as if he had been expecting to hear the word "Sasquatch" since he arrived, and now that it had been spoken aloud he could relax.

Turk reached above the fireplace and lifted a glossy, crimson red, wooden box from the mantel. It was a perfect square, large enough to store a bowling ball inside. He gently set it down on the burgundy felt of the table and all the guests' eyes fell upon it.

"Tomorrow morning we'll begin the expedition. I'll take you out over the ridge to get a good look at the bowl. You'll see then you've not been swindled."

Everyone's gaze was glued to the shiny, red box as Turk spoke. Even David had now given over his full attention. Like the floor in the foyer, the box was polished to where they could see their reflection in it.

Turk rested one hand atop the lid as he continued, "But to give you some peace of mind that we here at the Caliber Lodge have not taken advantage of you, and to keep Mr. Blackwell from wasting anymore good brandy…"

Betty could no longer contain herself. "What is it?"

Turk lifted the lid of the crimson box, revealing the blue velvet lining inside. He reached in and gently removed something with both hands.

Taking a slow step back, Betty reached blindly for her husband's hand. Jimmy's mouth hung agape. Kristian's eyes grew wider.

Cradled in Turk's open palms was a dome-shaped object covered in what appeared to be gray fur—but upon closer inspection wasn't gray at all, but a blend of white and brown strands, like human hair. It was roughly three quarters the size of a watermelon and around its flat base appeared to be frayed pieces of dried flesh.

"This, the soon to be christened Mrs. Blackwell, is the scalp of a Sasquatch."

Later that evening, after Turk had assured them all that more excitement was in store after everyone got a good night's rest, Kristian asked Gregory the butler to make him a Very Old Fashioned. He had wanted to give it a try since he first saw Jimmy sipping on one earlier, but was too proud to ask for one of his own at the time.

He walked to the lounge and took a seat in one of the high-backed leather chairs positioned in front of the fireplace. As he raised the glass to his lips he became lost in deep thought and almost spilled down his chin. His head snapped around, making sure he was still alone in the room.

One of Kristian's constant and conscious goals was to make sure he was never seen doing anything embarrassing. He was a stoic man, concerned immensely with other peoples' opinions of him. He did not want to be liked. He wanted to be feared. He worked hard to exude an aura of mysterious danger and felt there were few things worse than being thought a fool of. Even then, after seeing the scalp, his image was still a concern.

He considered the possibility that the macho man in the safari outfit could be telling the truth.

Could there truly be an ape-man wandering the Alaskan mountains?

That would certainly be worth the fee he'd paid to come to the Caliber Lodge, and it explained the amount of secrecy behind everything.

Kristian had seen things before.

Things that he could not explain. Things he was apprehensive to share with others for fear of ridicule.

He had kept those things to himself for years and had often times almost convinced himself they didn't happen. Turk's revelation in the game room, however, had shaken the foundation of his memories and he dwelt on the images of his past experience.

One of the logs in the fireplace sparked and crackled as the embers burned white hot. He thought for a moment that he could hear something within the flames. A soft whisper of a voice. He leaned in closer to the hearth as the whisper grew louder. The voice sped up to a frantic, frightened pace.

The volume of the shrieks swelled, and the echoes of screams blasted from the fire. Kristian leaned away, as far back in the chair as he could get. His eyes focused on the dancing flames.

Then everything was silent again.

Kristian relaxed into a slouch in the chair. He exhaled deeply, relieved, and took another sip of his cocktail.

Meanwhile, on the third floor of the Caliber Lodge, David lied on his back in the lavish, four-poster bed in their honeymoon suite. Betty was straddled on top of him, riding him hard. He looked up at her, but her eyes were closed, her head arched back, lost in thought. David wondered who she was thinking about but quickly tried to pull his mind elsewhere when it became all too apparent who was intruding in his wife's head.

He didn't mind all that much. So long as Betty was in his room, it didn't really matter who she dreamed about. David was still the one reaping the benefits. That's what he told himself, anyway.

Though both of their families were wealthy, Betty's held the esteem of having the larger bank account. He needed to keep her happy. At the very least, he needed to keep her family happy.

He felt maybe he overreacted in the game room when he threw his brandy against the wall. It was an embarrassing moment of weakness on his part, and he didn't like the way it made Betty look at him. He was on his honeymoon after all, and a vacation was a vacation no matter how you sliced it—but it would still feel good to make that khaki-wearing, strong jawed ladies man look like a fool in front of Betty if he could prove it was all a lie.

He tried to stay hard as his mind drifted back to the sight of that dome-shaped scalp that Turk had shown them. It looked real, but there was no way for David to say for sure. He'd seen some strange sights during his travels, and he'd heard tell of obscure oddities the likes of this Sasquatch creature, but never had he believed any of it. To see the pointed, hairy flesh in Turk's hands jarred him. He attempted to think of ways he could disprove its authenticity in the morning.

On the other side of the third floor, Jimmy sat in his room at the end of the bed, staring out the window at the snowy mountain wilderness surrounding the lodge. He'd come there to determine whether Kristian Beckett was truly Wilhelm Stengl, the Nazi war criminal he'd been trailing since South America, and this new development was taking up more of his attention than he was comfortable with.

He'd been morally against joining in on a big game hunting expedition since Levi first brought it up back in London, but he was willing to play the part because he knew it could mean finally brining Stengl to justice. While hunting a Nazi was commendable, hunting and killing a helpless animal wasn't sporting, and he knew there was no enjoyment or sense of accomplishment in it either. The thought of murdering a creature that was so rare that most people were unaware of its existence was even less appealing to him.

He put a stop to his wandering mind when he realized he was already accepting the possibility that the creatures Turk told them about actually existed. It was far-fetched, but Jimmy had certainly seen unbelievable things before.

The sun rose above the mountain peaks. It never got warm enough that time of year to melt away the snow, even in the hottest part of the day, but the icicles that hung from the gutters along the roof of the Caliber Lodge dripped rhythmically every few seconds.

David, Betty and Kristian sat at the kitchen counter finishing their caribou steak and eggs as they sipped on fresh squeezed grapefruit juice.

Igak, the portly Inuit cook, was cleaning up the prep area as the guests conversed. He understood minimal English, but he was well versed in the culinary world. It was his art form, and while most of the nuances of his cooking went unnoticed by the under-developed palettes of the guests who visited the Caliber Lodge, he would easily impress any five star chef.

Though steak and eggs seemed simple enough, Igak had taken it several steps further as he had done so with the moose the night before. The guests dined on house-smoked, thick-cut bacon, fresh eggs whose yolk drained slowly over expertly seasoned Filet Mignon cut caribou meat. Sprigs of rosemary and thyme graced creamy grits that rested atop buttery, crisp, hand-cut hash browns cushioned below the steak.

Jimmy still avoided the meat and satiated his hunger on the grits and potatoes while enjoying a cup of freshly ground coffee he assumed had been imported from the most posh area one could import coffee beans from.

"What are your thoughts?" David asked, chewing a mouthful of caribou steak as if it were any other. Kristian sipped his coffee as he poked at the grits.

"I'm not well versed in animal skins," Jimmy answered.

"It didn't look like anything else I've seen before. The crested dome shape. Gray hair." Kristian said.

"Could be gorilla," Betty offered.

"So you think it's fake?" David asked.

"Do *you* think it's fake, Blackwell?" Kristian asked David as he continued eating.

"Do I think the supposed Sasquatch scalp that Mister Safari

showed us last night was fake? Undoubtedly. I can't say I'm buying their ruse," David spouted off. He turned to Jimmy. "Mr. Knotts?"

"Well, I'm uncertain we can rule anything out. They've been in business for over ten years. They must have something worthwhile to hunt."

Jimmy looked over his shoulder to see Turk entering the kitchen carrying five large rifles across his arms. He set them all down, letting them clatter atop the marble island countertop.

"Those are big guns," Betty remarked. Turk smiled.

"Elephant guns," he said as he picked up one of the five identical weapons to show them. It was a .577 Nitro Express, a side-by-side double barrel, large bore center-fire rifle designed for bringing down big game. "You'll be glad you had something of such a high caliber when you see our friends in all their glory."

"Beautiful," David said as he pushed his plate aside. Turk handed him the rifle to examine. The stock was a polished Cherrywood, the barrel glossy and spit-shined. The weight and the balance impressed David as he gripped the mammoth rifle with both hands.

"You don't wanna piss 'em off. You wanna put 'em down," Turk said.

Gregory approached with an urn of coffee and asked if anyone cared for a top off. Kristian waved him away, but Betty took him up on the offer.

"I hope you all got some good rest last night. Finish up and get your gear on. Gregory's delivered everything you'll need to your room, minus the guns of course," Turk said as Igak handed him a full plate he'd set aside earlier.

Gregory poured Turk a cup of coffee. The khaki sporting man immediately chugged it all down and said to the guests, "Meet me out back when you're ready."

Jimmy was the last to finish his breakfast. The others had already retreated to their rooms to collect their winter climbing gear as he tried to help clean up. Igak refused to accept the help and warmly turned Jimmy away in his native tongue.

On his way back to his room, Jimmy stopped in the foyer, his gaze lingering toward the closed doors of the game room. He strolled across the mirror floor and opened the double doors.

The taxidermy animals all seemed to watch him as he entered. He noticed a collection of African tribal weaponry that hung along the walls beneath the caribou and antelope. He ran his hand along the shaft of a long, heavy spear mounted on a pair of brass hooks. Near the double-edged blade were a collection of short feathers from some flightless African bird.

Mounted just past the spear was a stubby, double-barreled pistol that looked like an antique sawed-off shotgun. He read the plaque beneath the gun.

"Howdah Pistol."

He glanced over his shoulder before lifting the weapon off its hooks. He popped open the breech and raised his brow when he saw it was loaded with two .50 caliber rounds. He snapped the pistol shut and placed it back on the wall.

The crimson box was back atop the mantle. Jimmy walked over and stood before it, staring, debating whether or not to reach out and take it down. He wanted to see inside it again. He wanted to see with total clarity of the mind the object they'd all seen the night before.

His hands extended out, and as they touched the sides of the red box, the vibrato of Turk's deep voice startled him.

"You're about to see something a lot more amazing than that piece of dried out skin, cowboy."

Jimmy's hands went back to his sides as he turned to face Turk, who stood leaning against the doorframe behind him. "That's the second time you've called me that, Mr. Turk."

"I apologize if the term offends you."

"I wouldn't say I'm offended. Confused by your choice to apply it to me is all."

As Turk walked further into the room he said, "You're American. Like me. That's what they call us overseas. Just something I picked up while I was in Africa."

"The Blackwells are American."

Turk chuckled. "That they are."

Jimmy made a leap with his next statement. "And Kristian." Turk didn't react.

"I guess you just seem like a cowboy to me." He walked around the pool table and stopped beside Jimmy. The two men looked at the box. "I killed this one, you know? It was my first actually."

Turk lifted the box off the mantel and set it back down on the edge of the pool table. "I spend a lot of time in this room. All these animals, these are my most prized trophies. They remind me of the great distances I've traveled."

"You spent a lot of time in Africa?"

"Oh, yes." Turk's gigantic hand clasped the lid of the box. "You ever been to Africa, Jimmy?"

Jimmy hesitated. He had been in Africa while he was documenting the war, but he was playing a character right now. He wasn't a war photographer; he was an oil tycoon heir, and oil tycoon heirs don't spend time in war zones. He imagined they sat in their family's estate, drank wine and talked about polo. So, he replied, "No, but I've always wanted to go."

"You really should have gone before you came here. Nothing's going to measure up after this expedition. Elephants and lions are child's play compared to what's waiting for you up in those snowy cliffs."

Turk closed the lid of the crimson box.

Chapter Six
THE EXPEDITION

Turk paced back and forth like a drill sergeant outside the back door of the Caliber Lodge. He watched Jimmy, Kristian and the Blackwells secure the crampons to their boots. The sharp spikes would make traversing the snowy terrain much easier than bare rubber treads. They strapped on their harnesses, hoisted the heavy climbing packs onto their backs and adjusted the straps so they were cinched appropriately.

Turk slid a pair of ice axes onto the side of each of their packs, then demonstrated how the quick-release holster for their elephant guns on the opposite side worked.

"Leather and metal. A much smarter man's invention, but modified by yours truly to accommodate the size and weight of the elephant guns. You can latch them in safely and unlatch them in three seconds or less."

Kristian, Jimmy and David latched their rifles into their holsters. Betty commented on how heavy hers was as she inspected the cannon in her hands. David offered to carry it for her, but Betty said, "No, no. I've got it. I can carry an elephant gun just like you boys." It was her first hunt, and she wanted to do it right.

Turk led the way out into the mountainous wilderness beyond the lodge, and the group followed him closely. Though the sun was out, it did little to warm them as the powerful wind blew the snow sideways across their path. Jimmy could feel the chill already beginning to burrow through his clothing, and for the first time in years he wished he was back in the damp, sweaty heat of Argentina.

The group trudged up to the top of a crested hill and gazed upon the full expanse of the seemingly endless terrain.

"This ridge is the dividing line. Past this point is their territory. From here on out, I cannot guarantee anyone's safety. If you do as I say, however, it'll reduce the likelihood that anything bad befalls you."

Turk inspected the members of his group. "You all signed the waiver, but you're still free to turn back." He paused a moment then asked, "Anyone want to take me up on that offer?"

Betty and David looked at each other, both of them full of mixed emotions—nervousness, excitement. Kristian stood stoically as he normally did, while Jimmy glanced at the others and said, "I think we're all good."

"This mountain is their home. We don't know how many of them there are, but we believe there's a substantial population, at least enough to be continually breeding. We believe they're omnivorous. We've seen them hunting caribou and other animals but assume they must also be eating vegetation to sustain their numbers and keep from completely decimating the other wildlife."

Hw gestured widely. "This ridge—no one crosses it—except for the guests of the Caliber Lodge."

Turk grabbed a pre-anchored line of rope from the edge of the crest and connected it to his harness. He grinned, then repelled down the other side of the ridge to the ground forty feet below. Kristian didn't hesitate to hook himself up and follow Turk down. With every springing kick he loosened the line for a moment, then tightened it again to keep a steady decline. His boots landed softly into the snow and Turk helped him detach the rope.

David assisted Betty, and they both descended to the other side of the ridge with the others.

Jimmy was the last to go. He took a moment to survey the

horizon one last time before running the rope through his harness. Though he wasn't consciously afraid of heights, the slickness of the ice, the wailing wind and the forty-foot drop were in the forefront of his mind. He imagined himself fumbling with the line and either losing his grip and breaking a leg, or just stumbling and embarrassing himself in front of the rest of the group—but his trip down to the bottom of the ridge went without error and he kept a confident face as he unstrung himself from the rope.

As the team traversed further, weaving through the dense pines, Betty asked how much longer it would be until they'd find one of the creatures they were hunting. Turk imparted some wisdom.

"Part of hunting is being patient. Isn't that right, David?"

"That's correct," David answered.

"When you were out in Africa, hunting lions with your uncle, sometimes you had to lie in wait—anticipate the animal's movements—and when the time was right, that's when you'd strike," Turk coached.

"Yeah. That's right."

"But before that you'd need to pick up a trail," Turk explained. He looked over his shoulder at Betty and said, "That's what we're doing now, Mrs. Blackwell."

Jimmy brought up the rear of the group. He kept a watchful eye behind them as he asked, "You hunted lions, David?"

"Yeah. My uncle and I."

"You shot one?"

"Got the photographs to prove it."

"He got it with his first shot," Betty piped up proudly.

"Better believe it. Right in the side. Blew it right off its legs. Damn thing didn't know what hit it. We skinned that beast and nailed it up on our wall at home. My uncle said it was the biggest one he'd ever seen."

"Bigger than the one in the game room?" Turk inquired.

"Sorry to break it to you, Mr. Turk, but yeah," David shouted over the rising wind. Turk smiled, amused by David's bravado.

David looked back at Jimmy as they continued to hike and asked, "How 'bout you, Jimmy? You ever kill a lion?"

"No, sir. I'll admit I've not killed much of anything."

"A virgin hunter. You and my wife have something in common then." David put his arm around Betty as they continued on and kissed her on the top of her head.

Jimmy watched Kristian from behind. He'd been silent since they left the lodge, and Jimmy wanted to get him talking again to see if he could pick up any remnants of a German accent that hadn't bled through before.

"Kristian," Jimmy started. The sullen man groaned at the sound of his own name. "You ever kill a lion?"

"I have not," Kristian answered. Jimmy still didn't hear any indication of a Germanic tongue.

"What all've you killed then?" David probed.

"I've killed my fair share of animals. Let's leave it at that." Kristian shoved past David and moved alongside Turk at the front of the group.

They trekked further through the dense pines, and as they came out the other side of the cluster they stood at the base of a steep rock face covered in ice, which led hundreds of yards straight up at a ninety-degree angle. None of them could hide their reservations about the towering climb ahead of them.

"We aren't going up that, are we?" Betty asked.

Turk grabbed a coil of rope off the ground that he had left there at an earlier date. He twisted and pulled it, cracking crystals of ice off, which showered down at his feet.

"This is the only way to reach the next level. You want to see one of them? We need to scale this. Those mountain climbing courses you all took are going to pay off tenfold."

Jimmy felt embarrassed to have been nervous about repelling down the measly forty foot hill earlier. This looming rock face completely dwarfed that. Just the thought of scaling this monster forced his stomach down into his bowels. He knew the others felt the same as they silently gazed up at the icy challenge before them. They each waited for someone else to make the first move.

David saw this as an opportunity to ensure his wife's impression of him as a fearless adventurer and took the first step up beside Turk. He adjusted his goggles, looked Turk in the eyes and confidently said, "Let's get to it." He did his best to be casual when he looked over at his bride, and he could tell that his faux bravery had resonated true with her.

Turk instructed each member of the expedition to check that their crampons were still securely attached to their boots. While the sharp points had made it easier in traversing the simpler parts of the terrain until that point, they would be essential to make it up the ice-covered slab of rock.

Turk double checked that their elephant guns were all still locked into their holsters, then directed them all to pull out their pair of ice axes. He cinched the leather leashes that connected to the end of the ice axe shafts around each of their wrists.

Though just tools, Jimmy felt that the axes were rather formidable with their curved metal handles and razor sharp heads. He thought they looked like a pair of ninja weapons in his hands, and right as his imagination swelled, the crack of David's axe piercing into the ice jolted him back to reality.

"It's gonna be a gas!" David said.

An hour later, the group was only halfway up the formation. Turk was in the lead, followed by David, then Betty and Kristin. Jimmy was bringing up the rear, as he had been for the duration of the trip. Anchors and tie-in points had already been secured from a previous expedition, and they used them to ascend safely up the rock. Everyone was harnessed to the same rope, all spread out with thirty to forty feet between them.

The rock was slick and the sharp points of the crampons around Jimmy's boots dug into the ice as he pulled himself upward. He looked down at the ground over a hundred yards below, then closed his eyes and took a deep breath, mustering what little courage he had left. He had been in dire situations before, but this moment took the cake.

He imagined what would happen to his body should he somehow fall from this height. It would smash upon the ground below, splattering across the frozen soil. It would be an explosion of crimson against the stark white, and Jimmy found some solace in the thought that his demise would at least be visually stunning.

Even through the *thwakkk, thawkkk, thwakkk* of the ice axes stabbing into the frozen formation as the group ascended, the wind still carried David's voice downward, and Jimmy heard him say to Betty, "This remind you of anything, baby?"

She smiled brightly, her red cheeks pushing her goggles up.

"Our second date," she shouted back.

Turk paused a moment and looked at the four of them below. He hollered down, "Mountain climbing on a second date?"

"Yessir!" David yelled.

Turk chuckled and continued climbing. "No kidding."

"Tell the truth, David," Betty said as loud as she could so her voice was sure to clear the breeze.

"It was this big ol' fourteener out in Colorado where we first met—Mount Elbert—but we didn't actually end up following through with the climb. Got too nervous. Good thing, too. Probably would've gotten ourselves killed with as amateur as we were. Don't know what I was thinking."

"You were trying to impress me!" Betty coached.

"It worked, didn't it?" he asked. She smirked as he continued, "We ended up in a little tavern instead. Drinks. Dinner. Then the hotel. That was the first time we—"

"David!" Betty interjected.

Jimmy grabbed hold of the rock above his head and pulled himself up higher. He shouted up, "So this reminds you of the time you *didn't* climb a mountain?"

David laughed. "Yeah, I guess—"

David's crampon slipped from its groove, throwing off his balance.

He scrambled, losing his grip on one of his ice axes, which swung loose and dangled from his wrist by the leash. His gloved fingers latched onto a rough spot jutting out from a patch of ice, and he dug the spikes of his crampons into the crust just in time to catch himself.

"Baby!" Betty wailed.

David sighed in relief as he pressed his body tightly to the rock. He took a moment before yelling back to her, "I'm all right."

Turk looked down at David to be sure. "David?"

"I'm good. I'm good."

"Everyone stop!" Turk shouted. The group froze.

"Boot just slipped. I'm good now."

"Everyone double-check your harnesses," Turk instructed.

They did.

Betty and David locked eyes and David could read the overwhelming emotion in her face. He reassured her, "I'm all right."

Turk gave them all time to let the adrenaline die down a bit before they resumed their ascent.

Another hour passed before the group made it to the summit of the rock face. Jimmy was the last to complete the climb and Turk helped pull him up to his feet where the others were waiting for him atop a snowcapped plateau. He watched as Betty hugged her husband like a vice before kissing him deeply. Her lips stayed on his face as she quietly murmured about almost losing him. She explained to him he had nearly fallen to his death as if he hadn't been there to experience for himself. He let her work through her emotions while holding her close.

Jimmy stepped forward, looking out over the other side of the plateau where a massive bowl-shaped valley glistened in the sunlight fifty yards below. Kristian and Turk walked up beside him, and Turk quietly motioned to Betty and David to join in. With a flattened hand he guided everyone to crouch down low, and as Turk lied out flat on his chest in the snow, they all followed his lead.

He lifted his goggles up and put a pair of binoculars to his eyes. Again, Jimmy, Kristian and the Blackwells followed suit and stared out into the valley. They could see a herd of caribou grazing on the freshly sprouted vegetation poking up between patches of heavy snow. Jimmy considered how different they looked compared to the taxidermy busts he'd seen in the game room. They seemed peaceful, relaxed, and completely unaware of his group's presence. Their cloven hooves stamped lightly in the snow, digging deeper to reach the hearty parts of the protruding plant-life.

"Caribou. This is an excellent sign. You see caribou, and soon enough…" Turk spoke in a tone just above a whisper. "They herd them down into these valleys. Trap them in the bowls. Makes them easier to catch."

Jimmy watched intently, unsure of what he was about to witness, but expected it would be something he'd never experienced. They all lied there in the snow together, waiting, watching.

"You know, the caribou are the only Cervid species in which both the males and the females grow antlers," Turk shared. He looked at Betty and smirked. "Nature's equality."

Betty smiled. When she felt David's heated gaze she asked him, "Is this what it's like? On your other hunts?"

"Usually a bit warmer," David answered. "But yeah. Though my uncle usually brings along a bottle of something to sip on."

"No alcohol on my expeditions, Mr. Blackwell. But there will be plenty back at the lodge to cheers with after the day is through." Turk lowered his binoculars and rolled onto his back. He stretched methodically, readjusting his body from the climb.

Jimmy's eyes stayed glued to the binoculars as he asked, "These… Sasquatch—are they fast?"

Turk rotated his shoulder, massaging it. "Not faster than a bullet." Jimmy asked for confirmation of their speed and Turk explained, "Long legs. Good for sprinting. Their stride is wide, almost double what ours is."

"So they're fast," Jimmy said.

"This is a common area for them. Most likely some tracks down there," Turk educated. Jimmy scanned the ground around the caribous' furry legs. He couldn't see any tracks other than the ones made by the grazing creatures' hooves.

Turk glanced over at his party and admired the expressions on everyone's faces. They were all transfixed on the valley, even Kristian, whose steely gaze was fully focused. This is how the members of all his expeditions looked at this stage. Idealistic. Imaginative. Full of expectation.

Down in the valley, one of the caribou raised its head. Its ear twitched, listening. It paused for a moment, and through the binoculars Jimmy felt as though he could read the animal's every thought. The caribou's head tilted to the side, angling its ears to hone in on whatever had alerted it, then as if it had suddenly forgotten the phantom sound, the caribou returned to eating the stubby grass.

For twenty-three minutes they watched the herd in silence until Kristian grew impatient and said, "I'm starting to think—"

Turk immediately cut him off, unwilling to let Kristian's attitude infect the rest of the group. "Let's head down there." Turk jumped to his feet, helped Betty to hers.

"I thought you said distance is our friend." Jimmy, David and Kristian stood and gathered their things.

Turk explained, "We must have missed them. Come and gone before we got here. Let's head down so you can get a good look at the tracks."

Moments later, Jimmy was once again the last person to descend into the valley. He untied himself from the rope and turned to the others. Turk unlatched his elephant gun from his holster. He didn't have to tell the others to do so. Quickly, they all reached along the side of their climbing packs and unlatched their guns.

The brisk movements startled the caribou, and the herd scattered as they noticed the humans approaching. They galloped away, struggling to leap out of the bowl. Some of them tripped and fell, but eventually they leapt and bound their way up and out, and as the last caribou made its escape, Turk led the way to the center of the valley.

Jimmy kept his eyes on the tree line at the top of the bowl, readying himself for whatever may befall them. His gaze shifted as he heard Turk say, "Here."

Turk crouched down in the snow and Kristian, Betty, and David gathered around him. Jimmy walked up behind them slowly as a nervous chill crept across his skin. They were all staring at the ground, at something in front of Turk, something that Jimmy could tell amazed them all.

Turk looked over his shoulder at Jimmy and said, "Come, Mr. Knotts. Take a look."

Jimmy moved in closer. He looked over the expedition leader's shoulder, down at the sight the others were so mesmerized by. It was a footprint, human looking, but significantly larger. By Jimmy's estimation, it was around twenty-four inches long and eight inches wide. He searched for words and was relived when David spoke first.

"My God."

"Closer to a brother, actually," Turk quipped. With that, he looked at Kristian and said, "But still an animal."

Jimmy took a few paces forward past the others and stopped beside a second track in the snow. He looked at the enormous size of it compared to his boot.

Betty said, "They look human."

"Humanoid. 'Look' is the key word," Turk explained. "They look, but they aren't."

"Five toes," Betty breathed. She reached down and grazed the footprint with her heavily gloved middle finger.

Kristian was alert. His sights moved to the trees, and he gripped the elephant gun tightly in his hands. This track had increased his acceptance. He knew that an animal that made a track of this size would be a formidable prey, and if they were not careful, perhaps a predator instead.

David looked at the next track, the one Jimmy stood by, then looked further to the third track, and furthermore to the series of tracks beyond that. He trudged through the snow, following them, excited to see where they would take him. The tracks led to the edge of the bowl and up into the forested area in the distance.

"David!" Turk called. David stopped and turned around. "We stay together. We move when I say we move."

Impatiently, David whined, "Is this a hunting expedition, or isn't it?"

Turk stepped forward into David's face. He put his hand on

his shoulder and assured him, "It's *the* hunting expedition. And we'll continue on, but we do it on my word. Understood? Attacks are less likely when we stay in a group."

The wind picked up, and Betty pulled the collar of her outer coat tight against her neck. Jimmy could see the frustration growing in David's body language as he pointed out that the tracks would lead them to the creature they were hunting.

David tugged at his coat, adjusting it as if it were a snake constricting him. Betty tried to calm her husband, but David brushed her aside. She tried again to ease his irritation, but he would have none of it. He wanted to be upset for a moment, to linger in the anger. To Jimmy, David looked like a child, pouting, stomping his feet because he couldn't get his way.

Turk let David have his moment, one that ended when David noticed Betty looking at Turk in a way that made him uncomfortable yet again. David could tell Betty was attracted to the man, and he considered that his tantrum would be seen as an expression of weakness to her, so he pulled himself together and rejoined the group.

Turk pat him on the back without another mention of the outburst and gathered the group together around the tracks. He pointed out at the forest along the edge of the valley and told them, "The woods beyond the valley bowl—going in there is a death sentence. One of them could come down right on top of us and we'd never see it coming."

Jimmy listened as Turk explained that they would need to go around the forested area and pick up the tracks on the other side. He was relieved to hear that they would not be venturing into the woods. While the sun reflected off the snow, bathing everything in a blistering white glow, the woods looked like a shadowy realm concealing a dreadful secret. As he imagined what danger lied within, he noticed that Kristian was also entranced by the clustered pines.

His gaze had never broken from the tree line.

The wind had died down by the time the group climbed out of the valley bowl, and Turk led the way along the border of the woods, keeping them a few yards away.

As they trudged onward, Jimmy was unsure if his drying eyes were playing tricks on him, or if he was seeing movement inside the forest. He knew the caribou herd was likely making their way through those trees, yet he wondered if the brief glimpses of motion may have in fact been the animal they were hunting.

"They live in the forested areas?" David asked.

"Some. Some live in mountain caverns." Turk made a wide gesture with his arms. "Like I said, this is their territory."

Kristian stopped, pulled a canteen from his pack, and took a long drink. He secured it, then pulled his goggles off to let his face breath. Jimmy studied him from a distance, always watching. He imagined the climbing gear replaced with an SS uniform, gray and black, adorned with patches and medals.

Kristian noticed his gaze and said to him, "Wish you had one of those Old Fashioneds right now, Knotts?"

Jimmy smiled and nodded. "Two would be better."

Turk hollered back at them, "Come on. Keep up." He waved them along, and they continued forward around the forest perimeter.

As they reached the other side, David came to an immediate realization. "The tracks never left the forest." The others looked around to verify David's claim. "We need to go in to find the beast."

"We need to do nothing of the sort, Mr. Blackwell," Turk scolded.

"If it went into the woods, and it didn't come out of the woods, then that would mean it's still in the woods," David growled through clamped teeth. "Hunting is about picking up a trail and following it to the source. You're saying we should do the opposite?"

"Mr. Blackwell, I'm saying we should be smart and not get ourselves killed. I assure you there will be another opportunity to see one of the creatures that won't lead to our certain demise." Turk gestured for the group to continue following him. "We'll catch one out in the open. Close proximity to one of these things—it's a nasty situation."

Kristian, Jimmy and Betty followed Turk's lead and marched away from the tree line. David stood his ground. He stared defiantly at Turk, willing the man to visibly lose his temper. Instead, Turk walked over to David and gently placed his arm around his shoulder once more. He leaned in close so that only David could hear the next few words that whispered out in an eerily calm fashion.

"Either you start following my lead, David, and stop putting the lives of the other guests at risk—one of which is your own goddamned wife for Christ's sake—or I will beat you black and blue with the butt of my rifle."

David looked into Turk's eyes and could see that every word he had uttered was sincere. The fire in David was immediately doused, and he nodded sheepishly at Turk, who in turn gave him one of his ear to ear toothy smiles and patted him on the back.

"Well, all right then," Turk said cheerfully, before walking back to take the lead of the group again.

He led them over the top of a tiny hill where a log cabin with an arched roof came into view—an oasis in the frozen mountain desert.

"Tell me there's a sauna in there," Betty wheezed as she leaned over her knees to catch her breath.

"We use it as a supply cache. Weapons. Ammunition. No food, though. Don't want to be attracting any wildlife." Turk put his hand on Betty's back. "And some comfortable furniture to take a load off." He looked at David and said, "We'll take a few minutes to rest, then we'll get back to the hunt."

They traversed down the hill toward the cabin, and though no one said so, they were all relieved to have a safe moment to recharge. Turk had made this journey many times over the past ten years, and each time arriving at the cabin was his favorite part. It was his personal bachelor pad out in the treacherous wilderness, surrounded by rocks, and snow, and vicious winds. He always felt safe there, and the release it gave the other members of his expeditions always made him feel accomplished.

As he approached the cabin this time, however, things were abnormal. The front door was ajar, and he could see the latch was shattered and strewn across the dusty floor of the interior. He gripped his elephant gun with both hands and raised it to his shoulder.

Chapter Seven
THE NEST

Kristian, Jimmy and the Blackwells all raised their elephant guns, unsure of what was happening or what had spooked Turk. The expedition leader held up a firm fist in the air and the group halted immediately. Looking down the sights of the massive rifle, Turk aimed through the doorway. He couldn't make out much detail inside the cabin. The reflection of sunlight bouncing off the snow partially blinded him. He took a deep breath and with a kick from his tank tread boot, the door slammed the rest of the way open and he stomped inside.

He scanned the room. It was a disheveled mess. Something had been in there, rooting around. The heavy wooden table was overturned and the handmade chairs were scattered about. He sniffed the air and as his nerves calmed, he lowered his weapon.

The air was fresh. He could smell no wild scent upon its breath. Whatever had made the mess had been gone for quite some time.

Turk waved the others inside and they lowered their rifles upon entering. He closed the door behind them and began tidying up. Throwing few logs into the stone fireplace, he brought the flames to life.

"Did one of the—did a Sasquatch do this?" David pulled Betty in close as they watched Turk stoke the fire.

"Could have been," Turk answered. His calmness relaxed them and when he nodded at the cloth couch at the other side of the room, the Blackwells moved over to it and sat down together, snuggling into each other's warmth.

Kristian noted a gun rack beside the window filled with various hunting rifles and shotguns. He ran his finger across the engraved stock of a 30-06 which read, "For Jonathan Turk. My Hero." He scoffed and lifted it off the rack to vet it. The weapon looked unused, polished and pristine, as if it were merely there for decoration.

"Mrs. Everly gave that one to me." Kristian looked up and saw Turk looking over his shoulder at him from the fireplace.

"And what did you do to earn such a hyperbolic sentiment?" Kristian inquired.

After getting a good blaze going, Turk picked up one of the chairs and sat down at the table. He leaned back, and the chair creaked beneath his weight.

"Saved her life."

"Wouldn't want anything to happen to the person who cuts your paychecks."

Turk couldn't help but chuckle at Kristian's comment.

Jimmy spoke up. "Speaking of paychecks, Kristian—I've been curious to find out who cuts yours." Kristian turned to Jimmy, who stood near the door, casually leaning on the frame. "You never did tell us what bank you worked for."

"My personal details are no business of yours, Mr. Knotts. You're here to hunt a beast. Same as I. Let's not allow ourselves to become distracted."

Jimmy didn't intend to.

Turk raised a leg and let his boot crash down on the table. Betty jolted in David's arms. Turk quietly said, "This is rest time, team. So, rest."

Betty leaned back against David's chest. Jimmy took a seat at the table opposite Turk, and Kristian dragged one of the chairs to the other side of the room and sat down. They all waited in silence, doing what they could to ease their minds. Kristian's gaze gradually drifted over to the fire. He watched the flames flickering, dancing. He focused on the various hues. Red and yellow. Orange and white. There was a quiet hiss and Kristian thought he heard that soft whispering voice again, the one he had heard coming from the fireplace back at the lodge. He looked at the others in the room and it was clear he was the only one hearing the sounds.

Betty and David closed their eyes, leaning their heads together. Short of passing out back to back after their late night romp the evening prior, this was the first time either of them had let their guard down, and it was the first time since arriving at the lodge that they had truly taken a moment to just enjoy one another's embrace.

Betty thought back to their wedding ceremony and how handsome David had looked in his perfectly tailored suit. She recalled him standing at the altar, rigid and nervous. She had seen his eyes tear up a bit when he'd watched her walking toward him down the aisle, arm in arm with his soon-to-be father-in-law. She was the last of her close friends to get married, and she smiled as she thought about telling them all about her outrageous honeymoon at the Caliber Lodge—then quickly realized that because of the contracts she'd never be able to brag about it in any detail. She pouted a bit, her eyes still closed, and nestled in closer to David's shoulder.

As Turk picked ice off of his boot, he casually observed Jimmy, who was simultaneously observing Kristian. As though he could feel the gaze, Kristian turned from the fire and looked over at Knotts. Neither of them spoke. In the silence, they each tried to figure the other one out.

Turk felt the tension. He leaned across the table and put his hand on Jimmy's shoulder.

"These expeditions can get a bit grueling at times. Though

the excitement of the hunt and the payoff of seeing these beasts well warrants the troublesome parts, there's no denying that scaling a mountain like this, in all this heavy gear—it's a challenging task."

Jimmy smiled and replied, "Good thing we have—"

The walls of the cabin reverberated with a bellowing howl from outside. It was a deep, guttural roar that echoed through the air, bouncing off the rocks and trees surrounding them. Everyone froze and Turk's toothy smile overtook his face. The creature they were hunting was near.

Everyone was on their feet, rifles in hand. The ominous, deep howl from the snowy wilderness outside had reignited their spirits.

"What was that?" Betty asked.

"That was one of our furry friends, Mrs. Blackwell," Turk answered.

"Sasquatch," Kristian said. For him and David, the urge to continue the hunt was overwhelming. Kristian took a step forward, but before anyone else could react, David slipped from Betty's arms and headed toward the door without a second thought. He gripped the broken handle and pulled the door open, spilling a gust of wind inside, blowing a barrage of snowflakes into the cabin.

Turk shouted, "David!"

Before anyone else could make a move, Blackwell disappeared out into the white. Turk slung his pack over his back and said to the others in a hasty tone, "Quickly! He can't be left alone!"

Jimmy, Kristian and Betty followed Turk out of the cabin where they saw David's tracks leading back up the hill toward the dense forested area they had earlier avoided. Turk saw him crest the hill, then vanish from sight once again.

"Damned fool."

"David!" Betty screamed. She rushed past Turk, chasing after her husband.

On the other side of the hill, David crossed the tree line and entered the forest. His eyes searched for the creature that had growled out the terrifying howl only moments earlier, but all he could see was the foliage of the pines. He weaved in and out of the trees, his elephant gun close to his chest.

HARRRRROOOOOOOO!

David stopped in his tracks as an identical howl echoed through the woods. It didn't sound like a wolf's howl. It was heavier, fuller. It sounded almost human, but he knew of no man that could project a sound at that volume.

He turned in all directions, looking for the source, then stopped and stood in silence, hoping to hear it again so he could lock onto its location. Behind him he could hear Betty's voice yelling from a distance, begging him to come back. But he couldn't. This was why he was there. To hunt.

David pushed on through the trees, moving quietly, but with purpose. The sunlight barely punctured the tops of the trees, leaving only splotches of light between the heavy pines. He noticed movement to his right and without much thought he spun and almost pulled the trigger blindly. He steadied his nerve and squinted through the shadows and could see something large moving through the trees. His finger lingered on the trigger, ready to squeeze at any moment.

He relaxed a bit.

Just a caribou.

The animal looked at him, unafraid, then continued along its way through the woods.

On any other day David would have put a bullet through the doe and been proud of his clean kill, but he wasn't hunting caribou. He was hunting something much grander, much more rare, and the doe meandering away brought him nothing but frustration.

He could hear the others enter the forest, snapping branches and brushing through the pines. They weren't concerned with staying quiet. He knew all they wanted to do was to find him, and stop him, and drag him out of the woods. Betty's voice rang out, echoed by Turks, each calling for David to come back, but David pressed on deeper as stealthily as he could.

He could see sunlight up ahead and thought he may have reached the perimeter of the woods, but instead stepped into a small clearing in the trees. Light floated down and warmed the circular ring where a large mound of severed branched and twigs were piled in an enormous heap. Pine needles covered almost every inch of the ground like a carpet, distorting the usual glaring reflection of the snow. David wasn't sure what he was staring at. It looked like a mud hut, but composed of pieces of discarded tree limbs and bark. It stood around eight feet tall and on one side there was a sizeable hole tall enough for David to walk through without crouching down.

As he moved in closer, he could see that the branches that made up the outer shell of the structure were woven together, tightly threaded back and forth in a knit-like formation, much like a wicker basket.

David held his rifle to his shoulder and neared the entrance. He balanced the elephant gun in place with one hand as he reached for his pack with the other and pulled out a flashlight. He clicked it on and held it along the barrel of the rifle, shining light through the hole into the dark structure. All he could see inside were more branches, more bark, and a continued flooring of pine needles.

Then something stirred beyond the branches, within them, beyond the shadows. David froze. Silence. He strained to see through the dead foliage, his eyes taking in all the detail of each limb that engulfed the interior. His eyes grew wide as he came to the realization that he was standing in the entryway of a nest.

One of the branches deep within the structure moved, though only slightly. Then the one beside it bent back. A few more, all from the same cluster, twisted and peeled away in unison. David gripped his rifle and flashlight. He didn't want to waste a round.

Take your time. Wait for your shot.

The branches in the cluster spread apart and two large, fur covered hands slid out from between them. They would have looked human if not for the thick hair and massive size. The fingers were long and thick, easily three to four times longer than the average man's, and while at first the fur appeared to be gray, he soon distinguished it as a combination of both white and dark brown strands.

David couldn't speak. He took a step back as the broad hands spread the branches apart, creating an enormous hole in the entanglement. There in the center of the hole was a face, long and rimmed with the same wispy fur. It had a sagging jaw lined with crooked teeth, most of them flat, but with jagged, razor-sharp incisors. It had a prominent brow like a gorilla, but beneath it were big round eyes. Blue eyes—they looked human, but twice the size.

As David stared at the face, he was filled simultaneously with fear and fascination, but when the creature let out a bellowing howl that shook the nest, only one of those emotions remained. He jumped back, dropping the flashlight.

He held out his hand, as you would to a dog that was too excited. His palm shook as he extended it outward toward the face in a halting gesture. With his other hand he did his best to hold the elephant gun, but it was heavy and sagged toward the ground.

The flashlight was laying atop the needles, still shining its beam across the interior of the nest, pointing at a spot just a few feet below the face which panted in the darkness, almost snorting. The face moved slightly and all the branches in the nest rustled. David's free hand snapped back onto the barrel of the rifle and he took aim.

"David!" Betty's high-pitched voice was close.

The distraction was just what the face needed, and before David could react, the full glory of the creature burst through the branches and charged at him. David staggered backward, trying to keep his rifle in position, but the heel of his boot snagged on a root and he fell backward, landing hard on his back. His rifle discharged with a loud *BAARRROOOOOM!*

One of the massive furry hands swatted the rifle from David's grip, sending it clattering against a tree a few yards away. All David could see before he covered his face with his forearms was a mess of grayish fur.

HARRRRROOOOOOOO! The howl was nearly ear shattering at this proximity.

"PLEASE! NO, NO, NO!" David shouted, his eyes squeezed closed. He expected to feel the tear of teeth piercing into his flesh, or the crunch of his own bones breaking under the pressure of one of those big hands, but as he lied there, his back upon the pine needles, no pain befell him.

"Please, please, please, please. Don't hurt me. Don't hurt me." He was whispering now, begging. He could hear the heavy breathing above him as it slowed to a calmer pace and lowered his arms to get a better look.

The creature stood over him on two legs, its body covered in the white and brown blended fur. Its posture was poor. It stood hunched, its disproportionately long arms hanging down, fisted knuckles almost touching the ground. David imagined that if it were to stand fully erect, it would be nearly eight feet tall. The most striking feature, however, was the enormous belly, round and bulbous. From David's view, he could not see the creature's head past the protruding stomach. He looked to the side and saw the creature's brawny feet. They were large enough to have made the twenty-four inch tracks they had seen leading out of the valley bowl.

The creature knelt down to where its belly almost rested atop David's chest, and it leaned forward so it could make eye contact. David could see his own reflection in the large blue orbs.

"Please," David whimpered. "Please don't hurt me."

The creature cradled its belly with one giant hand, which brushed against David's coat. It sighed and its hot breath rose into the air and dissipated. Its face contorted into a weak smile, and David furrowed his brow in disbelief.

This is no mere animal. Its emotions are clear and readable.

David forced himself to smile back at it.

The creature then stood, stepped over David, and meandered toward the tree line.

David rolled to his side and watched in awe as the hairy Goliath continued to lumber away. He gently got to his knees, then to his feet, and walked over quietly to collect his rifle. The animal had spared him. It could have easily ripped him apart or ground him to a pulp, but it didn't. It just smiled at him. In all his years of hunting, he had never seen a wild beast behave in such a manner. He had invaded the animal's territory, took it by surprise, and still the creature took pity on him. He couldn't understand it.

The lack of understanding, however, frightened him even more, and as his thoughts muddled together, David slowly and instinctually raised the elephant gun to his shoulder and took aim at the pregnant creature's back.

Turk's voice rang out, "NO!"—but David squeezed the trigger and the deafening crack of the elephant gun's blast filled the air. The bullet hit the creature below its left shoulder blade and a puff of red blood dusted across the snow.

David heard Betty yell out, "David! God!" The creature dropped to its knees, then fell to its side.

Turk charged David and tackled him to the ground. Jimmy, Kristian and Betty entered the clearing and skidded to a halt at the sight of the wounded animal.

Betty covered her mouth in shock. The view of the dying animal horrified her. Her eyes watered as she noticed the round belly and the red stain seeping across the snow. This is not how she expected it to be. All those grandiose tales of her husband's hunting trips with his uncle, the fanciness of it, the class, none of that was here. There was nothing attractive about their current situation. The dying animal before her was clinging to life, and the life of its unborn child.

David's face was smashed into the pine needles beneath Turk's elbow. As he stared out through the tussle at the dying creature, his eyes locked onto those blue orbs once more and he could see that the creature's breath was fading.

"Why?" Turk shouted, but David didn't know how to answer. "WHY!"

Betty trudged through the snow and shoved Turk off of her husband. David gasped for air as the pressure from Turk's weight lifted. He saw the creature use the last of its strength to raise its hand in the air defensively.

Turk looked over his shoulder to see Kristian standing behind him, his elephant gun at the ready.

"Kristian!"

BARRROOOOOOM! The bullet hit the creature just below the collarbone, and the labored heave of the animal's chest ceased. Betty covered her face as she sobbed. Kristian walked past them and approached the dead creature. They all watched as he stood over it and nudged one of the long ape-like arms with his boot. He crouched low and grabbed one of the animal's wrists, then turned it to inspect the massive hand.

Jimmy tried to hide his disgust at the violent display. Shooting this pregnant creature in the back, then again while it lay there bleeding out, was too brutal for him to handle. He turned away and his guts churned and spewed vomit across the pine needles.

David got to his feet and scowled at Turk. "You've grown rather accustomed to manhandling me, Mr. Turk, and I've had quite enough of it to say the least."

"And I've had quite enough of your insubordination, Blackwell."

While David and Turk stared one another down, Kristian admired the creature's face. Its jaw was sagging to the side, a stream of blood oozing out. The bright blue eyes were fading to gray.

"Magnificent," Kristian whispered as David walked up beside him and unsheathed a curved hunting knife from his pack, then crouched down over the dead creature's legs.

"What the hell do you think you're doing?" Turk growled.

"This thing's too big to cart all the way back. I'm taking a trophy." David sliced into the creature's ankle. The sharp blade cut easily through the thick fur, deep into the flesh.

"No trophies!"

"What?"

Turk grabbed David by the collar of his coat and pulled him up. "How much clearer do I need to be, Mr. Blackwell? You can't take anything back that might expose this place." David ripped himself free of Turk's grasp.

"Are you telling me you brought us all the way out here and we won't have anything to show for it?" David let the butt of his rifle rest on the animal's protruding belly. He posed, gripping the barrel, and said, "Look at this. Perfect moment for a photograph. Can we at least get that?"

Betty looked at her husband and tried her best to hide how ashamed of him she was at that moment. Turk grabbed David by the back of the neck and forced him to look down at the animal's body. "Look," he said. "Do you see that? It was with child. What you did —" he looked at Kristian, "What the two of you did—"

Turk shoved David forward at Kristian, who instinctively caught him, keeping him from falling face first into the snow.

Turk pointed at them and shouted, "These actions will have consequences!"

"Are you going to take us back to the lodge and spank us with your rifle?" David challenged.

"I'm the least of your worries at this point." Turk checked his rifle to make sure it was in a fully operational state.

"What do you mean by that?" Betty asked him, her empathy mutating back into concern.

Turk looked at the group, then at the carcass in the snow and said, "We need to get out of these woods."

Chapter Eight
THE ROCK FACE

The group hurried up the hill, the dense forest of trees behind them. Jimmy could not get the image of the dead creature out of his mind. The grayish fur, the primate arms, the enormous feet. Just the overall size of the beast had caused him to rethink everything he preconceived on his journey out to that frigid frontier. It may have been the belly that put him over the edge. He imagined it may have been only days away from giving birth. He considered cutting the baby out in an attempt to save its life, but had quickly disregarded the thought because of his lack of any medical experience and the fear of what further horrors may befall the newborn creature in the presence of David and Kristian. The fading of life inside its mother's declining warmth was a far more merciful ending. That's what Jimmy told himself, anyway.

He glanced over his shoulder at the cabin in the distance. They had stopped back by there and grabbed some extra ammunition on their way out of the woods. Turk was convinced that the killing of the pregnant female would result in its mate tracking them down, so for everyone's safety the expedition was ending for the day.

He assured them all that they would return to the hunt in the morning. It was already mid-afternoon and there was only a brief period of daylight left on the mountain which they'd need to safely return to the Caliber Lodge.

As they lowered down into the bowl-shaped valley, they passed by the Sasquatch tracks from earlier. They were still deep, perfectly formed, and Jimmy thought about how thick his skepticism was only a few hours ago.

He stayed in the middle of the group as they traversed through the snow. Having brought up the rear for the first half of the trip, he decided it was time to let someone else have the honor. They climbed out of the bowl and up to the plateau where the pre-existing anchors that Turk had prepared on his previous expeditions waited. Jimmy imagined how much more challenging that initial adventure up the mountain must have been for the very first expedition party.

As the group readied themselves for the climb back down the steep rock face, Kristian commented, "We should have waited it out in the cabin."

"You'd be dead by now if we had," Turk assured him. "We all would."

Kristian ran the rope coil through his gear and said, "That beast went down without a fight. How dangerous can they be?"

"It'll be dark soon. The temperature will drop beyond what you can survive. You'll be slow. Weak. Easy prey. If you want to stay out here and freeze, be my guest, Kristian." Turk cinched his rope as a form of punctuation.

Moments later the group was making their way down the towering ice-covered rock face. Just as before, they were all on a shared rope, each of them roughly thirty feet apart. Kristian was the furthest down, followed by Jimmy, who made it his business to stay as close as possible to the dour man for the rest of the excursion. If he was indeed Wilhelm Stengl, Jimmy knew that he'd need to do everything in his power to keep him alive long enough to get him to Levi and the rest of the team to tear the information they needed out of him.

Turk was in the center of the group, just below Betty. David was the highest up, just a few yards down from the top of the plateau. Turk called out, "Everyone be careful. I don't want anymore close calls this time around."

The wind picked up, blowing snow hard across their bodies. Jimmy looked at the ground far below him. He recalled David losing his grip during the ascent and how close he came to falling from the rock. He took a deep breath, tried to wipe the memory away, and forced himself to continue moving downward.

Betty was conscious of every move she made. Her eyes locked on her feet as they extended lower to the next foothold. She paced herself. Left foot, right hand, right foot, left hand. Repeat. The spikes on her crampons and the picks of her dual ice axes cut into the frozen sheets draped over the rock.

David wasn't concentrating much at all, at least not on his foot and handwork. He was thinking about the creature in the woods, and about the nest, how intricately constructed it was. He thought about the mercy the animal had shown him.

Mercy gets you killed.

He considered that if the species as a whole held the same morals, then that would explain their minimal numbers. Survival of the fittest. David knew that only the strong survive in this world. He thought of himself as one of the strong. He thought of himself as a survivor.

A metallic jingling sound from above caught David's attention, and he looked up toward the top of the plateau. He listened, trying to hear through the whipping winds. He heard the jingle again.

What's making that noise?

Before he could wonder anymore, the shared group rope was yanked up a few inches. It jerked David.

"What the hell?" he whispered to himself.

"David? Everything all right?" Turk hollered, glancing up past Betty.

David held himself in place. He stared at the rope, waiting to see if it would move again. It did. The rope yanked upward, this time a few feet, violently jerking everyone below.

"What the fuck?" Kristian shouted.

Turk was the only one who realized what was happening, and in his baritone voice he muttered to himself, "My God."

David let the ice axes dangle loosely from the leashes around his wrists, and gripped the rope with both hands. He yanked it downward, but it was taut, and he could not move it.

A mighty force pulled the rope out of David's hands, and with a snap the anchor at the top of the plateau ripped out of the rock. David fell backward through the air, hurtling past Betty, who screamed out in horror as her husband flew by. The second anchor held, and the rope went taut again, sending David slamming into the side of the rock face. His head smashed against the ice, immediately knocking him unconscious.

"David!" Betty screamed. He dangled limply between Betty and Turk, swaying on the rope, his head and legs brushing back and forth against the icy rock.

"David! Wake up, David!" Turk shouted. Jimmy stared up at the scene above him in absolute terror. He didn't completely comprehend the full scope of what was happening yet. He just heard the shouting and saw David's limp body swinging from the rope.

At first, Turk's eyes locked on David as he hung above him—then he looked past David, past Betty, at something moving above her. It was a creature, similar to the one the men had killed in the woods, but this one was a much larger male. It was crawling over the edge of the plateau, moving downward toward them.

"Betty! You gotta keep moving! Keep coming down!" Turk

hollered.

"David! Baby, wake up!" She had yet to see the creature above her.

"Betty! For Christ's sake, keep moving!"

Betty realized the terror in Turk's face. She turned, looked up at the creature coming down the rock face at her and screamed.

"Betty, move!"

She scrambled down to David's level as fast as she could without losing her hold on the ice. She shook him violently, trying to wake him.

"David! Come on, baby! David! David!"

"Betty, you gotta leave him!"

"David!"

"You gotta leave him. There's no other way. You have to keep moving!"

The creature continued to climb slowly down the icy cliff, growing closer. Its knife-edged fingernails dug into the ice even more efficiently than the teams' ice axes had, allowing the animal to descend with ease.

Betty yelled at Turk, "I can't. I can't leave him." Her eyes were full of tears as she shook David again and again. He hung there unconscious and unaware of their dire situation.

Below, Kristian planted his feet against the rock face so he was standing almost perpendicular to it. He unlocked his elephant gun and took aim. Above him, past Jimmy, Turk hadn't moved and was still trying desperately to persuade Betty.

"Betty, goddamnit! You're going to fucking die!"

Jimmy looked below him and saw Kristian trying to get a clear line of sight. For a moment, he thought Kristian was aiming the rifle directly at him. His mind raced, *Should I draw my weapon in response?* He was a sitting duck there on the rock face, tied to the shared rope with the others. The barrel of Kristian's rifle tilted slightly and Jimmy leaned as far as he could out of the line of sight. He hoped Kristian was an expert shot because poor aim could easily result in Jimmy losing a limb.

The creature reached the level of the second anchor, and it grabbed hold of the rope again. With brute strength, it pulled the rope, hoisting everyone a few feet back up the rock face. Kristian squeezed the trigger of his elephant gun and the rifle blasted out a shot that that hit the rock beside the creature's head and sparked off the ice. The creature ignored it completely and scooped one arm around David's limp body. It laid him out over its shoulder and with its jagged fingernails it cut David loose of the rope.

"David!" Betty screamed.

With one giant hand still holding onto the rock face, the creature used its other to fling David down at Kristian.

"No!" Betty pleaded as David plummeted downward, barely missing her as he careened past. Jimmy kicked against the ice, swinging himself out of the way as David fell past him. Kristian pulled himself tightly against the rock, flattening himself enough to avoid a collision.

Betty shrieked as David disappeared through the heavy snowfall and fell to the icy rocks below. The creature howled out in victory, then began pulling on the rope again, hoisting Betty, Turk, Jimmy and Kristian closer to its grasp.

The force of the tug caused Kristian to lose hold of his weapon—the elephant gun tumbled through the air and disappeared into the white.

"Turk! Do something!" Kristian yelled. Turk's mind raced. "Cut us loose! Do something!"

Turk quickly set a fresh anchor and detached himself from the shared rope so he couldn't be pulled any higher. He tied off the first rope to the new anchor and cut it just above the hinge so that Jimmy and Kristian were safe and unable to be hoisted anymore. He secured himself to the new anchor and steadied with both legs against the rock face as Kristian had done before.

The creature pulled Betty up with ease now that the rest of the weight had been cut loose. Betty dug her crampons into the rock face, trying to slow her ascent.

"No! No! No!" she cried.

The creature yanked harder and Betty lost her footing, causing her face to hit the ice.

"Betty!" Turk unholstered his elephant gun and took aim. Betty blocked his view as she was being pulled—he couldn't get a clear shot.

Jimmy watched in vain as the creature grabbed Betty by the arm. She screamed out for help one last time as the creature extended his arm out, dangling her in the air. Turk took the shot—*BAARRRROOOOOOM!*—but the bullet missed and the creature pulled Betty into its furry chest. It climbed back up the rock face and flung her like a rag doll to the top of the plateau.

Turk fired again, only seconds too late, missing the creature as it crawled out of sight over the ledge. The sound of Betty squealing in agony filled the air, slicing through the violent gale. The three remaining men could hear the crunching and ripping as they hung there on the rope helplessly, unable to save Mrs. Blackwell.

Turk locked the elephant gun back into the holster as the wet, gurgled screaming continued for another brief moment. Soon the only sound was the wind, and the men saw Betty's blood run over the edge of the plateau, streaming down the icy rock face.

Jimmy closed his eyes, and Kristian lazily turned away. He looked down below but couldn't see the base of the cliff through the snowfall. He knew his rifle and David's body were both lying down there, both shattered to pieces.

Turk sighed and climbed further down so he was side by side on the rock with Jimmy.

"We have to keep moving."

"We can't just leave her out here."

"You wanna climb back up there for whatever's left of her?" Jimmy searched for words as Turk said, "There's nothing more we can do."

The sound of ice cracking echoed above them, and all three men turned to look up at the plateau. An icy rock the size of a dinner plate flew through the air, forcing them to move and dodge it. Another rock, twice the size, fell past, narrowly missing them. The howl of the creature echoed through the air and Turk shouted, "We need to get off this rock face. Keep moving down. Quickly!"

Jimmy and Kristian obeyed and continued descending. Another rock, even larger than before, sailed down at them from above, almost hitting Kristian.

"Christ!"

A barrage of icy chunks rained down from the plateau.

"Move! Move!" Turk yelled.

One of the rocks hit Kristian in the shoulder and he lost his grip on the rock. He fell several feet before the rope snagged on the anchor, swinging Kristian across the cliff.

The anchor ripped from the rock and Kristian fell further. His weight pulled the rope and flung Jimmy away from the rock face. The two men dangled, trying to latch themselves back onto the mountain with their ice axes. They spun and swung wildly. The weight of the two men pulled on Turk and strained the other anchors.

Turk's eyes locked onto the anchor in front of his face as it began to buckle. He scrambled to get a fresh anchor from his belt and he screamed down at Kristian and Jimmy, "Hold on!" The anchor in front of him warped and bent. "Stop moving! You have to stop moving!"

Kristian and Jimmy continued to try to get a firm hold of the rock face. Turk got his fresh anchor free of his belt and just as he was about to lock it tightly into the ice, something pelted him in the face.

At first he thought it was a rock, but quickly realized it was too soft. It slathered him with warmth as it bounced off of his head, smearing his goggles with fresh blood, distorting his vision. He only caught a glimpse of the object before it fell from sight, and through the red he could see that it was Betty's severed arm.

Turk lost his balance and the existing anchor snapped loose. Turk, Jimmy, and Kristian plummeted toward the ground. Another anchor caught the rope, and the three men were jerked to a halt, but only for a brief moment before that anchor snapped under their weight as well, and the men fell again.

Another anchor caught hold and held just long enough for Kristian to grab hold of the rock face and cut himself loose from the rope with his ice axe. Jimmy and Turk tumbled past Kristian as the rope tore the anchors from the ice as they dropped with a repeated *SNAP—SNAP—SNAP!*

Finally, one of the anchors held again. Jimmy and Turk were both slammed into the side of the mountain.

"Fuck!" Turk yelled. Jimmy looked up at Turk for direction and Turk told him, "It'll hold! It'll hold!" Turk pulled another anchor from his belt and secured it into the rock face.

He looked up to see if he could locate Kristian. The snowfall had become too thick to see much of anything. He called out to him, but the distance between them was too great to communicate. Jimmy glanced down. Even as far as they had descended, a fall from this height would still be fatal.

"Where is he?" Jimmy yelled to Turk.

"Must have cut himself free!"

"We have to climb back up to him!" Turk hesitated a moment, prompting Jimmy to shout, "We can't leave him! Not if he could still alive!"

Turk nodded at Jimmy and said, "We don't have enough slack for you to stay behind! Better stick together!"

High above them, with no rope to secure him, Kristian was clinging to the rock for dear life. He looked down but couldn't see Turk or Jimmy through the blinding snow. He shouted out to them, but the wind stole his voice. He pulled an anchor from his own belt and secured it into a notch in the rock. The rope connecting him to the anchor was only two feet long—not enough to climb with, but enough to keep him from falling. He tried calling for Turk again, but stopped when he heard a crunching sound overhead.

His eyes darted up to see the creature moving down the rock toward him. Its massive hands gripped the mountain side with ease and its long legs extended fluidly to find footing. Kristian reached for his rifle but soon recalled that he had dropped it into the abyss below. The creature caught sight of him and it howled out ferociously. Kristian tried to move downward to flee, but he was tethered in place to the anchor. The creature scurried across the rock face at him, giving Kristian little time to form a plan.

He had two options: let the creature kill him, or risk falling.

He unclipped himself from the anchor and extended his leg out to find his footing. The creature was nearly upon him when Kristian's foot found a rock, but the spikes on the crampon slipped and Kristian fell. He dropped through the air only a short distance before he landed hard on his back atop a small ledge barely large enough to hold him. The back of his head hit the ice and his vision blurred for a moment before everything went black.

Further down the rock face Jimmy could see movement above him and Turk. He squinted and quietly said, "Turk," but the wind was too loud and Jimmy had to yell out, "Turk!" as the movement took the shape of the creature climbing down toward them.

Turk looked back at Jimmy and saw him pointing. Turk's head whipped around to see the creature drop through the air and effortlessly grabbed hold of a jagged rock. It swung itself across the rock face like an Orangutan, landing with a firm grip on the ice only a few yards from them.

"Aw, hell," Turk groaned.

The creature howled menacingly at Turk, taunting him. It used its free hand—the one not clutching the rock—to pound its chest and even through the wind Jimmy could hear the dull, wet thuds with every hit. Betty's blood was slathered all across its primitive face, and its grayish fur was stained red from the neck down to the groin.

Turk pulled his elephant gun from the holster and took aim. He squeezed the trigger—*CLICK!* Empty. Turk spun to Jimmy and crowed, "Jimmy! Shoot it!"

Jimmy fumbled for his weapon while Turk dug into his pockets for more rounds. The creature scrambled across the rock face at them as Jimmy raised his rifle.

"Shoot it!"

Jimmy fired. The bullet hit the creature in the hand, blasting it off the rock. It yelped out in pain and toppled from sight into the void.

Jimmy could hardly believe his luck. One shot and he had momentarily saved their lives. The single bullet, perfectly placed, was enough to cause the creature to lose its hold of the mountain. Jimmy couldn't have pulled that off again if he had a million attempts. Though he was no stranger to firearms, never had he needed to use one while hanging off an icy mountain.

They took a moment to catch their breath, and Turk patted Jimmy on the shoulder.

"Well done."

Chapter Nine
THE ICE CAVERN

Kristian's eyes peeled open, and he gently touched the back of his wounded head. He looked up, expecting the creature to be hanging over him, but he was all alone. He nearly rolled over the lip of the ledge when he moved to his side, and as he did, he looked down at the seemingly endless fall below him. Gently he pulled himself to his feet, and as he stood he found himself at the entrance of a dark cavern that led inside the mountain.

He pulled a flashlight from his pack and clicked it on. Through the darkness he could see the narrow corridor leading from the mouth, lined in wet, icy rock, glistening in the flashlight's glow.

He contemplated his options, of which again he saw only two: try to descend the rock face with no rope, or take his chance in the cave. The creature had seen him out here, though he wasn't sure how long ago that was. The light outside hadn't changed much from what he could tell, so it may have only been a few minutes since his head cracked against the ledge—but the creature may have still been in pursuit, and with no rope and no rifle he wouldn't stand a chance against it there on the ledge.

Kristian gripped his dual ice axes and walked inside the cavern. The wind howled through the passageways of the cave like a constant echoing moan as he forced himself through the tight corridor. He felt his chest squeeze in on itself as he brushed against the icy walls on both sides.

Something on his coat snagged. He tried to tug it loose, but the tightness of the cave didn't allow for much flexibility. He pulled again. It wouldn't budge. Then again. His breathing was getting quicker as he panicked. If the creature entered the cave behind him, he was still close enough to the entrance that he would be in range of the long hairy arms. He tried to push those thoughts out of his mind and gave one final, hard pull. The force was just enough to break him free.

He squeezed further down the corridor, all the while being mindful not to catch his pack or coat on anything else. The passageway opened up into a wider space, like a crystal lobby inside the mountain. Stalagmites and stalactites lined the floor and ceiling. There was no snow inside the cave, due to the curvature of the corridor he came through, which was enough to keep any flakes from fluttering in. Other than a few bits of exposed rock, the entire cave was solid ice.

The baritone call of the wind still hummed around him, and for a moment Kristian thought he may have heard the creature's guttural howl. He quickly dismissed it, however, as a simple inflection in the wind's scream.

In front of him, he could see three more corridors leading out of the icy lobby. Two of them looked narrow, like the one he had just come through, but the third was wider and looked much easier to traverse. He assumed at least one of these might lead to another way out of the mountain, something lower perhaps, an exit that would allow him to skip the rest of the climb down the murderous rock face. He chose the wider corridor and continued on.

Kristian started out walking normally, one foot before the other, his shoulders squared, but several yards down the passageway he felt as though the walls were closing in on him. The corridor was narrowing and Kristian had to turn to his side and once again squeeze his way forward. Another dozen yards further, the corridor widened again, and Kristian was able to breathe normally. He continued on, and again, the walls tightened. It was as if they were alive, constricting around him. He pressed forward, and the corridor widened once more, only to close right back in. Kristian imagined he was in the throat of a giant wolf, tightening and lurching to swallow a hunk of meat.

Light bounced off the wet walls near the end of the corridor. Kristian hastened his pace and slipped out into the belly of the cave, which opened up wide into a great hall of icy stone. He could see a series of ledges and rocky platforms that seemed to spiral down toward the base of the cave where a dim beam of sunlight flared from the outside. Kristian grinned at his fortune and took a step forward, preparing to leap to the first ledge—but he froze when a grunt echoed through the cave.

As if it were an unconscious reflex, Kristian clicked off his flashlight and tucked it away. He crouched down low heard another grunt, this one longer, straining. He leaned over the ledge and stared down at the bottom of the cave where the beam of sunlight was creeping through. In the glow he could see two of the hairy creatures huddled together over a caribou carcass, tearing at the flesh with their massive hands and three-inch incisors. Kristian gripped his ice axes tightly and watched in awe as the animals continued to feast.

The larger of the two creatures grabbed the dead caribou's head and tore it from the shoulders. Its jaws locked over the top of the caribou's brow, covering its lifeless eyes. It began to suck, suctioning the eyeballs from their sockets. Kristian heard them pop inside the creature's mouth as it chewed. It grunted in satisfaction before ripping the tongue from the caribou's mouth.

The smaller creature reached for the tongue, but the larger swatted him away. The smaller creature reached again, and this time the larger grunted aggressively, and the smaller creature scooted back. The larger creature held the tongue at both ends and took a bite out of the center. It chewed, staring the other creature down. The smaller creature kept back until the larger held out the two ends of the tongue as an offering. It grunted gently, assuring the small creature that he was allowing him to come closer. With a thankful grunt, the smaller creature took the tongue pieces gently from his alpha's palms and shoved them into its mouth. It bobbed up and down, ever so slightly, the way a chimp does when it's excited.

Kristian saw the warm blood oozing from the caribou, freezing to the icy floor. The creatures had most likely drug the animal inside through the crack in the cave wall where the sunlight bled in. That was his way out, the exit from the mountain he was hoping for. He wasn't sure that it would take him out to the base of the mountain, but either way it was further down than the entrance he had come in through, which meant a shorter distance for him to climb down to get back to the lodge. He knew that in order for him to get out, he'd need to make it past the two hulking beasts that were currently devouring the three-hundred and fifty pound buck.

If he still had his elephant gun, he would have been able to gun them both down. He had the perfect vantage point, high above them beside the highest ledge—but his rifle was gone. All he had were his ice axes and the spit-shined hunting knife on his hip.

Taking the creatures head on would not get him anywhere but pulled apart in a gruesome display of brutish violence. He'd need to be stealthy. He'd need to creep past them somehow. The ice axes and the knife were his last resort, a way to get a few digs in should his plan fail.

He looked at the series of ledges that led down to the bottom of the cave. If he were to jump down, ledge by ledge, the creatures would spot him. He'd need to distract them, get them to move, to leave the area. Kristian looked around for something he could throw, a loose hunk of ice or a rock small enough for him to pick up. He spotted a baseball-sized stone frozen to the ground, the perfect size and weight to lob across the belly of the cave and draw their focus away.

Kristian dragged his hunting knife from his belt so he could wedge the stone from the ice. The dull sound of the metal blade rubbing against the leather sheath sent the softest of echoes bouncing off the walls of the cave, and the creatures below perked up. Kristian was still.

The alpha creature stood, arching its spine, tilting its head backward. It sniffed the air, its thin ape-like nostrils flaring. It closed its eyes and its head rolled to the side as it inhaled deeply. As its eyes peeled back open it stared directly up at Kristian.

Kristian took a step back as the smaller creature stood and looked up at him as well. They glared at him and the alpha let out a bellowing howl that reverberated across the walls of the shimmering cave.

Kristian backed away from the ledge out of sight. He looked around frantically for somewhere to go, but the only option he could see was back the way he had come, and as far as he knew the creature from the rock face was still pursuing him from outside.

He heard an icy crack followed by a scraping sound, and he peeked over the edge to see the alpha climbing up the cave wall to the lowest ledge. The creature then leapt up to the next ledge and used its long apish arms to heave itself upward to the third.

The smaller creature spit out a small chunk of the caribou tongue and chased after the alpha. The alpha howled again and Kristian instinctually reached to cover his ears as the sound bounced off the walls, rustling loose bits of ice from the stalactites above his head.

As one of the ice chips slid across the ground, Kristian saw it fall and disappear into a hole he hadn't noticed before. He hurried over and saw a narrow chute in the ground barely large enough for him to fit through. He looked back and saw the two creatures ascending the ledges up the cave belly toward him.

They were almost upon him.

Without another thought, Kristian unclipped his pack and lowered his legs down through the chute, sinking into the ground. Going feet first, he couldn't see where he was headed—the narrowness of the chute didn't allow him to look past his legs. He guided himself with the toes of his boots and shuffled downward.

As Kristian's head sank from view into the earth, the alpha hoisted himself up from the final ledge. It sniffed the air, searching for Kristian's scent. Kristian wasted no time continuing to shimmy down the chute. The alpha heard the rubbing of Kristian's coat and stomped over to the hole. Kristian was only five feet down when he looked up to see the creature standing over the hole above him.

The creature dropped to its knees and as it shoved his massive hand down into the chute, its long fingers came just shy of ripping Kristian's face off. Kristian squeezed his eyes closed as the middle and index finger strained to reach him. When he opened his eyes again, he saw the animal's hand retract back up the chute, then the creature looked down through the hole again and the caribou's blood leaked over its slack jaw, dripping down across Kristian's face. He groaned as the warm liquid oozed over his cheeks.

The alpha began digging at the hole, trying to widen it so he could reach further inside. Its fists pounded the ice, cracking it away piece by piece. Kristian wormed his way further down and the passageway curved in an "L" shape so that soon he was laying flat on his back inside the thin tunnel.

The creature broke further in and reached out his long arm once again to grab Kristian, who was just beyond his grasp. Kristian took one last look at the creature above him before he inched his way out of sight.

The sound was even more deafening within the chute when the alpha howled again. Kristian growled back menacingly, then all went silent. He grinned at the thought his scream may have intimidated the creature.

Stupid animal.

Then something locked tightly around Kristian's ankle and he was pulled further through the chute and yanked upward out of the ground. The smaller creature had dug its own hole and grabbed Kristian's leg, jerking him back up to the surface. It flung Kristian through the air and he slammed against the wall of the cave.

The alpha grabbed Kristian by the scruff of his coat and hoisted him up so that the two were eye to eye. Kristian slashed at the creature with the ice axe in his left hand, slicing through the animal's cheek, then sunk the tip of the other ice axe into the animal's thick, muscly neck. The creature yelped and his fingers tore through the coat, dropping Kristian to the ground.

Kristian turned to run toward the passageway he entered through, but the alpha's clawed hand raked across his back, tearing through what remained of his coat, digging into his flesh. Kristian screamed and tumbled to the ground. The alpha howled again and beat its fists against its broad chest.

BARRRROOOOM! The blast from a rifle hit a stalactite hanging from the ceiling of the cave. It cracked and part of it broke off. The alpha had no time to move before the icy cone crashed down and impaled it through the shoulder blade, nailing it to the ground. Kristian looked up to see Turk and Jimmy standing behind him, elephant guns in hand.

The smaller creature leapt away and landed on the highest platform ledge. In unison, Turk and Jimmy both fired at the animal, but they missed and the creature fled down into the belly of the cave.

Turk hurriedly helped Kristian to his feet, and as he rose, Jimmy could see that his coat was flayed and bloody.

"He's hurt."

Turk looked over Kristian's shoulder at his wounded back. He gently spun Kristian around and pulled off what was left of the coat so he could get a closer look at the damage.

"Keep an eye out," Turk said to Jimmy as he began inspecting the four long claw marks across Kristian's back. "You're losing a good amount of blood," he muttered to Kristian. "I gotta wrap this up."

Turk reached into his pack and pulled out a roll of gauze that he began to unspool and wrap around Kristian's torso.

Jimmy winced at the sight of the cuts as the blood gushed out of them.

"What's wrong?" Kristian asked Jimmy as he clocked his expression. "Is it bad?"

"It's—" Jimmy started.

"It'll be fine," Turk interrupted as he finished the wrap. "But your coat's in shreds. You won't be able to last long in this cold."

"The other exit," Kristian said.

"What?"

"Down the belly of the cave. I saw another way out." He motioned down over the ledge where the scattered caribou carcasses were strewn about.

"The other Sasquatch went down there," Jimmy noted.

"Then we'll need to be ready for it," Turk replied.

Moments later, Turk had secured a line and the three men repelled down to the bottom of the cave. Turk and Jimmy held their rifles at the ready while Kristian gripped his ice axes tightly. The belly of the cave was lined with numerous tunnels and corridors, spreading out in all directions. Sunlight flooded in through the wide crack in the wall, a rift large enough for someone to walk through.

"There," Kristian whispered as he gestured toward the light. The howl of the smaller creature echoed through the belly of the cave and the three men spun around, trying to identify what direction it was truly coming from.

Even in that intense moment, Kristian could feel the

overwhelming cold constricting around him. His chest tightened, his extremities growing numb.

The three men made their way past the dead caribou toward the crack in the wall. As they moved stealthily across the belly of the cave Jimmy could sense the third creature's presence. He imagined it was watching them from one of the shadowy tunnels.

He kept his rifle aimed behind them even after the moment they stepped out of the cave into the fading daylight. The expedition had gone horribly awry, and Jimmy thought about all the bloodshed that had occurred in such a paltry amount of time. He imagined how many others had suffered a similar fate upon the mountain and wondered how many lives had been lost in relation to the Caliber Lodge.

Chapter Ten
IGAK & SHISHMAR

Alaska, 1951. Fourteen years earlier.

Mr. and Mrs. Everly had come to Alaska by way of the great white north in search of truth behind murmured legends of a beast that dwelled in the uncharted mountains of the frozen wilderness. They had heard tales of the ape who walked upright—the fur-covered Wildman. Though they knew the likelihood that the creature was nothing more than folklore, they nonetheless made the journey hoping to find a diamond among the ice.

They stopped in a small coastal fishing town and indulged themselves with a basket of prawns. The modest building looked as though it could topple over if the wind were to blow against it from the wrong direction. They struck up a conversation with a group of men and women on the opposite side of the room, who claimed to be from the U.S. Geological Survey. They said they were working on an exploration program in search of oil deposits, which had been ongoing since 1946. They noted that the U.S. Navy had become involved in the project, and there was talk that the discovery of substantial oil deposits would be justification for statehood for Alaska.

The Everlys engaged with the scientists for a short while, pandering to their interest in government affairs. When the time felt right, and he didn't think it would be too abrupt of a turn, Charles inquired whether any of them were hunters. One spoke up, stating he'd killed a reindeer the previous season. Charles then asked if they'd heard rumors of any uncommon prey in territory. The scientists rambled off the usual lineup of moose, fox, and bear before Charles came out with it.

"We're looking for a large primate of sorts."

The scientists were silent a moment, looking at one another before assuming that Charles was attempting to be humorous. Charles clarified that he was asking in sincerity, which drove most of the scientists to slowly turn their shoulders and remove themselves from the asinine conversation. One of them, however, a ginger-haired woman with oversized spectacles, offered a single speck of advice.

"The natives believe in the sort of animal you're alluding to. If you want to do some digging into their folklore, I would start by visiting some of the villages. There's one about ten miles down the coast." Charles thanked her and the Everlys packed up their gear and headed out.

Over the next several weeks they trekked across the Alaskan frontier, stopping into each village they passed. They had only learned a handful of Inuit words and had been having a troublesome time finding any information on what they sought. They began to lose faith that there was anything worth finding, assuming the rumors may have spawned from drunken sightings of Kodiak or perhaps Polar bears.

Halfway through the third week in the Far North, the Everlys came upon an Inuit settlement inhabited by an inland tribe of fur traders. It was summer, and the people of the camp had erected tents made of tightly pulled caribou skin for shelter. Fox and bear pelts were in abundance, sorted and organized on handmade racks staked into the frozen earth. They greeted the Everlys, welcoming them into their camp in the native Inupiaq tongue.

The sight of the Everlys' expensive clothing and gear was

enough to tell the Inuit people that the visitors may be prime customers to sell to or trade with. Several of the women approached them, laying their best furs over their forearms, showcasing the fine condition. Mrs. Everly removed her gloves and ran her fingers through the thick hair of the pelt.

She smiled and nodded to the women, approving of the quality. She made her way down the row of eager sellers, inspecting the furs, touching them, allowing first her thumb and index finger to roll the strands back and forth, then sliding her full hand across, letting the strands brush against the spaces between her fingers.

One of the tribesmen approached Charles Everly and gestured for him to follow. He led him over to one of the tents and motioned for him to sit down on the stump beside the entrance flap. The Inuit poked his head inside the tent, said something in his native tongue, then backed up as another man, this one a few years younger, emerged from inside. The first man pointed at Charles and said, "English," then walked away.

The younger man took a seat on the stump across from Mr. Everly, patted his chest and said, "Igak. Translate."

Charles touched the breast of his posh winter coat and replied, "Charles. Thank you."

Igak nodded as the two men sat together beside the small fire where a makeshift spit was slowly cooking up a skewer of seasoned meat. Igak offered Charles some water, then tore off a hunk of the meat and handed it to him. Every outsider who visited the village came hungry. It was a lengthy journey to and from the next cropping of civilization, and Igak felt it was his responsibility to provide sustenance for weary travelers.

As he chewed on the flesh, Charles attempted to inquire about the mysterious animal they were seeking. He was relieved that this Igak from the village could speak at least minimal English.

"We're looking for an animal. A large beast," Charles said as he stood and raised his arms in the air, stretching as tall as possible. Igak looked at him, cocking his head as he tried to understand. "Monkey. Ape." He mockingly scratched at his armpits and did a small hop.

"No apes," Igak said as he chuckled at the sight of the grown man impersonating a gorilla.

Mrs. Everly approached wearing a fox stole over her shoulders, which she had just finished bartering for with the native women. She ran her hand across the fur, then motioned to the rest of her body as she said, "It walks on two legs. Fur everywhere."

Igak's smile faded. He understood now. He nodded and replied in broken English, "Not ape. Not Animal. Much strong mans. Big mans." He pounded on his chest. "Strong," Igak repeated.

"No, we're looking for an animal. A primate of sorts," Charles elaborated.

Igak shook his head, offered Charles another piece of meat from the skewer, and then handed a cut to Mrs. Everly. She examined it. It was fully cooked, a bit charred on the edges. She pulled it apart with her fingers, revealing the pinkish core, and sniffed.

"Bear?" she asked. Igak nodded. Her eyes lit up as she took a bite. She chewed quicker, almost ravenously. The Inuit man smiled and handed her another piece. Besides being the local translator, Igak was revered as the best cook in the village. It wasn't saying much as there were only twenty or so other people who lived there, but it meant something to him. He learned to season game meat and fish. He learned how to pair flavors and entice the palate, all this with only the bare essentials available to him in the little hamlet.

Mrs. Everly looked at Charles and exclaimed, "This is amazing." Though not as immediately taken with the flavor as his wife had been, he agreed that it was indeed impressive. His attention, however, was on the task at hand.

"You look for much strong mans. Tornit," Igak said.

"No—," Charles started but was immediately cut off by Igak.

"Tornit."

Mr. and Mrs. Everly looked at each other, wondering if the other had understood. "Tornit?" Mrs. Everly echoed.

Igak nodded once more. He gestured for them to keep eating and after hesitating a moment they both finished the bear meat that Igak had provided. Igak grinned and pointed over at the mountain range in the distance.

"Tornit. Big mans. Strong."

"Big man?" Mrs. Everly asked. Igak stood and reached his arms as high into the air as he was able, just as Charles had done.

"Tornit. Big mans," he repeated, straining to reach higher. "All fur. People like us." He poked his temple. "Much smart. Much smart. Much strong. Not animal."

"Not animal?" Mrs. Everly clarified. Igak shook his head again.

"Can you take us to see this big man?" Charles asked.

"Shishmar," Igak answered. "No, no, no." He did slight warning waves with his open palms. "I make food." Igak gently shook the skewer of dripping meat.

"Please? We came all this way to see the big man." Mrs. Everly casually pleaded.

"Big mans in Shishmar. Danger in Shishmar."

"Shishmar is a place?" Charles inquired, his patience starting to run thin.

"Shishmar. No, no, no." As he spoke, he continued to shake his head and wave his hands, one of them still holding the meat skewer. An expression of great worry had overtaken his face and the Everlys immediately knew that wherever this Shishmar was, it was where they needed to be. "Shishmar people, no good."

"Why no good?" Mrs. Everly asked.

"Shishmar and big mans—" Igak pressed his fingertips

together rapidly, shaping his hand like a squawking duck. "Talk. Trade. Live as one."

"They live with the beasts?" Charles asked, unable to hide his look of disgust.

"Tornit live in mountain. Shishmar below. At base. Tornit come down, trade with Shishmar. Equal." Igak turned his palms upward, lowering and raising them like a balancing scale.

"Outsiders not welcome at Shishmar. Shishmar protect Tornit. Shishmar dangerous."

Charles helped himself to another slice of the bear meat. He shoved it into his mouth and as he chewed he mumbled, "We need a guide. What will it cost to convince you to take us to this Shishmar?"

"Not about money."

"Then you'll take us?"

"About safety. My people not go Shishmar. No like."

Charles looked over his shoulder to gesture at all the furs on the village racks. "This is how your people survive, yes? You sell the furs to travelers. You take them into the towns to sell to white folks."

"We try to sell, yes."

"If you agree to take us to Shishmar, we will buy them all. All the furs you have."

"Too many furs for you to carry."

"I don't intend to take them. I'll buy them and leave them here. You can sell them off again to the next passerby or take them into the closest coastal town. Twice the profit for your people. All we want is to go to Shishmar."

Igak stood from the stump and quietly observed the people of his village, some of whom had been watching the interaction with the visitors in silence. He looked at a man skinning an arctic fox over an almost perfect oval boulder. His eyes drifted to a young mother with a child as she tried to teach him how to properly roll up a tent flap. He looked at the women holding the pelts and they stared back at him, not understanding anything of the conversation that just took place.

He turned and looked at Charles and Mrs. Everly. "All the furs?" Igak clarified. Charles nodded with a grin. "I take you to Shishmar."

The walk through the wilds of Alaska was not a short one. Though the summer climate made it an easier trek than it could have been, there was no lack of struggle for the Everlys as they followed Igak across the white terrain. For four days they trudged up snowcapped hills and frostbitten fields, each night stopping to camp in a single caribou hide tent that Igak would assemble from the bulky pack he carried on his shoulders.

It was already dark on the fifth day when they reached the hamlet of Shishmar at the base of the towering mountain. The villagers assembled and approached them as a group. In their hands they held long spears that stretched ten feet into the air. Similar caribou skin tents were setup in a semi-circle around a hearty fire encompassed by large stones. There were no racks of animal furs as there had been at Igak's village. Instead, the area was filled with strange, primitive structures that look like enormous coffins standing on end.

The Everlys could immediately sense the hostility and aggression from the villagers, none of which uttered a word as they gripped the body of their jagged weapons. Igak stepped forward between the Americans and the Shishmari and greeted them in his native tongue.

The Shishmari did not respond. Igak glanced at the Everlys, then turned back to the spear wielding natives. He spoke to them further, Mr. and Mrs. Everly unable to understand a single word.

Regardless of their lack of verbal comprehension, the body language could convey all they needed to know. These people, the Shishmari, they would not allow them into their camp, much less share any information on the so-called Tornit with them.

"Please. We'd like to see the Tornit," Charles said, stepping past Igak. "I can pay whatever you'd like."

One of the Shishmari stepped forward and lowered the blade of his spear to Charles' throat. He shouted something at Charles, spewing a spray of saliva across Charles' face in the process. Charles' hand moved toward the holster on his hip, but before his fingers could even graze the butt of the pistol sleeping within, the remaining natives encompassed him with their pointed spears.

"Wait!" Mrs. Everly shouted, raising her hands in the air. "We'll leave. We'll leave."

The tallest of the natives, whose moose skin clothing was adorned with bear claws on woven tassels, raised his spear and walked over to Mrs. Everly. Judging by his somewhat elevated attire, she assumed this was the chief of the village. He spoke with a snarl, words she could not decipher.

She pointed at her husband and replied, "Don't hurt him. We mean no harm."

"Tornit," the chief said, shaking his head slowly. He stared at her with blank eyes. He didn't wear the same anger his fellow tribesmen displayed. He was eerily calm, void of emotion as he uttered, "Never for you."

Charles and Igak were as surprised as Mrs. Everly to hear the English words escape from the chief's mouth. He spoke once more with the same level voice.

"Never for anyone." He motioned to the other Shishmari, and they immediately raised their spears and backed away from Charles.

Mrs. Everly took Charles by the hand and they walked away

with Igak, leaving the villagers behind them. They put forty-five minutes between them and Shishmar before setting up camp for the night.

"It's up there," Charles said as his eyes stared up at the massive peak. He stoked the fire as Igak prepared some raw meat from his pack.

"Through Shishmar is way up mountain," Igak explained.

"We can traverse from the other side," Charles corrected him.

"Very dangerous path. Don't have gear."

"We'll free climb. The outcropping is rough enough to scramble. We can make it up to the first level at least."

Mrs. Everly was quiet as the two men discussed the route to take up the mountain to avoid being seen by the Shishmari. Her mind dwelled on the primitive structures they saw throughout the village. In the low light they resembled monoliths, though she could not be sure if they were stone or a very smooth wood. What she was sure of, however, was the images that were carved into the structures terrified her. They were creatures, standing upright, long arms pressed tightly to their sides, with etchings to resemble fur. The most startling piece were the faces. Thick brows, sharp fangs, and overly large bulging eyes.

She recalled, in the moments proceeding the Shishmari surrounding her husband, she had been much more intimidated by the inanimate carvings than she was by the armed villagers.

"We leave at dawn," Charles said as he took a piece of the seared meat from Igak. He looked at Mrs. Everly for approval. She nodded and gave him a weak smile, all the while her mind imprisoned by the thought of those terrible faces.

The climb, though treacherous, went without incident. Igak and the

Everlys ascended the mountain from a bulbous outcropping of rock protruding from the side. They avoided the icy areas and chose instead to take the slower, yet somewhat safer passage. At one point they could see Shishmar far below them and quickly relocated as not to be spotted.

They trudged through the snow alongside a dense forest that bordered a vast valley bowl. Mrs. Everly raised her flattened hand above her brow to shield her eyes. On the other side of the valley, she saw a massive rock face with an almost ninety degree drop leading toward the side of the mountain where Shishmar was located.

"Glad we didn't come up that way," she said. Charles touched her on the small of her back and pointed down into the valley.

"Caribou," he whispered.

She looked down at the grazing herd, smiling at the sight of the unbothered animals.

Igak had no interest in the herd. He kept his eyes moving, scanning the forest at their back for any sign of movement.

"Must be careful," Igak said in a hushed voice. "Tornit loves caribou."

Mrs. Everly clocked something in the snow. A footprint, like a man's but several times the size. She drew Charles' attention, and they inspected the track. There were a series of them, leading in all directions.

"Is this—," Mrs. Everly began to ask.

"Tornit. Yes," Igak said as he stood over one of the prints. "Adult male. And those," he said, pointing to a line of smaller tracks. "Youth."

The Everlys turned to him with surprised expressions.

"There are two of them?" Charles asked.

"Two? No. Many. Many big mans. Many Tornit."

Charles looked at his wife. "I thought it was just his poor English when he said big *mans*. I didn't think he meant it as a plural."

Igak stepped past them and pointed out at the rock face on the other side of the valley bowl. "There."

The Everlys stood from the crouched position they were in and each raised a hand to shield their eyes.

"Holy lord."

Fourteen years later, in 1965, Igak was still on that same mountain, albeit in the quiet confines of the ritzy Caliber Lodge. The Everlys had offered him a job to be their full-time chef after their shared adventure. He had led them to the creatures they sought and to repay him, they not only paid his village for the furs they chose not to take, they committed to him a lifetime opportunity to service the wealthy elite. That day on the mountain, the Everlys knew they found a goldmine. They had found their niche. That day on the mountain, they put in motion the needed steps to purchase the land legally and stake their claim on the wild beasts that inhabited it.

The only roadblock that had stood in their way were the Shishmari. The dangerous tribe had no intention of leaving the mountain. They saw it as their duty to protect the beings that resided there and would not allow a pair of Americans, regardless of the legalities, to take control of the land. This, however, was not much of a challenge for the Everlys to overcome. They hired a group of rough-neck drillers under the table to make the village of Shishmar disappear. A dozen shotguns, a dozen shovels, and few cans of gasoline later, the people of the tiny hamlet were nothing but a story among the other Inuits.

Chapter Eleven
THE MARBLE STAIRCASE

By the time Turk, Jimmy and Kristian had reached the lodge, the sun had set behind the mountain and the temperature dropped to an unbearable degree. Their journey out of the ice cavern had been mostly uneventful, save for the sight of David's body that was pulverized at the base of the rock face. Jimmy couldn't keep himself from heaving and vomiting into the snow a few feet away. He had seen dead bodies before, but the height from which David had fallen, and the force of the impact, had reduced his body to a pulpy mess of blood and organs barely recognizable as a human being.

Kristian had no reaction at all to Blackwell's remains. He was completely focused on the pain in his own throbbing back. The gauze wrapped around him had helped slow the bleeding from the long gashes inflicted by the creature's claws, and Turk had assured him he'd be able to fix him up properly once they returned to safety.

The glow from the light inside the lodge looked like an oasis to all three of them. It was a haven in the snowy distance, which they rushed toward as quickly as possible while the freeze numbed their bodies.

Upon reaching the back door of the lodge, Kristian's legs went slack and Turk had to all but carry him inside. He called for Igak to come and help lift Kristian and bring him to the elevator.

As Turk closed the ornately woven gate and pulled on the lift lever Jimmy was surprised to see the elevator descend into the floor. He was, until that point, unaware of the basement level's existence.

He wondered if there was some sort of medical unit down there, but before he had an opportunity to ask, the elevator and the three men inside were gone.

"Mr. Knotts," a voice said from behind him. Jimmy turned to see Gregory, the butler, standing in the middle of the foyer with his arms extended out. "May I take your things? I'm sure after the exciting hunt you're ready for a nice hot shower." Jimmy looked at the old man—his professional smile, his pristine tuxedo, his perfectly slicked white hair—it was a jarring sight compared to all the mess and violence he had seen earlier in the day.

"What's below us, Gregory?"

"Below us, sir?" Gregory was confused by the request. He looked at the ice caked all over Jimmy's climbing gear and the restless expression on his face.

"Turk just took Kristian to a lower level."

"There's a recovery bay down there for injured parties," Gregory replied.

"I need to speak to Mrs. Everly," Jimmy stated plainly.

"Wouldn't you like to relax from the journey?"

"I intend to, after I speak with Mrs. Everly."

"What are you needing to speak to Mrs. Everly about, sir?"

Jimmy snapped into character and pointed at Gregory, his index finger inches from the butler's nose. "Explain to me how that is any business of the resident butler."

Gregory took a step back, lowered his head and said, "Of course, sir. Pardon me. I believe she may be down in the medical bay. When she saw the three of you returning, with Mr. Beckett being carried, she immediately went down to prepare." He backed away further and before he turned away he said, "Shall I take you down there, sir?"

The squeak of the elevator caught Jimmy's attention. Mrs. Everly stood behind the gate as it rose back up to the foyer level.

"Mr. Knotts. How are you holding up? Jonathan just filled me in on the tragic details of the expedition," she said as she stepped out and approached him. Gregory took his leave as Jimmy turned his focus to Everly.

"Tragic details is a mild way of describing what happened, Mrs. Everly."

"I don't mean to make light of the situation. It is terrible, to say the least."

"Two people died on your man's watch."

"Mr. Knotts, this was all in the agreement that you and the others signed. Safety was not guaranteed. To insinuate that it was Mr. Turk's fault that the Blackwells died is—"

"Mrs. Everly—"

"Sir, I fully understand the state of mind you must be in right now. Trying to comprehend not only the existence of those animals out there but also the death of the Blackwells—their fate, it is a tragedy for sure—but the agreement you signed stated that this was a dangerous expedition."

The ice on Jimmy's gear began to melt and pool on the floor beneath him. "In circumstances such as this, what is the protocol? What do you tell the families?"

Mrs. Everly took a step closer as she replied, "What we tell the family Blackwell is not something you need be concerned about, Mr. Knotts. Let it escape your mind. Relax. Enjoy yourself. Don't dwell on others' misfortune."

"Others' misfortune? Nearly mine as well."

"You need to decompress," she said. "Take a few minutes. Get out of your gear. We can talk when you've had time to calm down." She walked away into the kitchen, leaving Jimmy alone in the foyer.

He looked down at his distorted reflection in the wet, glossy floor. He considered that she may have been right. If there was ever a time that one would need to decompress it would have been after the day that he just had. He'd seen creatures he'd only hours before questioned the existence of. He'd seen a woman torn apart and her husband flung to his death. He wrestled with his emotions in that moment and settled on the understanding that he had an obligation to push them aside. Jimmy was a professional with a mission to carry out, one he wasn't willing to risk botching a second time.

He made his way to the lounge and found the telephone sitting atop an end table made of antlers and pine. He stood as he dialed and as it rang, waiting for the recipient to pick up on the other end of the line. Jimmy kept his eye on the door.

The ringing eventually stopped with no answer. Jimmy dialed again, only to be met with the same outcome. He decided he would try to reach Levi at a later hour and take Gregory's suggestion to relax for a spell.

When he got into the elevator, he debated taking it down to the basement level to see how Kristian's recovery was going, but decided to first get out of his thawing clothing.

Once in his room, he stripped down, and as he folded his jacket and pants over his arm, the ice covering them crunched and chipped apart. He turned on the shower and closed himself in the bathroom to let the steam fill the room. He breathed deeply, trying to clear his mind as the heat warmed his core.

He let the water run over his face, and with his eyes closed, the day's violent images flashed through his mind. He thought about the murder of the pregnant creature, and Betty's blood oozing over the edge of the cliff, and David's mashed body, and Kristian's slashed back.

His eyes snapped open.

Kristian's back.

How could I have been so short-sighted?

This was the opportunity Jimmy had been waiting for. It was

a known fact that Wilhelm Stengl had been stabbed in the back, just above his right kidney, and therefore would have a sizable scar. It was the only tangible identifier they had to go off of, yet during the chaos in the ice cavern, it had not even occurred to Jimmy to get a glimpse of what lied beneath Kristian's shredded coat.

He quickly finished in the shower and as he dried off, he popped open his suitcase and removed the hidden Ballester-Molina. He checked to be sure it was still loaded. It always was.

As he sat down on the edge of the bed, he contemplated his next move. He'd need to go down to the lower floor when no one else was around. If the staff of the Caliber Lodge caught him down there inspecting Kristian's body, it would raise a flag. Even worse would be if Kristian himself were to catch him sneaking a peek. Jimmy knew he'd need to wait for the right moment, but there was no way to be sure how big a window he had.

Would Kristian be returning to his room? Would Turk or Igak be staying down in the recovery bay with him all night?

The only thing Jimmy was certain of was that he had about an hour to kill as the staff tended to Kristian's wounds. After that, he'd take the next steps. This was his chance to rest, to decompress as Mrs. Everly had said.

He set the alarm on the golden clock perched upon the end table, tucked the pistol beneath his pillow, laid his head upon it, and closed his eyes.

It was seven at night when Jimmy awoke to the sound of the clock's alarm. He sat up in bed, his eyes adjusting to the dimness of the room, and he gave himself a moment to collect his thoughts as the nightmares he was having slowly faded from memory. He tucked his pistol back into his suitcase and pulled out a slick suit. His hunger had kicked in and if breakfast had been any sort of indicator, he knew that Igak could cook up something to satisfy.

As he took the elevator down to the foyer, he scanned his surroundings. He knew he'd need to identify the location of all the staff members before he could make his move and take the elevator down to the basement level.

It didn't take more than a few seconds before he located Igak. The cook was slicing up thick cuts of raw, pink meat in the kitchen. Jimmy poked his head in and cleared his throat. Igak turned to him and Jimmy said, "If it's not too much trouble, I was hoping you'd be able to whip something up for me."

Igak nodded at him and answered, "Vegetarian?"

"That would be lovely. I'll be back shortly." Jimmy turned and left the kitchen. Igak went back to slicing the meat.

Jimmy made his way across the foyer to the lounge where he found Turk picking out a record to play. The expedition leader was back in his khaki outfit with a rocks glass of whiskey in hand. He hadn't noticed Jimmy yet, and Knotts tried to back out of the room without him hearing, but his movement caught Turk's attention.

"Mr. Knotts, I thought you had retired for the evening," Turk said as he held up his glass.

"My stomach woke me," Jimmy replied, approaching the man in the safari getup.

"I'll have Igak get something started."

"No need. I already spoke with him."

"He understood what you asked him?"

"Pretty certain."

"Can I have Gregory make you a drink?"

"No thank you, I think I'll just—"

"Aw hell, I don't need Gregory for that. Come on, I'll pour you a whiskey."

"I really just wanted—"

"I insist," Turk said with a waving hand.

Jimmy gave in and followed Turk to the barroom where Gregory was polishing bottles. "Gregory, my dear friend, would you have Igak start dinner?" The butler nodded and hurried off to the kitchen to complete the request.

"I told you I already spoke with him," Jimmy said in an increasingly frustrated tone.

With Gregory gone, Turk walked around behind the bar top and selected a bottle of American whiskey from the display shelf. As he poured a glass of Federal Club 90 Proof for Jimmy, he said, "You really impressed me out there."

Jimmy didn't know how to take the compliment. It was odd to think about his own heroics when the other two guests that had arrived just after him had met their demise. He took a sip of the whiskey and nodded a thank you to Turk.

"I thought we were done for when that beast was coming at us on the rock face," Turk said, his elbows on the bar top, his sleeves rolled, showing off his hairy forearms.

"It was a lucky shot," Jimmy admitted.

"No reason to deny your gun skills, Mr. Knotts."

Jimmy quickly changed the subject. "How's Kristian?"

"He'll be fine. Already talking about going out hunting again tomorrow." Turk could see that Jimmy was in no mood for a light discussion. "I'm sorry about how all that turned out. But you see the reality of it, right? Now that you've had time to think?" Jimmy swirled his whiskey and his lack of an answer made Turk feel obligated to continue. "The Blackwells were killed by those animals out there. Not by me. And not by Mrs. Everly."

Still, Jimmy was silent. He took another sip of his whiskey and Turk said, "We have someone you can talk to after you leave here. A therapist we employ. She can help you work through everything you're feeling right now."

"It's a common occurrence then?"

"Common wouldn't be the right choice of words. But we have lost people before, yes."

"You don't seem bothered."

Turk sighed deeply and took a moment to choose his next words carefully. "You've heard the excuse that 'This is my job,' or 'I was just following orders.' People like to pass the buck to someone higher up to justify the things they do. I'm not one of those folks. Yes, this is my job, but a man chooses his work. I'm no slave. This is a choice I made to work here for Mrs. Everly and her husband before he passed. I don't enjoy seeing people die, but I live for the hunt, the thrill, and all the danger in tow. It's my passion. We do all we can to make sure that the guests understand the risks of going on the hunt. That's a choice that they make, just like the choice I make every day to stay here. I liked the Blackwells, they had spunk, vigor, and I mourn for them, I truly do, but I can't let myself dwell on the decisions others have made."

Jimmy finished his drink and slid the glass across the bar top to Turk. "As expedition leader, your job is to ensure the safety of your team. If you look at your job performance objectively, can you really feel good about it?"

Jimmy got up, scooted his barstool in, and walked out into the foyer. Turk watched him leave, knowing that if Jimmy wasn't a guest of the Caliber Lodge, he would have busted his nose for a comment like that.

At the very least, Jimmy intrigued him. At first Turk had taken him as green, an amateur hunter who wanted to play adventurer. When he had read that Jimmy Knotts was an oil tycoon heir, he assumed he would be the same as the other men of that upbringing. Spoiled, entitled, and underneath the facade, weak.

Since the mountain, Turk had reassessed his opinion. Though Jimmy had been reserved during the hunt and had shown no sign of wanting to kill one of the creatures, he was not doing so out of fear or boredom as Turk initially thought. He could see now that Jimmy had been watching, observing, not the creatures and their habitat, but the other guests and maybe Turk himself. To what purpose Turk was unsure, but he could feel the disdain for the killing of those creatures resonating from every part of Jimmy's being. Even when confronted with certain death, Jimmy still hesitated before firing at one of them. Those were not traits of a true hunter, nor of a man wanting to become one. Turk considered that perhaps they were the traits of an activist. He knew that rich men often took up causes to fill their time, and if Jimmy Knotts were indeed there at the lodge to gather information, he would be more dangerous than any of the beasts on the mountain.

He poured himself another glass of whiskey and contemplated the effect a wealthy animal activist could have on the lodge, on Turk's employment and livelihood. Jimmy had signed the confidentiality agreements, and up to that point none of the guests before him had dared breach it, but a man who came from wealth, who had never been poor, who had never wanted for anything, would not understand what the loss of his fortune would mean. That lack of understanding coupled with the urge to make a difference, to prove himself for a cause, that could be the recipe that would lead a man to break the contracts he had agreed to.

The paranoia continued to build up in Turk's mind and as he finished another glass of whiskey, he planned his next course of action.

Jimmy was lost in thought as he sat at the kitchen island countertop. While Gregory and Igak were likely to stay on the main floor, Turk was a wild card, and he'd yet to locate Mrs. Everly. Either of them could go down to the lower level at anytime. Jimmy knew that if he wanted to get a clear look at Kristian's back, he'd need to take a chance and just go for it.

Igak kept one eye on him as he prepared all the ingredients for Jimmy's dinner. The two men shared the space for another fifteen minutes in silence, as Igak finished grilling up an assortment of vegetables. He drizzled truffle oil over them, then sprinkled crushed rosemary. He let them sit for another moment before plucking them off the burner and displaying them beside steaming scalloped potatoes on a lavish piece of china for Jimmy. Igak cleaned the grill and the countertops, then left Jimmy to eat the meticulously prepared meal in solitude.

As Jimmy took the first bite of the roasted endive, he noticed a closed door at the far end of the kitchen. He could tell by how far inset it was, that it did not lead outside. He stood and quietly walked over to it, checking to be sure he was still alone in the kitchen before pulling it open.

Behind the door was a staircase leading both up to the second floor, and down to what Jimmy could only assume was the recovery bay. He glanced over his shoulder once more before seizing the moment and descending the steps.

Even after closing the door behind him, the stairwell was still supremely lit by a series of copper sconces. The walls were made of large, white marble slabs, layered upon one another, spiraling downward like a medieval castle.

When Jimmy reached the base of the stairs he was confronted by another door, and he only hesitated a moment before pushing it open. Beyond the trespass was a severely dim room. The only light seemed to come from the illuminated stairwell behind him, and when he closed the door it took several seconds for his eyes to adjust to the darkness.

Slowly, he made out the details. A series of medical monitors and cabinets full of pharmaceutical supplies were arranged in a neatly organized fashion. In front of them was a hospital bed, and upon the bed was Kristian. He was asleep, or sedated, Jimmy was unsure which. He was lying on his chest, his head turned to the side, a stream of drool draining from between his lips. His bare back was wrapped in fresh gauze, and other than his pants, the rest of his clothing had been removed.

Jimmy approached slowly, not wanting to wake his potential prey. His oxfords clicked lightly on the tile floor and the sound echoed through the cavernous dark. It wasn't until that point that Jimmy realized how deep the room was. He had initially only seen the immediate medical area but could eventually make out hints of the rest of the room that remained shrouded in shadow.

He startled himself when he caught his own reflection in a glass barrier on the far end. He could not tell what was beyond it, nor did he have much interest. He was down in the basement for a singular reason.

He regained his composure and walked up alongside the bed. He stood over Kristian staring down at the gauze and wondered how was he going to see beneath it, knowing that if he pulled on the fabric too much, it could wake him.

To the left of the bed he saw a stand with a metal tray containing a pair of medical scissors and a partial roll of gauze. He quietly scooped up the scissors and ever so gently, slid the tips to the edge of the wrapping along Kristian's spine. He leaned over to get a better look at Kristian's face to ensure he was still unconscious.

Jimmy made a minor cut in the gauze, then paused. Kristian did not stir. A few more snips were enough to pull a flap of the fabric up to see beneath. The fresh cuts from the creature's claws were slathered with ointment. The surrounding skin was red and puffy, and Jimmy could feel the heat rising from them. He winced at the gruesome sight.

Then he noticed another wound, a much older one. It was a scar just above Kristian's right kidney. This was it—the infamous scar he'd been hoping to see. It was the confirmation he had needed to know for certain that the rumors were true.

Kristian Beckett was Wilhelm Stengl.

Chapter Twelve
INCIDENT NEAR THE BERGHOF

Germany, 1938. Twenty-seven years earlier.

In Bavaria, close to the border of Austria, overlooking the small town of Berchtesgaden, was the mountainside retreat of the Obersalzberg, where Hitler's Alpine home was perched. The Berghof was a popular destination for German tourists hoping to get a glimpse of the Führer as he came and went from the residence. The visitors, crowded near the gate at the end of the lengthy driveway, gawked at the approaching Mercedes-Benz and accompanying motorcycles, expecting to see the mustached dictator. They were disappointed by the face of someone they did not recognize and therefore had no interest in.

The Leibstandarte SS Adolf Hitler, the Führer's personal bodyguards, pulled the gate and allowed the motorcade to enter. It traveled up the drive and came to a stop outside the renovated building. The driver of the Mercedes came around and opened the back door, allowing twenty-seven-year-old Wilhelm Stengl to step out, a black leather satchel slung across his chest. He stared up at the large terrace decorated with pastel umbrellas.

"Just the way it looked in Homes & Gardens," he murmured to himself.

The front door opened and a woman with pale blond hair, cut short, and striking blue eyes, walked out past the SS guards. She saluted to Wilhelm and said, "Heil Hitler."

"Sieg heil," Stengl replied with his own matching salute.

"You must be Wilhelm," she said.

"Ma'am." Stengl gave a subtle nod.

"No need for such formalities here. You may call me Eva," she encouraged him. "Come."

She gestured for him to follow her inside. He obliged her and the two strolled side by side through the entrance, past a large assortment of potted cacti. They entered the great hall where an array of 18th century German furniture was arranged around a red marble fireplace.

"You have a beautiful home here," Stengl observed, admiring the jade green color scheme.

"Isn't it?"

"The Führer has excellent taste."

"Are you still referring to the Berghof?" Eva quipped. Stengl was taken aback. He didn't know how to respond appropriately. She grinned at him and touched his arm. "Relax, my friend."

Stengl glanced around to see if anyone else had heard her comment. Only the young housekeeper passing through on her way to the kitchen could have been in earshot. It seemed all the officers were stationed outside, well out of range.

A soft warble caught his attention and Stengl turned to see an ornate bird cage housing a yellow Harz Roller canary on the other end of the room.

"Her name is Fay," Eva said. "Like the actress. The Führer loves King Kong."

"I've yet to see it," Stengl replied.

"I often find him in here with his face pressed to the cage, just watching her, listening to her sing. I imagine he's pretending to be the ape in the film, staring through the woman's window."

"And where is the Führer now?"

"He's gone out," Eva said as she approached the birdcage.

"How do you mean?"

"He does not tell me where he is going, nor is it my business to ask. But he made sure I knew you'd be arriving today and asked that I accompany you while you wait for him to return."

"Which you expect to be when?" Stengl inquired.

"Not till tomorrow, I'd imagine." Eva snapped her fingers at the housekeeper as she walked back out of the kitchen into the hall. "You there! Are you not going to offer our guest a drink?" The housekeeper froze in place, a terrified expression across her face.

"Of course. My apologies, ma'am," the housekeeper whimpered as she scurried over to Stengl. "May I bring you something to drink, sir?"

Stengl looked at the youthful woman, her straw-colored hair pulled back into a bun. She dared not look him in the eyes. Her gaze was on her own feet and nothing more. He wondered whether she'd ever even seen the spectacular decor of the residence with her narrowed vision, or if she kept her blinders on at all times.

"Perhaps later," he replied. The housekeeper nodded and hurried away. Stengl watched her as she disappeared around the corner.

"Pretty little thing," Eva commented as Stengl turned to her. "I can see how much you appreciate the views here. Let me show you best one."

She led him down the hallway and out onto the terrace he had seen when he first pulled up. They stood beneath the resort-style umbrellas and gazed out at the snowcapped alps.

"It's truly a sight to behold," Stengl said.

"Those were my exact thoughts the first time I laid eyes on it. I was just an assistant at Heinrich Hoffmann's photography studio when I first met the Führer. So strange how much life can change in just a few short years." Stengl glanced at her. She caught his eyes and asked, "You've met Heinrich before, yes? He's the Führer's—"

"Official photographer," Stengl interrupted. "I have. The man is always trying to get me in front of his lens. Avoiding him is no easy feat."

"Don't enjoy having your picture taken?"

"I leave the spotlight to the actual heroes of Germany." His comment made Eva grin again.

"Do you ski, Wilhelm?"

"Yes, ma'am. I enjoy it immensely."

"And have you ever skied on the Obersalzberg?"

"No, ma'am."

"Well then, you must. I'll have the men prepare a set for you." Her offer made him uncomfortable. He could not allow himself to be seen partaking in recreational activities while he was supposed to be on duty.

"I don't know if that would be appropriate."

"Not appropriate?"

"I just came to deliver a report to the Führer."

"And as I said, Adolf is not here and likely won't be for at least another day. I insist you enjoy yourself while you wait."

"Perhaps I should just come back when he's returned," Stengl said as he spun to walk back inside the Berghof.

"My direction came directly from the Führer, Stengl," she said sternly. "He told me I was to accompany you while you wait for him to return. If you leave here, how can I follow those orders?" Stengl stood in the doorway, his back to Eva as he listened. "You would have me disobey his command?"

Stengl knew this was a dangerous game. One misstep and his career could be over. He turned back to face her. She was leaning against the railing of the terrace, a coy expression painted across her pale face.

"No, ma'am," he replied. "I would do nothing of the sort."

A few hours later, Stengl and Eva were cutting down the Bavarian slopes, carving through the powder, weaving gracefully through the hills in their two-piece, wool snow suits. Skiing was Stengl's favorite pastime. He had spent much of his youth on the German and Austrian hills and until his career overtook all his free time, he was still going on runs weekly.

He was enjoying himself so much that he'd almost forgotten who he was skiing with. He knew there were much worse ways to spend an afternoon. Coasting down a blue with the Führer's girlfriend as his host would be a story he'd remember the rest of his life.

They skied for hours, exchanging only a few words about the state of the snow here and there. Occasionally Stengl would catch Eva grinning at him as though she had some hidden agenda in store. He shrugged it off and assumed it to be nothing more than the playful banter of someone who'd spent far too much time alone up at the mountain retreat.

Eventually the sun lowered. There was only a short amount of daylight left, and Eva declared they'd do one more run before retiring. As they came to a cropping of trees, Stengl veered right, separating from Eva as she continued on to the left. The trees were grouped so tightly that Stengl lost sight of her completely. He tried to spot her through the gaps in the trunks but got only flashes of her as he sailed through the snow.

He preferred being alone, something that seemed increasingly rare since he joined the SS. He tried to savor these little moments, when no one could see him, when no one was watching. These trees were his barrier wall if only for a few brief moments.

When he turned his sights back to the path in front of him, he was startled by what at first appeared to be a man dressed in furs, standing in the center of the run. He almost lost his balance on the skis and had to catch himself to stay upright. As he slid closer, however, he realized it wasn't a man at all, but a hairy beast standing on its hind legs, its back slightly hunched, long furry arms sagging toward the snowy ground.

The setting sun was at the animal's back and it silhouetted it slightly from Stengl's view. Even in the light's obscurity he could gauge the size of the creature, and he quickly shifted his pose to slow his pace down the hill as not to approach it too quickly. As Stengl decelerated, the beast turned casually and lumbered into the trees, disappearing from sight.

Stengl reached into his wool jacket and whipped out a Walther pistol as he skidded to a halt in the section of the path where animal had been standing. Squinting in the sun and trying to shade his face with his free arm, he pointed his pistol into the trees in the direction the beast had strolled away in. He stood there on his skis, his arm extended out, the barrel of the Walther aimed into the shadows of the forest, waiting for any movement among the foliage. His eyes scanned every trunk, every branch, but he could not see the hairy creature anywhere.

He looked down at the snow-covered ground, expecting to see tracks, but the skidding halt of his skis had all but wiped them away. He contemplated walking into the woods, looking for the animal, or at least the tracks beyond the tree line, but couldn't move his legs. He was paralyzed by the image of the beast in his mind. The size of it, easily eight feet tall—and the long ape-like arms.

What could it have been?

He had never seen or heard of such a creature before. It had looked enough like a man from a distance to fool him briefly, but he knew with certainty that it was not human.

"Wilhelm!"

He could hear Eva calling him from a distance. She had no doubt grown worried when he didn't come out the other side of the chute when they separated on the run. He waited before answering, thinking his voice may scare the hidden animal away for good, or startle it into hostility.

"Wilhelm!" She continued to call for him until he shouted back, assuring her he was all right. He stared into the trees a moment longer before turning his skis forward and heading down the hill.

When he came out the other side, Eva was waiting for him. "I thought maybe you'd crashed into a tree," she joked. It didn't take her long to realize something was wrong. "What is it?"

Stengl tried to hide his worried expression. "Nothing. Everything's fine."

Eva looked up at the run that Stengl had come down. All she could see was the powder and the pines. She looked back at Stengl and said, "I think it's time for a brandy."

Stengl nodded. "That sounds like perfection." Eva hopped and pointed her skis downhill and zoomed away toward the base of the mountain.

Stengl lingered a moment, glancing back up at the cluster of trees. His eyes fixated on the foliage, and his imagination grew.

Eva instructed Stengl to leave his skis by the door so that the help could take care of them. She guided him to one of the many guest rooms in the house and opened the door for him.

"May your evening be as exciting as our afternoon, Wilhelm," she said as he walked into the room. He turned to ask her what she meant, but before he could speak, she stepped back out into the hallway and closed the door. He listened to her footsteps die off as she walked away down the hall.

Stengl removed his wool ski suit and hung it on the coatrack beside a framed watercolor sketch of a German shepherd. He rolled his eyes at the sight of the amateur art, and as he sat down at the foot of the bed, his mind went back to the mountain.

He questioned whether it had been a trick of the mind, or sunspots in his eyes.

Maybe it was the altitude. Maybe it never happened.

He tried to convince himself of the lie, but deep down he knew that what he had seen on the slopes was no normal animal sighting. It was something unique.

The sound of footsteps coming back down the hallway toward his room caught his attention. A knock at the door caused him to sit up straight, adjusting his posture to that of a soldier. He stood, cleared his throat and opened the door, expecting to see Eva again. His brow furrowed with surprise.

Standing in the doorway, as meek and mousy as she had been upon first meeting her, was the young housekeeper. In one hand she held a hand-blown brandy snifter, in the other, a decanter full of ruby-colored brandy. Stengl smiled.

"I was told to deliver this to you, sir," she said in a sheepish tone.

"And very grateful I am for that." Stengl opened the door wider and ushered the woman inside. "Set it over there on the desk if you would." She nodded and did as he said. She walked back to the door and just before she was about to leave, Stengl said, "You only brought one glass."

She turned to him, visible confusion on her face. "I don't understand, sir."

"I said, you only brought one glass."

"You are only one person, sir."

"There are two of us though. You and I."

"I'm afraid I don't follow you, sir."

Stengl sat down on the bed and raked his fingers through his hair, scraping his scalp with minor frustration.

"What's your name?" Stengl asked her.

"Amelia."

"I'd like you to drink with me, Amelia."

"I don't think I'm allowed, sir."

"Eva sent me two gifts just now. The brandy was only one of them. I insist that you sit and drink with me." He waited for her to respond as she contemplated her options.

"I'll get another glass."

"Good girl," he said just above a whisper. She walked out of the room, leaving the door ajar. Stengl went to the desk and poured himself a healthy amount of brandy. He took a sip, held it in his mouth a moment, then let it slide down his throat, warming his chest on the way down.

Amelia returned with a second glass and closed the door behind her as to hide her activity from the rest of the staff. She approached Stengl and handed him the other snifter. He smirked as he filled it for her, then handed it back. She hesitated before taking a sip.

He expected her to wince or cough from the burn of the alcohol, but she closed her eyes and smiled as though tasting a long-lost love. As her eyes peeled back open, they locked onto Stengl's with a dreamlike gaze. Her mousiness had faded—replaced with an unexpected bout of confidence.

"You're young," she commented.

"From a certain point of view."

"You're here to meet with our Führer, no doubt."

"I'm afraid I can't discuss the details of my visit here," he said, looking down at Amelia.

"You must be an important man." Her free hand grazed his undershirt and slowly slid up his chest. She took another sip of her brandy. He followed suit.

"I have my value."

"Yes," she said as her hand changed direction and made its

way below his SS belt buckle. "I'm sure that you do."

Amelia lied naked atop the sheets beside Stengl, who stared blankly up at the painted ceiling. She reached across his bare chest and grabbed her snifter, which sat next to the nearly empty decanter. As she scooted up against the carved headboard to take a sip, Stengl asked her, "How long have you worked here?"

"Just over a year, I suppose." Stengl paused a moment before asking his next question.

"Have you seen anything strange since you've been at the Berghof?"

"I see strange things every day," she answered. He rolled over onto his side to face her.

"Do you ever go up the mountains? To ski, or to take a walk? Anything like that?" She looked at him curiously.

"I suppose I take walks now and then. When I'm off duty, of course."

"Of course." He knew she was being careful not to present herself as an irresponsible employee. "And when you've been out taking your walks, have you ever seen any… wildlife?"

"Sure. Red deer, mostly. I saw a lynx once. There are wolves here as well, though I've never seen one." Stengl scooted up against the headboard beside her.

"Have you ever seen anything larger than a wolf? Larger than a deer?" He looked her in the eye, and as she stared back she tried to read the hidden words behind what he was asking.

"Did you see something out there?"

He cleared his throat and reached for his half-empty snifter. "I think I did." He took a long drink and his eyes drifted off into the abyss. "I think I may have, yes."

"What did you see?"

"I'm afraid to even verbalize it. It would sound too crazy."

She laid her spindly fingers across his chest. "You can tell me."

He turned to her again, wanting to trust her, desperately wanting to say out loud what he had experienced to someone, even if it was just the housekeeper.

"If the wrong people heard me talking about such things, it could be the end of my career." She saw his eyes becoming wet, a light swell of tears. They were red, though she was unsure if it was from emotion or too much brandy, or both. His words were slurred as he spoke now, and she decided it best just to comfort him.

"I won't utter a word. You can trust me."

He hesitated a moment longer, then nodded. He pulled her into his arms and held her so she could not see his face as he continued.

"I was on the slopes, with Eva. We became separated, and in that moment I saw the most otherworldly thing I've ever laid eyes on." Amelia listened, her interest piqued, her cheek pressed to his chest. She could feel his heart pounding as he told his tale.

"It was a colossal behemoth, covered in hair, gray or black. It stood upright, like a man. Mostly upright, because it had a hunch, but it was certainly on two legs. It looked at me, unafraid, and when it walked into the woods it did so at a meandering pace. It didn't scamper away like a deer or wolf might."

Amelia's eyes were wide, hanging on every word that Stengl spoke. "I should have shot it," he said. "I was so surprised by the sight of it, I waited too long to draw my pistol."

He finished the rest of the brandy from his glass and ran his free hand down Amelia's arm. "The next time I see it, I will not hesitate. No matter the circumstances, I'll put a bullet in the beast so I have proof of what my eyes truly saw."

The two of them sat in a moment of contemplative silence, then Stengl's fingers tightened around Amelia's elbow. "This stays between you and me, yes?"

Though her eyes were brimming with fear, he could not see them. She rubbed her fingers across his chest.

"You can trust me."

The next morning, Stengl readied himself for the day, donned his SS uniform, and entered the great hall. Eva was there waiting for him, cup of coffee in hand.

"And how was the rest of your evening, Wilhelm?" she inquired playfully.

"Much appreciated."

"I'm very glad to hear it," she said as she leaned in close with a snarky grin. "The little slut seems plenty satisfied herself this morning."

Her eyes led Stengl's to the other side of the room where Amelia was hard at work, polishing the red marble mantel above the hearth, having just finished shining up the expensive Cembra pine paneling.

Stengl cleared his throat. "Any word from the Führer?" Eva pulled back slowly and used her index finger to raise Stengl's coffee mug up to his lips. He took a drink.

"There was in fact. He's been delayed." Eva adjusted the collar of her blouse. "He asked me to reschedule your visit."

"Understood. I appreciate your hospitality."

"What am I if not a perfect host?" Stengl didn't know how to respond. "Enjoy your coffee. I'll call for a car to take you back."

Stengl nodded as Eva strolled out of the great hall and disappeared around the corner. She passed by one of the housekeepers, this one a tall, broad woman, who carried a bottle of oil over to Amelia at the fireplace.

Stengl watched from the other side of the room as the two women conversed quietly. Amelia stole a brief look at Stengl, smiled, then her eyes quickly darted back to the taller housekeeper, who giggled just before glancing over at him. When she saw he was already looking at her, she immediately lowered her eyes and hurried off to the kitchen.

Stengl sneered. He set his coffee down on the end table by one of the 18th century armchairs and stomped across the room. He grabbed Amelia by the arm, yanking her in close to him.

"What did you say to her?"

Amelia was shocked by Stengl's aggression. She looked around to see if anyone else was present, but the two of them were alone in the great hall. She looked up at Stengl and timidly replied, "Nothing."

"Nothing?" His fingers dug into her fair skin. "That didn't look like nothing."

"We were discussing our work."

"And which part of your work were you discussing? What you do out here, polishing the mantel? Or what you do in the bedrooms, polishing other things?" She winced, disgusted by his words.

"I wasn't talking about you, if that's what you are implying."

"She looked over at me—that Goliath of a maid you were yammering with."

"I don't control her eyes," Amelia hissed at him.

He grabbed her around the jaw, squeezing it like a vice. "Watch your tongue, bitch." Amelia tried to pull away, but Stengl's hold was too strong. "What did you tell her? Huh? Did you tell her about what I saw?"

"No," Amelia said sincerely. Stengl searched her eyes.

"You did. You told her, and she laughed about it."

"No. She wasn't laughing at you," Amelia whimpered through the pain. She could feel Stengl's thumb pressing hard through her cheek, against her molar, pushing it slowly from its socket.

Stengl took a breath and loosened his grip around Amelia's face. She reached up and massaged her jaw, a tear running down her cheek. She looked up at Stengl and whispered, "I told you that you can trus—"

Stengl grabbed her by the shoulders and threw her into the blazing fireplace. The flames exploded, snapping at her as she frantically tried to push herself off the glowing logs. She screamed in agony as the fire burned through her clothing and seared her flesh. Her hands gripped the outer edges of the fireplace, but as she began to lift herself out, Stengl kicked her back down onto the wood with his shiny black boot and held her in place with his heel as the flames devoured her.

Through Amelia's harrowing screams, Stengl heard the echoing clops of approaching footsteps. He backed away from the hearth and raised his hands to his face, pretending to be in shock. Eva, followed by three SS Officers, stormed into the great hall behind him. They stopped in their tracks, staring into the fireplace at the melting housekeeper.

"Christ!" Eva yelled. She turned to the SS guards and shouted, "Get the extinguishers! Put her out before she burns the whole damn house down!" The Nazis obeyed and doused the flames, quick enough to save the Berghof, but not Amelia.

Eva turned to Stengl, who slowly lowered his hands from his deceptive face. "What the hell happened!?" she demanded.

"She was upset—devastated when I told her I had no intention of—" he trailed off into silence.

"No intention of what?" Eva asked authoritatively.

"She's a Christian. Last night—what she did—she said her

father would disown her if… I'm not a man fit for marriage, Eva. Surely you can understand that."

Eva stared at him, reading through his lies. She looked over her shoulder at the smoldering body in the fireplace as Stengl picked up his cup of coffee from the end table and took a sip.

"How long on that car?" Stengl asked with an oozing smugness.

Chapter Thirteen
THE MOOSE'S ANTLERS

Jimmy could hardly believe his luck. Upon his arrival he wasn't sure how he would confirm whether or not Kristian Beckett was actually Stengl, short of jumping in the shower with him. The deadly creature in the ice cave, though it nearly killed them, helped unmask Stengl's true identity. Jimmy knew he would need to get in contact with Levi Aarons as soon as he could to let him know that the lead from the old woman in the travel agency had proven to be worth the trip. He prayed this time his partner would answer the phone when he rang.

Grabbing the roll of gauze, Jimmy cut off a few strips, which he laid across the open area on Kristian's back, covering the ointment slathered claw marks and the old identifying scar. He couldn't wrap them all the way around Kristian's torso without waking him, so he did his best to layer and tuck the new strips to mingle with the ones Turk had spun.

As he covered up the wounds, Jimmy wondered if the former Nazi had kept his infamous notebook that included dossiers on all the significant members of the high command and their subordinates. Though it would have been a risky item to keep on hand, he didn't deny himself the thought of such a providential possibility. Even without the book, however, Stengl was a treasure trove of information that could help them hunt down the other fugitive Nazis they'd been seeking.

The challenge now would be getting Stengl out of the lodge

and down the mountain to the rendezvous point without revealing his true identity as a Nazi hunter to Turk, or Mrs. Everly, or anyone affiliated with the Caliber lodge for that matter.

His non-disclosure agreements and confidentiality forms were, of course, all signed under false pretenses. Levi had forged the fake identity and background for Jimmy so he could get admission, and if Everly and her attorneys discovered that Jimmy had falsified the agreements it would be a maelstrom for Levi to sort out, and would no doubt take up valuable months, money, and resources, distracting from their hunt.

Jimmy had to continue to keep his objective a secret. Getting Stengl to the rendezvous point after they had both checked out from and exited the lodge was the only option he saw. Unfortunately, there was another day and a half left until checkout time, and Jimmy tried to stay hopeful that the Nazi's wounds were not serious enough to cause any detrimental complications before he could get him to Levi.

He finished with the gauze and put the roll and scissors back where he found them. Slipping off his oxfords, he held them in hand as he walked back to the door and pulled it open a crack, just enough to slide through, not wanting to wake Kristian with the light from the stairwell.

As Jimmy disappeared up the marble spiraled staircase, and the door clicked closed, one of Kristian's eyes peeled open, his pupil glazed, still foggy from the medication.

Jimmy poked his head out from behind the door at the top of the staircase. Gazing into the kitchen, the room appeared to be vacant. He was worried that Igak may have returned while he was down in the recovery bay, but it appeared the Inuit man had decided to leave Jimmy alone for an extended period to finish his dinner in peace.

Jimmy emerged from the stairwell, slid his oxford shoes back on, walked through the kitchen, and headed toward the foyer, but he stopped when he saw Turk from across the great hall coming out of the bar. Jimmy quickly turned and sat back down at the counter in front of his plate of vegetables as not to draw any attention.

Turk, passed by without a glance, pulled open the gate to the elevator and took the lift up. Jimmy listened to the sound of Turk's footsteps above as the expedition leader walked down the hall to what Jimmy could only assume were his quarters. The sound of the bedroom door opening and closing was barely audible, but as soon as it did, Jimmy jumped back up and hurried out of the kitchen, across the foyer and into the lounge.

With no regard to acting casual, he jogged over, lifted the receiver and dialed. After several rings Jimmy was about to hang up —that is until he heard Levi's voice on the other end of the line say, "Aarons." Jimmy could not have been happier to hear from his mentor.

"It's me," he said in a hushed tone.

Several miles away, near the harbor, in a tiny fishing village, sat the Moose Antler Motel. The single-story, ten-room establishment had closed down its kitchen for the night, and the vacancy sign glowed red beneath the cartoon-style moose image carved in wood beneath the welcome message.

Though the curtains were drawn, the hazy light could still be seen through the window of guest room number three. Inside, Levi Aarons sat on the edge of one of the two twin beds, holding the phone receiver to his ear.

"Jimmy. Thank God. Are you All right?"

It took Jimmy a moment to respond, and Levi imagined he

was checking over his shoulder to ensure the secrecy of the call.

"It's him," Jimmy replied in a hushed tone.

Levi's back stiffened. "You're certain?"

On the other side of the cramped motel room, Walt, the British strong-arm, sat cross-legged on the floor in the corner, drinking from a can of Old Crown. His attention hung on every word coming out of Levi's mouth. He couldn't hear Jimmy on the other end of the line, but Levi's responses filled in the details.

"I saw the scar," Jimmy said.

"Can you get him to the rendezvous point?"

"It will have to be after check out. I can't make it happen before that without alerting the staff here."

"Do you want me to send Walt up?" Levi asked as he checked the time on his Swiss Wittnauer Revue pocket watch. Walt tilted his head, watching Levi's body language, guessing what Jimmy's response would be.

"As much as I'd love the assistance, we can't risk blowing my cover. You put too much work into getting me here."

"Do you think he suspects anything?"

"I don't think so. We haven't exactly been chumming it up together, but that's more on account of his rather lone wolf demeanor."

"Does he have the notebook with him?"

"I haven't been able to—"

Jimmy stopped mid-sentence. Levi's brow furrowed and Walt could tell something was off.

"Jimmy?"

Levi heard the click of the receiver. He turned and looked at Walt, who stared back at him, understanding the situation.

"You want me to head up there?" Walt asked, setting his half-full can of beer on the carpet.

"Let's give him time. He knows what he's doing," Levi

assured him. He stood and walked to the window, pulling one side of the curtains open. Looking out at the bay, he watched the white caps swelling and fading across the dark sea.

It had been a stressful trip for Levi, not only because of the agonizing anticipation of hearing from his partner but also because of the close-quarters he'd been sharing with Walt. The Englishman's sense of privacy was non-existent, and while Levi had splurged for separate rooms, Walt still found his way into room number three to "enjoy some conversation." Levi was appreciative that the other member of their team, Zsolt Baranyai—the Hungarian interrogator —enjoyed his solitude and remained within the confines of his own room down the way.

Three plane rides and a turbulent boat trip had brought the trio to the great Alaskan frontier. A quick "Arrivederci" and Jimmy was on his way across the territory to the Caliber Lodge in the posh, black Bentley. Levi, meanwhile, remained with Walt and his aniseed twists in the modest motel.

"He could be in trouble," Walt cautioned from his cross-legged pose on the floor.

"In our line of work, we're always in trouble," Levi remarked, his gaze still focused on the tide.

"We have confirmation, right? That Nazi bastard's shackin' up in that fuckin' lodge. You don't wanna blow Knotts' cover. Makes sense. Not a financially savvy move. But there's no reason I can think of why I shouldn't waltz on in there myself, grab that kraut fuck by his collar and drag his ass outta there. What're a buncha hotel hospitality fucks gonna do? Right? Wag their fingers at me? Fuck 'em."

Levi turned from the window and looked at Walt. "What are you eating?"

"Aniseed twists."

"Aniseed?"

"They're fuckin' delicious, ain't they?"

"Aniseed. Anise. Black licorice?" Levi deduced. Walt nodded. "I hate licorice." Walt responded with a shrug.

"No offense intended, Levi, but what does your like or dislike of licorice have to do with whether or not I should go Sean-fuckin'-Connery on that Nazi fuck?"

Levi strolled back to his bed and sat down on the corner. He pointed at Walt's beer can and asked, "You have another one of those?"

Walt grinned, jumped up and walked over to the bathroom sink, which he had filled with ice and the remains of a six-pack. He pulled off a can of Old Crown and tossed it to his boss.

Levi delicately cracked it open, let the foam bubble up over the lip, and gently took a sip in the most dignified manner he could. "I want to tell you a story, Walt."

"I love a good fuckin' story, boss. I got a good one about wine, but you go first." Walt leaned forward over his knees.

"There was a hitman, hired by a wealthy politician to take out a rival. Now this hitman, he was one for the flare, liked to make a show of his kills. He decided that the best way to do away with his target was to poison him, but it wasn't enough just to poison him. He needed to make a show of it. So he purchased this novelty tea cup, one that had 'You've just been poisoned' written on the inside of the cup, the idea being that once the target had drank the poisoned tea, he'd see the revelatory message."

Walt chuckled. "Brilliant."

"Except, before the hitman could pour the poisoned tea into the cup, the target walked into the kitchen and saw the humorous message in the mug. Well that target, he didn't find the situation all that funny, in fact he'd been suspecting that he was in his partner's crosshairs for sometime. The target, he grabbed that tea cup, smashed it on the counter, then stabbed the hitman in the neck with it. Cut his jugular wide open." Levi made a throat cutting gesture. Walt leaned back.

"The point is, you get cocky, you get too gung-ho, you risk spoiling everything."

"I see your point," Walt said as he picked his beer back up off of the carpet.

"We trust Jimmy to do his thing," Levi said. Walt nodded in agreement. He held up his plastic baggy of candy.

"You're sure you don't want a twist?"

Moments earlier, Jimmy hung up the phone in the cradle when he saw Gregory enter the lounge. The butler strolled in, a cocktail in hand, and said, "Thought you could use a nightcap, Mr. Knotts." Jimmy turned to him and smiled.

"I think I've reached my limit for the time being, Gregory."

"Not feeling well?"

"The altitude, maybe. You lot don't shy on the alcohol."

"It's our job to keep the guests content." Jimmy took a moment to mull over Gregory's statement. 'Content' was not the way Jimmy would describe his feelings at the moment.

"What's that you have on the tray?" Jimmy asked. Gregory looked at the meticulously prepared beverage.

"I call it the Panama Premiere. It's a classic Panama, but made with Napoleon Premier brandy. Hence the name."

"A Panama?"

"That's right, sir."

"And what's in a Panama, Gregory?"

"Well, as I said, sir, Napoleon Premier brandy, that's a ten-year-old label, then I add white Creme de Cacao and a splash of light cream."

"Not really my style, Gregory. I'm not partial to creamy drinks."

"Have you tried a Panama before, sir?"

"I've not."

"Would you do me the favor of giving me your opinion?" Jimmy forced a smile as he lifted the drink gently from the tray and held it to the light.

Without tasting the drink he set it back down on the tray and said, "I'll let you know when I'm ready for another beverage, Gregory." Gregory pursed his lips, bowed, and backed out of the lounge.

Turk had kept a watchful eye down below when he took the elevator up, not to the second floor, as Jimmy had assumed, but to the third. He had seen that Jimmy was still in the kitchen enjoying the meal that Igak had prepared. His steps were light as he made his way down the open hallway toward Jimmy's room, and he pulled a ring of keys from his pocket, which he used to gain entrance inside. He gave one last look below to make sure he would not be seen, then he slid inside the room and gently closed the door behind him.

He didn't know exactly what he was looking for, something that stood out as unusual, maybe a pamphlet on animal rights or a photo of Jimmy at a rally—though he knew neither of those were likely to be lying around if Jimmy was undercover. He'd be a fool to have something so damning on him, and of all the things Turk considered Jimmy, foolish was not at the top of the list. Still, Turk held out hope that he'd find something to help confirm his suspicions.

The Ballester-Molina service pistol was the last thing that Turk expected to find, and when he pulled it out of Jimmy's suitcase his fear of an undercover animal rights activist faded away and was replaced with a much more foreboding possibility. Turk was an aficionado of firearms and this retired Argentinian pistol was an unusual choice for someone to carry. It wasn't an ideal weapon, there were far better options, both more affordable and more reliable. A collector might have one, but the only likely reason someone would carry that specific pistol on them for protection would be if it used to be their daily sidearm. Turk knew Argentine police and military used to use such models, but it was clear by looking at him that Jimmy was certainly not Argentinian.

Turk sat down on the bed and tried to make sense of it. He knew that something was amiss. He could see the warning signs but didn't know how to put the pieces together. He could go to Mrs. Everly, but without a convincing explanation for it all she could dismiss the entire thing as Turk having one too many drinks and letting his wild imagination get the best of him.

He thought, perhaps, that would have been an astute observation. Maybe he *was* letting his imagination get the best of him. Maybe the pistol held no significance at all. It could have been possible to get a pistol like that in a pawnshop or have it passed down from a family member.

He brushed it aside for the time being, tucked the pistol back into Jimmy's suitcase, took a few more looks around the room, and took his leave. He was careful not to be seen as he locked the door behind him and hurried back to the elevator. As he traversed down the hall, he could hear a muffled conversation in the lounge below, and recognized the voices of Jimmy and Gregory. What they were discussing, he could not be sure, though he was thankful for the timely distraction.

He yanked the lever and took the elevator down to the second floor where the staff bedrooms were located. His room was at the end, past Gregory's and across from Mrs. Everly's. It was a bold-looking room. Heavy, dark curtains lined the floor to ceiling windows. A Winchester rifle hung on the wall, held up by a set of curled kudu antlers.

An enormous bull moose head was mounted above the four-poster bed. Turk had killed it the same year that the Everlys hired him to run the expeditions at the lodge. He'd been on his own, further down the mountain near where the private road started that led up to the lodge—where the village of Shishmar once existed. He was tracking an arctic fox that he had eyed and wanted to add to his taxidermy collection, when out of the white, the moose appeared and charged at him. He had no time to think—his body relied solely on muscle memory to snap the rifle into place and pull the trigger. The bull immediately went down, skidding to a halt in the snow. It was unquestionably the largest Turk had ever seen, and he had to trek back up to the lodge to grab the pickup truck to haul the animal off the road. The severed head, he mounted above his headboard, often falling asleep at night while staring up at it.

Turk kicked off his heavy boots, and after he pulled off his belt, he hung it from the moose's antlers. As he unbuttoned his shirt, he felt the hairs on his back stiffen. Someone was standing behind him, having just stepped out of the bathroom.

"I thought the rule was we keep a professional distance from one another when we have guests in the house," Turk said as softly as his baritone voice would allow.

"I wasn't seen," Everly replied from behind him. A heavy fur blanket was wrapped around her shoulders, her feet bare on the wooden floor. "Did I tell you to stop unbuttoning your shirt, Mr. Turk?"

Turk turned to face her as he slowly undressed, all the while keeping his gaze on his employer and the grayish fur blanket concealing her body. He hung the rest of his clothing on the antlers and approached her. His big hands grazed the fur, gently massaging her arms beneath.

"It's still in perfect condition," Turk said as he rolled strands of the fur between his thumb and index finger.

"Good as the day you brought it to me." She spread her arms, holding the blanket out like wings behind her, and Turk lifted her off the ground, then dropped her on her back in the bed. As he lowered himself on top of her, Everly wrapped the fur around him, letting it consume them both.

Chapter Fourteen
GREAT WHITE HUNTER

Africa, 1953. Twelve Years Earlier.

The name Jonathan Turk was well known in the Nairobi region, and his infamy as an expert hunter and expedition leader spread even further than that. He was easy to spot in the villages by his green Land Rover, on which he kept his antique elephant gun mounted to the outside of the driver's door for easy access. His tent, a heavy-duty canvass pulled across shaved and polished, perfectly curved tree branches he had skinned himself, bore his recognizable black rhino logo over the entrance flaps. It was an invitation to the wealthy—and a warning to the wise. He was a man who made a good living and enjoyed how he made it. Though he wasn't the only game in town, many considered him to be the best, and maybe they were right.

It was that notoriety which brought the Everlys to his camp in the month of September. They had been disappointed with the safari they had just been a part of and were looking for an adequate thrill before their return to the States. They had heard that the 28-year-old American was the man to talk to.

Turk was at a lack of words when Mrs. Everly lifted the flap and stepped into his tent. Her perfectly tailored khaki outfit showed off her thin waist and curvy hips, and her brown leather boots—which looked as though they had been polished that morning—made their way up her long legs just below the knee. Her black hair was pulled up beneath her stylish pith helmet, and on her belt she wore a Smith & Wesson Triple Lock—a big, heavy handgun loaded with .44 Special shells stuffed with far more powder than was ever intended for that model.

For someone who had just spent weeks on safari, she looked extremely clean and groomed. Turk couldn't gauge her age. Her body was fit, trim, like a woman in her twenties, but her eyes were older, beginning to cloud, and the surrounding wrinkles were much too defined for someone in their youth. She was 48 at the time, though Turk never asked to find out.

Mr. Everly—Charles to his friends—walked in behind his wife. His attire was similar, a khaki safari outfit and boots with a matching pistol holstered on his belt. He wore his signature red ascot around his neck and a two-day stubble upon his face.

"Mr. Jonathan Turk?" Mr. Everly inquired as he removed the pith helmet from his head and cradled it to his chest.

"How can I be of assistance?" Turk sat in a small wooden chair that looked like it was ready to buckle beneath the weight of his beefy form. He leaned over a fragile looking wooden desk, upon which was scattered a mess of maps, logs and landscape sketches.

"My name is Charles Everly. This is my wife, Mrs. Everly."

Mrs. Everly smiled.

"Glad to meet you both," Turk said as he stood and came around to the front of his brittle desk. "What brings you to Nairobi?"

As Charles spoke with Turk, Mrs. Everly strolled around the inside of the tent, looking at the collection of safari gear and weaponry.

"We've just come from a safari with the Ruark party," Charles shared.

"Is that right?" Turk kept a leering eye on Mrs. Everly as she inspected his residence.

"It was—how did you put it, my love?" Charles asked.

"Disappointing," Mrs. Everly replied.

"Disappointing. Yes."

"Well, I suppose I'm sorry to hear that," Turk commented. "I'm not associated with Ruark or any of his men so—"

"Yes, we are fully aware of that, Mr. Turk." Charles sat on the edge of the desk and the wood moaned.

"Then what is it I can do for the two of you?" Turk would not have been surprised if the entire piece of furniture had collapsed to the floor.

"We've been told you provide a much more thrilling service for those willing to pay the price," Mrs. Everly said softly.

Turk turned to her and asked what she meant by that, to which she responded, "Hunting antelope and buffalo was a bore. We came here to this dark continent hoping to see the brutality of the land."

"The brutality of the land, ma'am?" Turk asked.

"We've hunted game all over the world. We had hoped Africa would provide something new. Something exciting. It didn't. So we've come to see the Black Rhino. That's what they call you around here, right? The Black Rhino?"

"Some call me that."

"Others call you by another name," she said. Turk waited for her to continue, assuming by her leading statement that they had heard the stories about him.

"Others call you the Feed Master," Charles finished.

Turk stared at them and said, "The services of the Black Rhino come at a high price tag. The services of the Feed Master are unaffordable for nearly everyone."

"Nearly everyone. But not us," Mr. Everly boasted.

"You know what you're asking of me?" Turk questioned.

"We wouldn't have traveled all the way out here if we didn't,"

Mrs. Everly interjected.

Turk searched their faces.

"May I ask why either of you would want to see such a thing?" Turk asked.

Mrs. Everly went to her husband's side and placed her thin fingers on his chest. The couple stared at Turk, their eyes telling him all he needed to know. These wealthy, bored tourists craved a depravity that Turk had become comfortable delivering. He had provided the service to others in the past and each time he had done so, what little humanity he had left chipped away in flakes. The first time he did it was on a dare, a challenge from a local tribesman. Turk, never wanting to appear weaker than those around him, crossed the morality line with a leaping stride. This encounter with the Everly's would mark the eleventh time he'd committed the atrocious act.

After the trio sorted out payment, Turk asked the Everlys to wait in his tent while he attended to the details. He set out to the other end of the camp where he spoke with one of the men in his company responsible to packing and unpacking the gear. The man joined Turk and the two of them saddled up in the green Land Rover and rolled out.

They voyaged across the swampy territory to the nearest marketplace, where the locals traded and bartered beneath brightly colored tents.

"Killing is like over-drinking. In the moment, it's a rush. But afterward you feel sluggish, regretful, and you say 'I'm never doing that again.' But then a bit of time passes and you forget the pain it caused you and you think about that rush once more. So you try it again and again and soon you realize that if you never stop doing it, then the pain and the regret never has time to set in."

Turk's words did not resonate with the man who accompanied him. He just nodded and said, "Yes, boss."

Turk waited in the vehicle as the man he arrived with strolled over to one of the tents and quietly haggled with the middle-aged man working beneath it.

Turk paid no attention to the interaction. He closed his eyes and leaned back in the driver's seat, letting the bustle of the marketplace act as his white noise. He was unsure how much time had passed when the man he arrived with jumped back into the Land Rover along with the middle-aged man from the tent.

"All good?" Turk asked. The man in his employ nodded. Turk revved the Land Rover and the three of them cruised back to the camp.

It was dark when they returned and Turk sent the two men off in the other direction on foot as he rejoined the Everlys inside his tent.

"Thank you for waiting," Turk said as he pulled open the flap and entered to find Charles and Mrs. Everly lounging among his things.

"No trouble at all," Mrs. Everly replied. She was lying atop his cot, reading from a leather-bound journal.

"I trust all went well?" Charles sounded off from behind the desk.

Turk could tell that the two of them had rummaged through every item he owned. There was surely no privacy left in the realm of the Black Rhino.

"As planned, yes."

"Good," Charles said as he stood. "And when will the festivities commence?" Mrs. Everly rolled to her side, her head resting in her open palm.

"Give me a few more moments to ensure everything is adequate. These things are best not rushed. Patience and anticipation is part of the enjoyment… for those who enjoy such things."

The rest of the camp was asleep when Turk led the Everlys up and over a sandy hill. He carried a long, wooden staff with him. It was clearly hand-carved, with nothing fancy or notable about it. Once on the other side they were welcomed by a row of torches staked into the ground, creating an illuminated pathway in the darkness which lead a hundred feet out into the open grassland. The vegetation had all been cleared away, leaving only the dirt along the path and the circular area it led to.

At the end of the path were two chairs which sat side by side, facing a large metal cage covered by black parachute fabric. Turk let the Everlys go first, strolling down the silent path, the glow from the torches bathing the immediate vicinity in an orange hue, while everything outside its perimeter dropped off into almost complete tenebrosity.

They approached the chairs, and Turk gestured for them to sit. The chairs were not made of the same splintery wood the ones in Turk's tent had been constructed from. They were polished African Blackwood, harvested from the dry savanna regions of the southern part of the continent. Mrs. Everly took a moment to admire the material, rethinking her decorating choices back at her recently constructed Alaskan lodge.

No one spoke.

The Everlys sat, and as they waited in silence, Mrs. Everly could see subtle movements through the thin fabric from inside the covered cage. Her heart picked up its pace and as though he could sense it, Charles reached over and softly put his hand upon hers.

The villager who had accompanied Turk to the marketplace approached down the lighted pathway from behind, carrying a tray with a pair of cocktails in stemmed martini glasses. He handed Mr. and Mrs. Everly their drinks and disappeared back down the pathway.

The Everlys clinked their glasses together. The sound was like a gunshot in the quiet of the field. They each to a sip and instantly recognized the beverage. Vesper Martinis. Gordon's Gin, grain-based vodka, and Kina lillet. They had first tried the cocktail only two months earlier after reading the recently published, popular spy thriller by Ian Fleming, which they had acquired during a trip to Cape Town.

Turk walked out to the cage beneath the fluttering parachute. It stood seven feet tall and was longer than the green Land Rover they had seen on their way into camp. It could only have been transported by one of the supply trucks in Turk's caravan. The light from the torches danced in the breeze, casting contorted shadows upon and within the rolls of the blowing fabric.

Turk stopped at the corner of the cage, turned to face the Everlys and crossed his hands in front of his belt. He looked at his guests, trying to remain expressionless, though they could tell he was feeling something. Apprehension perhaps.

They sat there, enjoying their martinis, quietly staring at the covered cage only twenty feet in front of them. Turk looked like a Queen's guard posted outside a royal residence. Once in position, he did not move. He waited for the couple to finish their cocktails and only then did one of his hands raise and gesture past them to an unseen presence.

The villager returned, once again carrying his tray with another pair of Vespers. This time, however, the villager was followed by the middle-aged man from the marketplace, whose dusty, drab clothing had been replaced by an ornate, visually pleasing tunic that looked as though it had been recently stitched together with the finest of silks.

After serving the Everlys their fresh drinks, and collecting the spent glassware, the villager motioned gently for the middle-aged man to walk over to Turk. The villager once again receded into the darkness and the middle-aged man walked past Mr. and Mrs. Everly in their pristine chairs, hesitantly approaching the cage.

Turk hospitably put his arm around the man and squeezed him tight. He whispered into his ear.

"You are a brave man. Your family will never have to worry. Your sacrifice will protect them for life."

The middle-age man turned to face the Everlys and they could see tears running down his cheeks. He was trembling, his arms pressed tightly to his sides, trying to hide the involuntary shaking. Charles and his wife sipped their drinks.

Turk grabbed the dark fabric with his free hand and tore it off the cage, revealing a lioness pacing back and forth in the confined space. The jungle cat emitted a low, rolling growl from her throat. Mrs. Everly's eyes gleamed with fascination. This animal, with its long yellow teeth and deep orange eyes, she could see it was ravenous. The outline of its ribs were visible through the dry fur along its lanky body, and its muscles were lean and weak.

With one of his large, meaty hands, Turk patted the ladder attached to the end of the cage. The middle-aged man looked to it and closed his eyes. He took a lengthy breath, likely reminiscing the fondest moments of his brief life before he ascended the ladder to the top of the cage.

The lioness stopped pacing. She sat and stared up at the African perched above her. Her tongue slid out of her parched mouth, sliding roughly across her upper jaw, rolling over her coarse whiskers.

Charles leaned forward, his forearms pressing into his knees. Mrs. Everly leaned back and finished her second martini.

Turk pulled on the ratchet lever, popping open a hatch on the far end of the cage ceiling. He quickly and viciously prodded the man in the back with the wooden staff, shoving him forward, down into the cage. Turk yanked back on the lever and the door slammed closed, locking the man inside with the predator.

The sounds that followed had surely awoken every man in the

camp, though none dared to venture over the sandy hill to the sacrificial site. Turk had measured the distance perfectly, ensuring that the blood splatter landed as close as possible to garner the upmost reaction without blemishing the Everlys' clothing.

As they watched the starving lioness tear the man apart, Turk continued to stand at the corner of the cage, blood and bile splashing against his motionless body. It was at that moment that the Everlys knew they had found their man.

Less than a month later, Jonathan Turk had transported the entirety of his belongings all the way to the Alaskan frontier on the Everlys' dime. He took up residence in the Caliber Lodge, decorated his bedroom, and filled the game room with his favorite trophies.

He had been given a similar spiel, as the Everlys would later give all their guests; that the best game in the world could only be hunted on the mountain upon which the Caliber sat, and only with the permission of Mr. and Mrs. Everly could the animals be tracked or killed.

Turk had asked on more than one occasion what type of animals he could expect to see. The Everlys, of course, told him he'd need to wait and witness their grandeur for himself. They required him to sign a contract forbidding him to tell anyone about what happened at the Caliber Lodge or about the animals on the mountain, and although it seemed strange and more than questionable, Turk was a man who favored money above all else and he knew a great financial opportunity when it presented itself.

On his first expedition up the mountain, it was only he and Charles Everly. It was a trip much like all that would follow it, beginning with going over the ridge, up the steep rock face, down and out of the valley bowl, around the perimeter of the dense forest and out to the cabin. It was there that Charles and Turk discussed in-depth the Everlys' thoughts on the rare creatures that they found.

"They may be the missing link," Charles had said to Turk as they enjoyed a bottle of brandy together in front of the hearth. "A transitional evolution between man and ape, frozen in time up here in this frozen forgotten land."

"Apes. You're saying you've brought me all the way from Africa to give guided tours to hunt apes?" Turk asked.

"Not apes, Mr. Turk. They are not human, but not apes either. Something much, much more impressive. Creatures strong enough to turn over cars, and intelligent enough to, well, do more than apes can."

"How many of these animals are there? What's the population size?"

"We don't know for certain," Charles told him. "The first one we saw, it was sitting at the top of the rock face we climbed on our way here. It was a cloudless day. It's long legs dangling off the edge, swaying a bit, the way a child does when sitting on a swing. When we looked through the binoculars, we got a better glimpse. It was lanky, like a malnourished bear. But its face… its face was that of a primate, and its eyes, large and blue. They appeared human. It looked down at us from the top of the peak and its curiosity was as thick as ours."

Turk sipped his brandy. He didn't even notice his fingers had been squeezing the barrel of his rifle as tight as they had been until they began to hurt. He casually loosened his grip, not wanting to give Charles the satisfaction that his story had been so captivating.

The glow from the fire seemed to dance across Charles' face, slithering from side to side, whipping back and forth like a cobra preparing to strike. Turk crossed one leg over the other and leaned back in his chair, pretending to be relaxed as Charles continued.

"Then the creature stood, and we were able to get a better gauge of its height. They're over eight feet tall, you see. It didn't run off. It had no reason to fear us. The only other humans they'd ever interacted with treated them as equals."

"Others have interacted with them?" Turk inquired.

"Those people aren't around anymore. The point is, they weren't afraid of humans." Charles poured Turk more brandy and said, "Have you ever pointed a gun at a dog? They know what it is, even if they've never seen one. They know. It's bred into them to be fearful of a gun pointed in their direction. They can sense the danger it poses to them. That day, the creature looking down at us, it wasn't fearful of us or the guns we carried."

Turk's grip had tightened again around the stock of the rifle on his lap. He let loose and swirled his brandy. Charles could read the man like a book. He grinned at Turk's lack of control over his body language.

"And what happened?" Turk asked.

"Well, they're fearful now."

Charles finished what brandy he had left in his glass and stood and stretched in front of the hearth. He walked to the other side of the cabin, to the gun rack, and picked up a heavy antique rifle. He measured the weight of it in his hands and turned to Turk.

"We ascended the cliff and when we reached the top, the animal was there waiting for us. It wasn't aggressive—not at first. It was sheepish, cowardly. It was strange to see an animal that large, and that capable of so much destruction, just hunch there, half excited, half apprehensive. If it had been a bear, it would have mauled us in seconds. But it wasn't a bear. It was this big, oafish, missing link. It wasn't a beast. It was human-like in the way it regarded us. There was no raw animalistic instinct in it. It was debating what to do. Debating. Not reacting the way animals do."

Charles raised the rifle to his shoulder and aimed it at Turk. The safari man froze. He had never been so lost for options. Even with his own rifle laid across his lap, even with all the dire circumstances he had previously found himself in, he simply sat there, staring down the barrel of Charles' gun, staring into the bored holes of darkness that drilled back toward the trigger.

"I raised my rifle to my shoulder like this. And I fired. Like this." Charles pulled the trigger.

CLICK!

All the air escaped from Turk's lungs as he sighed deeper than he had ever done before. He had been like a deer in the headlights, waiting to be run over. Charles set the empty rifle back on the rack.

"The creature's head came apart. Pieces of skull and brain sliding all across the ice behind it as it crumpled upon itself. It wasn't some mystical creature. It was flesh and blood. That's what they are. You can kill one as easy as you would a lion. Easier, perhaps. That's what you're here to do, Mr. Turk. Take rich folks up this mountain, show them these creatures, and let them slaughter them."

Had Charles shared that story when they were all three back in Africa, Turk may not have come. It sounded absurd. An animal no one else had proven to exist, living on a private mountain retreat, waiting to be killed by wealthy big game hunters—it would have been too fantastical for Turk to have accepted. There in the cabin, however, sitting in front of the fire, a quarter bottle of brandy in his gut, Turk absorbed every syllable that Charles uttered.

The two men spent the rest of night in the cabin, discussing Turk's adventures in Africa and Charles' conquests across the globe. They eventually passed out, and as they slept their bodies burned off most of the brandy flowing through their systems.

At dawn, the first light peeked through the shutters and crept across Turk's swollen face. The warmth woke him gently, and he tightened his grip around himself, capturing the body heat beneath his clothing. If having the rifle pointed at his face the night before wasn't enough to disturb Turk, the loud bang of something hitting the outer wall of the cabin startled him to his soul. He jumped up from the floor and both he and Charles, who had already been up and moving, turned in the sound's direction. They stood in silence, waiting, staring at the wall.

A second bang against the outside of the cabin made them step backward. The impact against the cabin was strong, heavy, but as a third bang crashed upon the wall, Turk sensed a lack of aggression. The pounding was somewhat random, with long pauses between each one, and when a fourth came it carried with it a feeling of curiosity.

"It's testing the strength of the walls," Charles whispered.

"It?" Turk asked.

"Pick up your rifle," Charles instructed him. "See the shadow blocking the light coming through the slats," he asked as he motioned toward the wall receiving the beating.

Turk nodded and raised his rifle to his shoulder, taking aim. When the fifth bang hit, Turk pulled the trigger and the elephant gun barked out a blast that blew a hole through the cabin wall.

"Damn fine shooting! Damn fine!" Charles shouted. He hurried to the other side of the room and peered out the hole into the snowy morning. "You got 'em, son."

Turk took a moment to compose himself before he walked over to Charles' side and poked his head out the hole. Lying dead in the snow on its back was a Sasquatch, just as Charles had described it, lanky, covered in fur, primitive. Its enormous hands grasped weakly at the gaping wound in its chest, its dark blood, almost black, oozing through its coarse hair and down into the powdery snow.

The two men walked outside and stood over the creature, and as they watched it lie there helpless and afraid, Turk noted the confusion in the animal's eyes. It didn't understand what had happened. At one moment it had been like a kitten, pawing at something that had piqued its curiosity, and the next it was in tremendous pain, breathing its last breaths.

That moment verified to Turk that he had made the right decision in taking the Everlys' offer. The beast, as he saw it, was unlike anything he had ever encountered before. Now he had killed one, and that old thrill of taking life was reignited in his soul. He couldn't imagine himself ever being happier.

Over the next year, Turk perfected the route in which he would lead expeditions up the mountain. He secured climbing anchors, stocked up the cache cabin, and tested every coil of rope. He selected the weaponry and verified the reliability. Once he was confident in his planning and execution he gave the Everlys his blessing to open the Caliber Lodge for business.

He led five expeditions in the first four years of operating with a zero percent fatality rate. The Everlys were beyond ecstatic. They had chosen their man well. Mrs. Everly in particular had grown quite fond of Turk, and as the years went on the two developed a friendship over late night cocktails and early morning coffees.

Charles was either blind to his wife's growing affection for Turk or no longer cared to concern himself with her actions. He had become obsessed with the creatures on the mountain and spent his days watching them from the plateau, or sitting in his study sketching crude illustrations of them.

Mrs. Everly, on many occasions, had tried to persuade her husband to join her in intimacy, but as time went on his interest in her completely faded. He came to see her as no more than a business partner. Their flame had been doused. After all those adventures, those trips down the Nile, the Amazon, through the Rocky Mountains and the Sahara, his attraction to her was gone, and as Mrs. Everly sat in her room pondering how the thrill had faded, she came to the sobering realization that Charles' attraction had never been for her. It had always been the hunt. She had been but a traveling companion, a witness for his spectacles, and nothing more.

It was that night, in the winter of 1959, that Mrs. Everly began plotting the murder of her husband at the hands of one Jonathan Turk.

It wasn't difficult to convince the safari man to buy in. An additional monetary bonus and an increment of flirtations was all it took. Mrs. Everly had suggested Turk simply poison Charles, or smother him while he slept, but Turk felt too many questions would arise from the rest of the Caliber Lodge staff. He knew that the best course of action was to make the event look like an accident.

On the eleventh expedition up the mountain, Turk was leading a pair of Japanese businessmen and a Croatian entrepreneur out to hunt the Sasquatch. Charles came along, as he always did, and as Turk had hoped he would.

They reached the highest peak of the mountain and Turk assisted the two Japanese men and Charles up, helping them get their footing. The Croatian man was still a ways behind, ascending the cliff slowly, and much more cautiously than the others. As Turk stood on the edge of the cliff, watching him, making sure he was all right, Charles and the Japanese men took a moment to catch their breath. None of them heard the heavy breathing of the massive creature perched on a rock above them.

The scream of the Japanese men alerted Turk, and when he turned around, he saw the grayish creature grab one of them around the skull, and with a mighty force it kicked the man in the torso, ripping the man's head from his neck, sending his body flying against an icy boulder.

Charles stumbled and crab walked frantically backward, out

of sight behind another massive rock. Turk raised his rifle to gun down the creature but stopped, realizing this could be his chance to let nature do his dirty work for him. He quickly lowered his rifle and followed after Charles, staying out of sight.

A bellowing howl boomed through the air and as Turk took cover he heard the gurgling screams of the second Japanese man as his spine was dug out of his back and torn from place. The creature reached in through the man's open back and pulled out his lungs, then immediately shoved one of them into its jaws, clamping down on the soft tissue, blood pouring down its chin and chest.

It was at that point the Croatian entrepreneur reached the top of the peak, his adrenaline high, preparing himself to rescue his fellow climbers from whatever had caused them to scream out. The wind had picked up and his visibility was low. He held his arm out in front of him, trying to block the battling snowflakes as they bombarded his goggles. From his hiding place, Turk saw the Croatian man slide backward across the slick ground as a powerful gust attacked him.

When the Croatian man looked up again he saw the creature crouched in front of him, the Japanese man bent over his furry knee, his back ripped open like a package, exposing blood and bone and organs that leaked out over the grayish fur of his killer. The Croatian man pulled his elephant gun from the caribou skin holster on his back and stared down the sights at the blood-covered animal before him. As the creature stood, the Japanese man's body slid off his knee onto the ice. In its hand it held one of the severed lungs, which it tossed casually at the Croatian man, slathering his coat with blood.

Turk peeked out from behind the boulder and saw the creature backhand the Croatian man across the face, sending him flying through the air. He landed hard on a steep hill of ice and slid downward, unable to slow himself. He reached for his ice axe, fumbling at his belt with his gloved hand. His finger finally locked around the handle and he ripped it from the leather. Desperately, he tried to stab the pointed end into the ice as he continued to slide, picking up speed, headed straight toward the edge of the cliff.

The ice axe chipped at the ice with a repeated *THWACK! THWACK!* The man looked over his shoulder at the ledge he was quickly sliding toward. He continued to swing his ice axe. *THWACK!* This time the tip locked into the ice, but the man lost his grip and it slipped from his gloved hand.

With nothing left to grab hold of, nothing to stop himself, the man met his end as he careened off the mountain.

From a distance it must have looked rather peaceful—a small, dark object slipping off the side of a mountain ledge, flying outward into white nothingness, softly turning, spinning, like a six-foot tall snowflake—but from the Croatian man's point of view, there was nothing peaceful about it. He launched off the edge of the cliff, his momentum sending him out a slight distance before gravity kicked in and sent him plummeting downward into the abyss below.

If Turk had been paying more attention to the safety of his team and less on the prospect of murdering Charles, he may have prevented all of this, but there was no time for mournful thoughts.

Charles readied his rifle while sitting in the snow behind the boulder beside Turk. He looked up at his assumed comrade and whispered, loud enough to cut through the wind, but soft enough to not draw the creature's attention, "You want this one?"

Turk swung his ice axe, and the blade pierced through Charle's neck.

"Yes," Turk whispered. "I do."

Charles grasped at the razor sharp metal jutting out of his throat, his gloved fingers dragging across the tip, fraying the fabric. Turk slid the axe back out of Charles' neck and shoved him out into view of the creature.

Charles stumbled to his knees, choking, coughing, blood

pouring out all over the white. The hulking beast stomped over to him and slammed its big, heavy foot down on Charles' back, hammering him into the ground. It stomped again, this time on Charles' head, pulverizing it into wet, red pulp.

BARRRROOOOOOM! The crack of Turk's gunshot blared out, and the creature took a bullet in the heart. It staggered, then collapsed beside the mutilated body of the lungless Japanese man.

Turk came out from behind the boulder, unsheathed his knife and began skinning the creature, head to toe. He wrapped himself in the bloody fur and kicked all the bodies off the edge of the peak, including Charles' and the skinned, muscly Sasquatch, which Turk thought looked even more human with its fur removed.

That was the last anyone would see of Charles Everly, big game hunting champion, co-founder of the Caliber Lodge, and husband to Mrs. Greta Everly.

Chapter Fifteen
THE POISON

Had the whir of the heater not kicked on, Kristian may have slept through the rest of the evening. He had been in and out of consciousness due to the pain medication Turk had injected him with. From what he could tell, the effects had mostly worn off, and the pain, though not unbearable, had indeed resurfaced. He sat up and dangled his feet off the edge of the medical bed. He winced, feeling the tight, fresh bandages constrict around his wounded back as he moved. He reached around and his fingertips prodded, feeling a throbbing warmth. He examined his fingers for any trace of blood.

A section of the gauze fell from his back and he gathered the pieces in his hand, trying to make sense of how they came loose from the rest of the wrap. He reached around behind him again and felt that the gauze had been cut halfway up his spine. Shaking his head in frustration, he snarled at the shoddy workmanship. He clocked the roll of gauze on the stand and used it to spin a few more layers around his torso.

Though he presumed that Turk had cleaned him up well, he didn't know what sort of bacteria or fungus may have thrived beneath the curved claws of the arctic beasts in the cave. It was a harrowing experience and one Kristian was lucky to have survived thanks to the care of the bulky safari man and the mysterious oil tycoon heir.

Looking around, Kristian saw he was in an unfamiliar room filled with an impressive collection of hospital equipment. It looked completely contrasting to the rest of the Caliber Lodge. The walls were a stainless steel. The lights were a dimmed, cold blue.

He stood, his bare feet pressing against the cold, sterile floor. His pants were all that remained of his clothing, and he searched around for the rest of his attire before deciding the staff must have taken it to be cleaned and mended.

He reached for the light switch panel and turned the dimmer knob up, fully illuminating the entire room, revealing the ghoulish collection that had hidden in darkness along the back wall.

Behind a glass barrier that ran the entire length of the room, were four, intricately assembled Sasquatch skeletons. They were posed in action stances, with one skeleton on the left, a knotted tree branch in its hand, raised over its shoulder like a club, and the other three skeletons on the right, facing off against the weapon-wielding rival.

Kristian walked across the room, the warmth from his feet leaving sweaty footprints on the dark tile floor. He stood at the glass, admiring the display. The skeleton bones were unnaturally white, all bodily fluid and stains bleached clean off them. He walked along in front of the glass barrier at an almost motionless pace, taking in every detail of the panoramic scene.

Then he saw it—a glass door within the glass wall. He went to it and pulled it open. A suctioning gasp squeezed out, the captive air escaping from the glass room and the Goliath skeletons within.

Kristian entered. He walked up behind the first skeleton, the one nearest the door. It was crouched, its shoulder blades hunched, its hands curled, knuckle bones pressed to the ground. Kristian ran his open palm gently across the curved spin.

He moved on to the second skeleton, this one, its knees bent, tail bone almost touching the floor. Its arms were extended high above its head, the wrists limp, gigantic hands hanging downward. Kristian thought both this skeleton, and the first looked like they had been modeled after typical primate poses—chimps, maybe. They seemed primitive in their stances. Wild and mindless.

Kristian approached the third skeleton. It stood on its hind legs, the knees only slightly bent. Both arms extended out forward, the long finger bones reaching menacingly. Kristian moved around in front of it, standing with his head centered between the two extended hands. He stared up at the open jaws of the Sasquatch. The teeth looked just the way they had in the mouth of the creature that almost devoured him alive—only whiter, cleaner. He remembered the face of the alpha, its blue eyes and stinking yellowed incisors that oozed a thick gelatinous saliva.

The memory of how close he'd come to death terrified him once more, but he quickly shook it off with a faux unimpressed grunt. He turned and looked at the fourth and final skeleton. This one stood erect, its knees locked, back straight. Its right arm raised over its shoulder, gripping the gnarly tree branch as though ready to bludgeon the other skeletons to dust.

Kristian grinned at the remains of the mighty animal.

"If only your brothers out there had a fancy club like that, they might still be alive."

His hand reached slowly up toward the skull of the skeleton that stood eight feet tall. He pinched his index finger and thumb around one of the fangs on the lower mandible, and with a forceful jerk, he popped the tooth from the jaw. Examining it in his palm, Kristian hissed, "Survival of the fucking fittest."

He slid the tooth into the pocket of his pants, took another look at the diorama and walked out of the glass-encased tomb.

On the opposite end of the medical recovery room, Kristian saw the elevator frame and made his way over to it. He pulled the lever and listened as the lift descended toward him from the main level up above.

While seeing the skeletons of the mighty creatures, the likes of which had nearly mauled him to death, brought about an overwhelming series of thoughts, something else was burrowing through his brain as he waited to board the lift. He had grown suspicious of the supposed oil tycoon heir, Jimmy Knotts, over the course of the expedition, especially during their hiatus at the cabin. Something about the way Jimmy had looked at him, and the questions he had asked, made Kristian uneasy, and he felt compelled to find out all he could about the man he was sharing the weekend with. True, Knotts had helped in his rescue, but there was a nameless presence that beckoned Kristian not to trust him.

He took the lift to the third floor, and as he walked down the hall to his room, he saw Gregory walk out of the lounge below carrying a tray with a creamy drink in a cocktail glass—the Panama Premier. He watched as Gregory strolled into the bar with an indignant expression plastered across his face.

Kristian unlocked the door to his room and went inside to don a full outfit. He cringed when he pulled on his suit coat, the bandages once again tightening around his slashed back. He pulled open his leather briefcase and removed a small black fabric case, which he unzipped to reveal a series of picklocks. He ran his finger across the intricate tools that were positioned side by side, before selecting the one he felt most appropriate for the task at hand.

He sauntered down the hall to Jimmy's room and knocked lightly, awaiting an answer that never came. He knocked again, just to be sure, then picked the lock and let himself inside.

He made quick work of his investigation in Jimmy's room, knowing that at any minute Knotts could walk in. He checked beneath the bed, beneath the mattress and the sheet, placing everything back in its original state as he went. He went through the bathroom cabinets and the armoire. He saved the suitcase for last, resulting in the discovery of the Argentinian pistol.

The last time he had seen a Ballester-Molina had been before he'd adopted the alias of Kristian Beckett, back when he was hiding out at the Residencia Inalco. It was before he'd murdered his cohorts and absconded with the Nazi treasure that he used to buy a new life in the States.

The sight of it in Jimmy's suitcase drew him to the accurate assumption that Knotts had acquired the weapon in South America. Jimmy wasn't Argentinian, and neither was he a German immigrant, which led Kristian to the next logical train of thought—that Jimmy had been in South America to hunt men like him—to hunt Nazis.

And surely his reason for being at the Caliber Lodge is no different.

He wasted no time. Tucking the pistol behind his back, beneath his suit jacket, he shut the suitcase, and closed the door on his way out of the room.

As he walked down the hall to the elevator, he thought he could hear a muffled moaning sound and a dull thudding from one of the staff rooms below him. He paid it no further attention, took the lift down to the foyer and made his way into the lounge where Jimmy was sitting in one of the leather chairs, listening to classical music on the record player. Jimmy turned as he sensed Kristian's presence.

"Kristian. How are you recovering? I didn't expect to see you up and about already."

Kristian strolled over to the record player and inspected the vinyl.

"I'll be fine." He considered the truth of his statement. He would be fine, and partially because of Jimmy.

Jimmy having went through the trouble of saving him from the beasts on the mountain, instead of letting them dispatch of him, told Kristian everything he needed to know about Jimmy's endgame. His intentions were to keep Kristian alive and attempt to have him stand trial.

Jimmy watched as Kristian walked around the room as if

seeing it for the first time. He ran his finger up the wood paneling, like an auditor performing an inspection.

"Can I get you a drink? Or something from the kitchen?" Jimmy offered.

"Did you become a member of the staff while I was out?"

"Just being courteous."

"You saved my life back in that cave, Knotts. That's enough courtesy for a lifetime."

"Is that your way of thanking me?"

"What are you listening to?" Kristian asked as he approached the record player once more, ignoring Jimmy's question.

"I think it's Vivaldi," Jimmy answered, ever watchful of Kristian's movements.

"Viv-val-di," Kristian repeated, annunciating every syllable with an Italian accent. "He was a Catholic Priest, you know?"

"I know nothing about him. I just saw his name on the vinyl cover," Jimmy admitted with a shrug. "Let me get you a drink."

"I'm fine."

"Far from it! You almost died out there. You should be resting. Here, have a seat," Jimmy urged as he gestured toward the high-backed leather chair across from the one Jimmy had been occupying in front of the blazing fireplace. "Let me grab you one of those Very Old Fashioneds."

Jimmy jumped to his feet and Kristian, knowing he would be unsuccessful in contesting Jimmy's insistence, said, "San Martin."

Jimmy stopped in the doorway.

"What was that?"

"San Martin. It was one of the cocktails listed on the bar menu."

"San Martin," Jimmy clarified.

"If you're set on getting me a drink, I'd like to try one of those."

Jimmy nodded and vanished from the room.

Kristian sat down in the chair and tried his best not to look over at the fire. He could hear the embers sizzling, popping. He leaned his head closer toward the record player, trying to drown out the sound of the hearth with the tune of "Four Seasons."

Moments later, Jimmy was back with a pair of drinks in hand. He handed the ruby red colored San Martin in the cocktail glass to Kristian, while Jimmy kept hold of the second drink, a clear cocktail in a martini glass.

"Thank God Gregory was in there. I couldn't imagine whipping these up myself."

"Thank you," Kristian muttered quietly.

Jimmy adjusted his suit jacket and sat down across from him, then nodded and raised his glass before taking a sip. He looked at Kristian, thinking about how odd it was to be sitting there in the warmth of the lodge, enjoying a casual drink with the man he'd been hunting all these years. The Nazi had committed such atrocities during the war, partook in such evil events, even murdered his own comrades back in Argentina, yet here in Alaska, in front of the fireplace, Kristian looked like any other man, stoic still, yet normal in every other regard.

"That butler knows how to mix a drink," Kristian said as he ran his tongue across his lips.

"Gregory has a talent," Jimmy said, agreeing.

"We all have talents, don't we?"

Kristian looked at Jimmy, and his eyes seemed to glaze over cold. A strange, subtle change of expression slid over his face, almost unnoticeable, like a wax coating over an apple, only visible in the right light.

"What did you order up there?" Kristian asked, motioning to Jimmy's beverage.

"Smoked Martini."

"Smoked?"

"He poured a splash of scotch into the glass, the peaty kind, then swirled it around and tossed it out before pouring in the vodka. Gives it a smokey scent without being too overpowering."

"What a description. You could write ads," Kristian remarked.

"If the oil market crashes, I'll keep that in mind."

Kristian chuckled and took another sip of his San Martin.

"If memory serves, the menu said it was made with Stolichnaya," Kristian said.

"Yes. Rare."

"Not just rare," Kristian corrected. "Illegal. Like a Cuban cigar."

"I suppose that's right," Jimmy said as he drank.

"You don't mind living beyond the law, Mr. Knotts?"

"Playful question, Mr. Beckett."

"If you're in the midst of a game, best to be playful. Yes?"

"A game?" Jimmy asked.

"You know, I'd seen one of them before I came here," Kristian said.

"A bottle of Stolichnaya?" Jimmy said with a grin.

"A Sasquatch."

Jimmy's brow furrowed.

"I'd seen one before I came here to the Caliber," Kristian continued.

Jimmy didn't know how to respond. *How could Kristian have seen one of the creatures before this weekend*, he wondered. It was not where he guessed the conversation would have gone when Kristian sat down.

"You've seen them before? Where?"

"I wasn't certain until now if it had been imaginary or not. Most people go their entire lives without seeing one of those beasts, yet somehow I've seen them twice, on two different continents."

Kristian took another sip. "What do you think the odds of that are?"

Jimmy began to answer, "How could—"

Kristian cut him off. "You see, I've been going to all the notable big game hunting and mountaineering expeditions I could find, hoping that I'd get lucky and see one of them again. And now I have. And now I know I'm not crazy."

Jimmy leaned forward over his knees and asked, "Where else did you see one?"

"The Obersalzberg," Kristian said calmly.

"That's in Germany," Jimmy uttered quietly.

"Yes. Where the Berghof used to be."

Jimmy couldn't believe what he was hearing. Kristian was openly admitting to have been in the area where Hitler's retreat once stood.

"When were you in Obersalzberg?"

"You already know the answer to that, Mr. Knotts. You know all about me. I'm sure you have a rather detailed timeline of my movements until this point."

The words made Jimmy squirm in his chair. The candor was unsettling. He couldn't comprehend why Kristian was being so transparent suddenly.

Kristian asked Jimmy a question, and as he did his American accent was replaced by a thick Bavarian brogue.

"Was it you that shot at my seaplane back at the Inalco?"

Jimmy couldn't speak.

Kristian grinned.

"Of course it was," Kristian said, answering his own question. He took a big swig of his cocktail. "The Nazi treasure that I took from the Inalco, I sold it to amass my fortune. It allowed me to change my identity and pay for my admission here, so I could continue my hunt for my sanity. I've regained that now."

"How long have you known about me?" Jimmy asked as he

sat back in his chair.

It was at that point that Kristian revealed the confidence behind his gall—Jimmy's Ballester-Molina pistol—which he laid across his lap and gently rested his hand atop. Jimmy eyed the weapon and sighed. He had brought it along with the intent that the pistol that failed him once would get an opportunity for redemption. It was a poetic thought that became more nostalgic to Jimmy since his time in Argentina. In retrospect, Jimmy now saw the pistol as nothing more than a bad luck charm.

"It took me awhile to sell off all the items," Kristian explained. "I would've drawn too much attention if I attempted to pawn it all off at once. It would have made it too easy for you and your friends to track me down."

"You've been in the States since?" Jimmy asked through closed teeth.

"A small Nebraska town just south of Lincoln."

Those words made Jimmy's heart drop. Nebraska. It was where Jimmy had grown up, where he got his start in the investigation world back when he worked for the private detective firm as a photographer. He hadn't thought of those days in quite some time, and to think the war criminal he had been searching for all those years had been hiding out in his home state made him nauseous.

"You're the scout. Is that right? The one they send in to confirm the identity of your team's targets?" Kristian asked.

Jimmy stared at him through a heavy brow.

"That's what I was too," Kristian shared. "I investigated people for the Führer. Germans. I confirmed their true identities, then I shared my findings with mein Führer, the same way you share your findings with *your* boss."

Kristian tapped the barrel of the pistol in his lap. "This here, it's not our weapon of choosing, is it?" Kristian asked. "Men like us, we use our eyes, our ears, our instinct. We are patient men who wait for the opportune moment to make our moves. We're not soldiers. No. We're above that. We're hunters, you and I."

"Comparing yourself to me won't gain you any empathy," Jimmy sneered.

"Have you killed men, Knotts?" Though Jimmy didn't answer, Kristian could read everything he needed from Knotts' face. "I've killed people in order to survive. I've done what I needed to do so I could continue to pursue the things I wanted. And that's what you've done as well, isn't it? You've killed people to continue your hunt."

Kristian took another drink of the San Martin. "I won't pretend to know you personally. I don't know where you grew up, what your grandparents' names were, your favorite dish, though certainly something vegetarian. I can't tell you about Jimmy Knotts, but I can tell you plenty about your class of human. I know people like you intimately, because I *am* one of you. The countries we were born in, the century we exist in, the education we received, the people who raised us—none of it affects who we truly are. Our primal core. And at our core, Mr. Knotts, we're doppelgängers."

Jimmy was silent for a long moment. He sat uncomfortably in his chair, his eyes narrowed on Kristian. The flames in the fireplace warmed his already heated skin. Jimmy leaned forward, his elbows on his knees. He looked straight at Kristian and in the most calm, confident tone, he responded.

"A doppelgänger is a lookalike, someone who resembles another person. You may think we're the same, Stengl, and on the surface it's easy to draw simplistic comparisons, but let me assure you, before you blind yourself even further with that cosmic fate bullshit —you and I could not be any more different. I've killed men before, yes. I did it in self defense and in an attempt to protect others. What were the circumstances of the murders you committed? If they were to protect someone, I'd assume it couldn't have been anyone other than yourself."

Stengl stifled his animosity as Jimmy continued. "You may have been an investigator, but a job title alone does not tell the entire story. I investigate in the pursuit of justice for those it's owed to. You investigated to create a kill list for a malevolent, mass-murdering dictator. You can pretend all you want that being a 'hunter,' as you labeled it, is some sort of ancient, noble way of living, but the truth is—," Jimmy leaned even further toward Kristian. "You're just a piece of shit Nazi."

Kristian smiled, trying to conceal the fuming rage behind his sharpening gaze. Jimmy didn't break eye contact. The two men stared at one another in silence, Kristian knowing that he had the upper hand with the Argentinian pistol in his possession.

The crackling fire drew his attention. Those same screams filled his mind, crescendoing to an overwhelming volume. They were the screams of Amelia, burning alive in the hearth of the Berghof. Kristian rubbed his middle finger against his temple, then slammed his fist down on the arm of the leathery chair. The sounds in his mind dissipated as Jimmy shifted in his seat ever so slightly.

As Jimmy settled, Kristian saw that his nemesis had pulled something out from behind his back. He was now staring down the double barrels of a stubby pistol that looked like an antique sawed-off shotgun. Jimmy's index finger was wrapped tightly around the worn, metal trigger.

"The plaque beneath it said Howdah Pistol," Jimmy quipped. "Turk did a marvelous job labeling everything in the game room."

Kristian grinned as he remarked, "The true purpose of you offering to get me a drink."

Kristian's hand grazed the trigger of the Ballester-Molina.

"Ah." Jimmy cocked the Howdah. Kristian withdrew his hand. Jimmy stood, keeping the African pistol aimed perfectly on

Kristian's chest and said, "You and I are going to go visit some friends of mine."

Kristian bit the side of his cheek. In the brief time Jimmy had known him, Kristian had always had a grim demeanor, but his aura there in the lounge had never been quite so austere.

"Stand up and let it fall off your lap onto the floor." Kristian paused a moment, trying to read Jimmy. "I want you alive," Jimmy started. "Surely you've figured that out by now—but if you try anything, I'll settle with taking in your corpse."

Kristian stood slowly and let the Argentinian pistol fall to the polished floor. "What happens now, Mr. Knotts? Are you going to march me out the front door?"

Turk's bellowing voice rang out, "I don't think anyone will be going anywhere right this moment."

Jimmy and Kristian turned to see him standing in the lounge's doorway holding a Winchester rifle, aimed at Jimmy's chest.

"Thank the Lord," Kristian muttered back in an American accent. He stepped away from Jimmy. "I think Mr. Knotts is at the end of his rope."

"It seems that way," Turk boomed.

"There's a bit more going on here than you realize at the moment, Mr. Turk," Jimmy said.

"How about you just set my pistol on the floor there, Mr. Knotts?"

"I can't do that."

"Oh? Did you incur an injury during the expedition that I'm unaware of? Are you unable to bend down?" Turk questioned condescendingly.

"You need to hear me out here, Turk," Jimmy urged him.

"I don't need to do anything of the sort. This is a Winchester rifle. 'The gun that won the west.' It's not going to have any difficulty besting the likes of you."

Jimmy's eyes never moved to Turk. They remained locked on Kristian like a vice. "Kristian isn't who he says he is."

"Put the gun down, Mr. Knotts," Turk directed.

"He's been lying."

"Put the gun down, Mr. Knotts," he repeated, his hands steady on the rifle.

"You need to listen to me," Jimmy pleaded.

"Put that fucking gun down, Jimmy," Turk demanded in an eerily calm tone. The vinyl continued to rotate, trilling out the classical music of Vivaldi.

Jimmy, in an effort to be compliant so he could further explain the circumstance, followed Turk's direction. He uncocked the Howdah and let the trigger guard spin loosely around his index finger as he raised his hands up as a sign of surrender. He looked over at Turk for the first time since the safari man entered the room and tossed the pistol onto the floor in front of the hearth. Kristian let out an almost unnoticeable sigh of relief.

"It's safe," Turk called into the foyer. A moment later, Mrs. Everly entered, her high collared black dress back in place.

"The excitement of the mountain wasn't enough for you, boys? Had to try to start a gunfight here inside the lodge?" Mrs. Everly quipped.

Jimmy gestured at Kristian and sounded off, "You see this man here, the one who's been calling himself Kristian Beckett—he's in fact a Nazi war criminal named Wilhelm Stengl. He's been hiding in the States for years, using a false identity. He needs to be brought to justice."

Turk kept his rifle up as Everly walked further into the lounge. She turned off the record player, and the room grew jarringly silent. She stared at Jimmy for a long moment before saying, "We know who he is. We are here to run a business, not to involve ourselves in worldly affairs. Stengl may have been operating under a guise, but we knew his true identity from the beginning. Knowing that our legal team is quite thorough, he was open with us, and as we only care about our secrecy here, we knew that if we kept his secret, he would no doubt keep ours."

Jimmy could not believe what he was hearing. He looked at Turk and his face told him that none of this was news to the safari man.

"The person I'm concerned with now, is you, Mr. Knotts. Clearly you are much better at deception than any of us. Turk shared with me his suspicion you may be an animal activist, but it seems clear now why you are truly here. I don't think it likely that an oil fortune heir would moonlight as a Nazi hunter. You forged your identity, breaching all the contracts you signed. You are a threat to the Caliber Lodge. You are a threat to me," Everly hissed in a dire tone.

"I'm not a threat to you. I'm just here for him," Jimmy stated sternly as he pointed at Kristian.

"You have no fortune. No collateral. You have nothing to lose. What is it exactly that will keep you from telling people about the creatures up on the mountain?"

"The creatures on the mountain? This is much bigger than any of that!"

"There is nothing bigger than that! Those creatures are the most valuable find in history! Our profit comes from their rarity, the secret of their existence. The world will ask where the infamous Nazi Wilhelm Stengl was apprehended. You will draw the globe's attention to the Caliber Lodge. Reporters, journalists, law enforcement—all of them trudging around my mountain. And how long after that does some sneaky photographer come across one of the creatures? You will expose us. You will ruin my business and everything I've built here."

"You're choosing money over morals!" Jimmy yelled at her.

"Morals?" She laughed. "You know nothing of me, Mr.

Knotts! My morals dissolved long ago!" Everly screamed back at him.

Jimmy took a step forward but halted as Turk pulled back the hammer of the Winchester. He searched for words to convince Everly to hear him out further, but he could see in her darkening eyes that she was a heartless shell that had no intention of listening to any more of his pleas.

"Mr. Turk," Everly said, "This man is a poison to us all. Please do away with him."

Turk adjusted his grip on the Winchester. Jimmy felt his stomach drop. He imagined this is how all those animals in the game room had felt, staring down the barrel of the antique rifle, peering into the black hole of their ultimate demise.

"If you wouldn't at all mind, Mrs. Everly," Kristian offered. "I'd rather enjoy the opportunity to dispatch of this liar."

Jimmy looked back to Kristian.

"Should you like the honor, Mr. Stengl, you have my blessing to take him out back and put an end to this circus."

With that, Kristian picked the Ballester-Molina up off the floor, checked it, cocked it, and pointed it at Jimmy's gut.

The wind blew violently against them as Kristian marched Jimmy out the back door of the Caliber Lodge. The Nazi didn't let Jimmy put on a coat before stepping out into the cold, and after the first few yards Jimmy could feel his skin tingling.

"You're a greedy man, Mr. Knotts," Kristian yelled over the howling wind. "You could have killed me. You could have won. Instead, you rolled the dice, hoping you could bring me in alive. You had every chance to end this during the expedition. Cut my rope. Friendly fire. Even just let one of those beasts tear me apart in the cave. But no. Not you. You're full of greed, just like those Jews you sympathize with."

Jimmy rubbed his upper arms, then his chest, trying to keep the blood flowing. His cheeks stung, and he was almost certain that the small hairs on his face were icing over. He thought about the things he could have done differently. Maybe Kristian was right. Maybe Jimmy should have killed him when he had the opportunity. He was no assassin, though. He was a hunter, not a murderer. His job was to bring the Nazi to justice, not exact some secondhand revenge.

"Who is it you work for? Mossad?" Kristian continued to prod as the two men walked farther out, perpendicular from the direction they took up the mountain during the expedition earlier that morning.

"If I could find you, others will be able to do the same. You'll get your comeuppance, sooner or later, Stengl."

Kristian laughed, a low, rumbly guffaw. He kicked Jimmy in the back of the knee, forcing him to the snowy ground. "Men like me —" he said with an oozing confidence, "Men like *us*, my friend—like I said, we are survivors. Men like us come out on top. But when you pair two doppelgängers against one another, unfortunately for one of them, someone has to lose."

Kristian stood behind Jimmy and pressed the barrel of the gun against the back of his head. Jimmy's body had grown numb. Everything felt prickly and phantom. On his knees in the victim's stance, the snow almost came up to his chest. Kristian applied pressure, pushing the barrel hard against Jimmy's skull, but Jimmy held strong, keeping his posture as best as he could.

"I'll give you the courtesy of last words, Knotts."

"Go fuck yourself, you Nazi prick."

Kristian grinned, and his finger tightened around the trigger. Jimmy closed his eyes and wondered whether he would hear the gunshot before he departed from existence.

The sound he heard next wasn't that of a bullet exploding

from the barrel of his Ballester-Molina, however, it was an echoing howl that tore through the blustering wind.

Kristian turned, and through the darkness he could make out fuzzy silhouettes galloping toward the lodge. He squinted, trying to get better clarity, but all he could see was moving shapes. They were a good distance away, coming down from the ridge and moving fast toward the glow of the Caliber.

Jimmy took advantage of the distraction and before Kristian knew what was happening, Jimmy snapped Kristian's wrist, wrenched the pistol free and cracked the Nazi across the scalp. Kristian collapsed to the ground and Jimmy rose to his feet, pointing the gun down at the murderer's face.

His adrenaline pumping, Jimmy was ready to end the entire ordeal. Fate had provided him with yet another chance to finish the bastard off, but as he looked down at his helpless enemy, Jimmy knew he had to complete the job he had taken on. He knew that he had to get Kristian back to the rendezvous point and bring him to Levi. He still didn't know where the infamous Stengl notebook was, and without that book, Kristian's brain was invaluable and necessary.

With no coat, no form of protection against the cold, Jimmy's body was shutting down. He only had a brief window of time to make it back to the lodge before his extremities completely gave out. He grabbed Kristian by the collar and began dragging him back toward the Caliber. Halfway there he had to look down to be sure that his fingers were still gripping the Nazi's coat as he no longer had any sensation in his hands.

He could see the silhouetted shapes charging toward the lodge in the distance. He couldn't make out the details, but he knew that it could only be one thing. The Caliber was about to come under attack by what looked like a coordinated assault.

Jimmy knew that the lodge wouldn't spell safety for him, but he couldn't think about that now. His only goal was to make it back before he froze to death, and to make sure Kristian made it back with him. He had no other option but to pull Kristian into the heat of the lodge, then decide his next course of action.

He heard another howl, then another, bouncing off the snow, ricocheting off the trees. He tried to focus, but all the wetness in his eyes had either evaporated or froze. His vision became blurred. He stumbled and lost his hold on Kristian's collar. His bare hands sank into the snow, but they were already so raw that he couldn't sense the iciness. His lungs felt as though they were on fire, hot and constricting. He clutched his chest, then his throat, but could not feel his own touch.

He tried to stand, but his knees immediately buckled, and he was back down in the snow. He crawled a few feet, gasping. If his body had been capable of producing tears at that moment, they would have been streaming down his face. He wasn't even sure if he was in pain anymore. He couldn't even trust his own senses as he began confusing thoughts and feelings, ideas and sensations.

Using the last of his strength, he forced himself back to his feet and looped his arm under Kristian's the way an usher would. He took a long stride with his left leg, then extended his right leg out and heaved Kristian along behind him. As he grew closer to the lodge, the glow from the windows became nothing more than a hazy halo of light that rimmed the outlines of his dying pupils.

Chapter Sixteen
THE ABOMINATIONS

To call what happened next "a massacre," would not do it justice. After Kristian escorted Jimmy out into the freezing darkness beyond the Caliber Lodge, Gregory entered the lounge where Jonathan Turk and Mrs. Everly were conversing about what had just transpired, as Dean Martin's "You're Nobody 'Till Somebody Loves You" played on the record player like a soundtrack.

Gregory offered to get each of them a nightcap and Everly, due to the stress, Turk due to his addiction, accepted. The three of them went to the bar and closed the double doors for privacy.

Mrs. Everly thought of the first time she met Gregory as she watched him prepare their cocktails. His skills as a master of flavors had only improved over the years and she continued to feel confident that for several reasons, he was the only man that could have filled the position at the lodge.

"Now, I know our dear friend, Mr. Turk here, is the owner of a set of taste buds that prefer the flavors of the whiskey and brandy varieties, however, I'm convinced that what I'm about to pour you both will satisfy even the most stubborn of dug in drinkers," Gregory quipped as Turk grinned at his showman's personality.

He reached into the refrigerator beneath the bar top and pulled out three frosted martini glasses, which he set side by side in the center of the bar. Stepping up on the stool, he pulled down a bottle of Cana Brava white rum from the display shelf behind the bar, along with a bottle of Luxardo Maraschino liqueur.

"The Hemingway Classic," Gregory said as he prepared to craft the cocktail. "It is, of course, named after the famous author who, after spending a great deal of time in Havana, became obsessed with daiquiris."

He flipped up a copper-lined cocktail shaker from beneath the bar and poured in a few glugs of rum. "Two ounces white rum. I've chosen Cana Brava. You'll hear people say, 'Rum is rum,' and to that I say, 'No, sir.' Is white cane sugar the same as brown? Though subtle as the taste may be, there is indeed a difference." Gregory splashed in the red liquid from the Luxardo bottle. "Maraschino cherry liqueur. One-quarter ounce."

Gregory raised the shaker to his nose and sniffed. "Gorgeous." He pulled a mason jar of grapefruit juice from the under-counter refrigerator and poured in a healthy amount. "Three quarters ounce of pink grapefruit juice. Fresh." Gregory stopped, the jar of juice still in hand and said, "The proportions, you've likely noticed, I've multiplied by three, as I'm simultaneously making each of us one of these delicious endeavors."

"Naturally," Mrs. Everly said with a smile. Gregory smiled back and with quicksilver speed, chopped up three plump limes and squeezed them into the shaker, leaving a fourth lime untouched atop the bar top.

"Lime juice. Again, fresh. This Roses Lime fad is utter rubbish."

"Wouldn't know. Never drink these fancy concoctions," Turk said lightheartedly as he waited patiently with Mrs. Everly while Gregory filled the shaker with ice.

"You shake it all up," he said as he slapped the lid on the shaker and rocked it back and forth over his shoulder. He popped the lid off and inserted a strainer over the top. "Then strain." He tilted the shaker over the frosty glasses one at a time, filling each nearly to brim.

"Looks perfect," Mrs. Everly said as she reached for the closest glass.

"Not yet," Gregory inserted. He reached for the untouched lime and quickly cut it into wheels. "Looks are everything, are they not? The garnish is not solely decoration. If you hang a lime from the rim of the glass, it not only looks pleasant, it smells pleasant, and it's more than likely the first scent you'll smell as you raise it to your lips."

Gregory slid a lime wheel onto the rim of each of the three glasses, then drug it around the lip, rolling the juice across the entire perimeter. "It's not so much that looks can be deceiving as it is they can be distracting. A pretty face, a fancy suit, first impression. It makes all the difference. It can convince someone that what lies beyond is just as kosher, but we all know, sometimes what lies beyond is total fucking bollocks."

Mrs. Everly and Turk listened calmly as Gregory made his point. "What you see is what you get. That's how it should be. That's how we operate. That's how this drink is. It looks tart, it is tart. The lime on the rim says it all. Judge the fuckin' book by its cover, because false advertising is the just a fancy name for bald faced lying."

Gregory slid Mrs. Everly and Turk their completed cocktails. He raised the third for them to cheers. "So fuck anyone who wears a fancy lime suit when the person beneath is nothing but rot-gut liquor."

Turk clinked his glass against Gregory's. Mrs. Everly smiled with appreciation and gently touched the lip of her glass against theirs. They all drank, and Gregory watched their expressions to gauge the quality of his cocktail. Turk raised his eyebrows in surprise. Though not the profile he was accustomed to, he quite enjoyed the citrus flavor.

"It's become an increasingly brutal business, has it not?" Mrs. Everly said as he swirled the foggy liquid in her glass.

"Life is brutality," Turk said.

Everly looked at him, trying to conceal the dull grin that spread across her porcelain face. In her mind she reminisced about all the years spent at the Caliber, and all those spent traveling the globe before it, the violence she had seen, the blood and vulgarity. For a moment she thought of her late husband, Charles, and the day he had been killed. Turk had brought her back the freshly skinned Herculean pelt of the creature that tore him apart. She kept it as a throw for her bed so she could be reminded every night before drifting to sleep that she had the power to achieve whatever she dreamed of. After all, it had been her idea to capitalize on the mountain's treasures. It had been her idea to open a luxury hunting lodge for the wealthy elite. It had been her idea to protect their find with ironclad legal documents. She was the one to lure Gregory into their employ. She was the one to entice Turk into leaving Africa with nothing but the promise of opportunity. She was responsible for it all. Not Charles.

Her husband had many admirable attributes, but creative thought had not been one of them. He was intelligent, brave, and shared her twisted passion for the violent macabre, but an entrepreneur he was not. That never bothered Mrs. Everly though, and she hadn't just been content with Charles, she had been happy. She had loved her husband dearly. The moment she realized her love was not reciprocated, however, she was the one to remove him from all she had dreamt up.

In return for Turk seeing to her husband's demise, Mrs. Everly had bestowed upon him a rifle with a personalized inscription that read, "For Jonathan Turk. My Hero." She recalled the look on the safari man's face when he read it. It had made him uncomfortable, being called a hero for murdering a man, but he didn't dare say so. He just smiled and thanked her.

The trio finished their Hemingway Classics and Gregory

mixed up another round. They clinked their glasses together ceremoniously, then Everly stood up and adjusted her dress before taking a sip.

"I'm going to need some sustenance," she said. She excused herself, pulled open the double doors and disappeared from the room. Turk and Gregory caught one another staring at their employer's backside as she strolled out into the foyer.

She concentrated on her footing, not wanting to sway and appear intoxicated to the men behind her that she assumed were no doubt watching. Her heels clicked atop the polished tile, echoing within the massive entryway.

When she pushed open the door to the kitchen, before her eyes had taken in the state of the room, Everly said, "I saw you seasoning some Sasquatch meat earlier, Igak. Let's get the stove fired up and—"

She stopped mid-sentence when she realized what she was looking at. The kitchen was painted with a splattering of angry crimson. The once white walls and marble counters, now covered in wet, dripping blood.

At first she thought Igak was nowhere to be seen, until she understood that Igak was… everywhere. The cook's severed arm was laying atop the island counter. His left leg was strewn in the corner, leaking out all over the floor.

Everly gasped, covering her mouth. She slowly backed out of the kitchen, her gaze locked on the blood-soaked cabinetry.

She quietly stepped out of her heels, leaving them sitting in the middle of the foyer. She glanced behind her toward the open doors of the bar, wanting to call for Turk but knowing that whatever had butchered Igak was likely still lurking nearby. The loud clanking of metal pans crashing across the kitchen startled her, and she veered away from the bar and hurried toward the elevator.

"You all right?" Turk's voice called from the bar.

Everly's head turned back toward the kitchen, expecting to see the beast emerge at the sound of the call. Somehow the coast was still clear.

Turk stepped out into the foyer.

"You headed back to your room?"

Everly held her finger to her lips, and Turk could see the pale fear that had glazed over her face. She pointed toward the kitchen and Turk only paused a moment before running to the game room to deal with the issue.

Everly ran to the elevator and pulled open the gate. The squeal from the metal echoed through the foyer. She froze and took a deep breath before looking back over her shoulder.

Standing in the kitchen doorway, its grayish fur stained red and dripping with Igak's innards, was one of the creatures, its long arms sagging, its jaw slack, and its blue eyes leering at her.

"JONATHAN!" Everly screamed as she threw herself inside the elevator and slammed the gate closed.

The creature charged at her, its long legs making easy work of the distance. Everly yanked the lever to initiate the ascent, but the creature grabbed hold of the gate, its long, wet fingers wrapping through the ornate weaving. As the elevator began to raise, the creature used all its strength to hold it in place. The motor chugged and reared, then sputtered out a thick cloud of smoke. It weaned to a halt and the elevator was stalled in place.

"JONATHAN!" Everly yelled again as she stared helplessly at the creature on the other side of the gate. She pressed herself against the back side of the lift and frantically looked for another way out.

BARRRROOOOOM!

The gunshot from Turk's rifle was even louder within the walls of the Caliber Lodge. The bullet hit the creature in the shoulder, spinning it away from the elevator gate. It howled out in pain and grabbed at its wound.

Turk took aim, ready to put a second shot in the animal, when a massive hand wrapped around the barrel of the gun and ripped it out of his grasp. The second creature backhanded Turk in the chest, sending him flying back into the game room against the side of the pool table.

All the air escaped from his lungs, and Turk doubled over, gasping for breath. He grabbed the edge of the table to help steady himself, and as he stood he could feel the sharp, piercing pain of broken ribs stabbing his insides.

He stumbled across the room and lifted an African spear off a set of hooks just as the creature stomped in.

"Come on, you son of a bitch!" Turk growled as he brandished the spear. The creature threw its head back and howled.

"Come on!" Turk yelled.

The creature took a step forward and Turk moved around the other side of the pool table, using it as a barrier between them. He poked at the animal tauntingly and the creature swatted at the tip of the spear each time it came near. Turk lurched forward over the table, thrusting the weapon, but the creature slapped it away effortlessly. He tried again—the creature grabbed the neck of the spear and pulled it, forcing Turk to release his grip or else be dragged across the table. The creature cracked the shaft over its leg and tossed both ends of the spear to the ground.

Turk reached for one of his mounted rifles and the creature stepped up onto the pool table behind him. With a ferocious swipe, the creature raked its claws across Turk's back, shredding his shirt and tearing through his flesh. Turk screamed, and the creature stepped down off the table and grabbed Turk by the ankle, pulling his legs out from underneath him. It lifted him into the air and let him flail and dangle there.

Turk strained, trying to reach any of the weapons on the wall, but all were just out of reach.

As he hung upside down in the animal's grip he saw another creature saunter into the room. It wasn't the same one that had been trying to break into the elevator—the one he had shot in the shoulder—it was a third creature, its grayish fur clean and clear of any fresh blood stains. The two creatures looked at each other and the clean creature gave a slight grunt to the one holding Turk, as if indicating a direction.

Turk reached again for the wall of weapons, but just as his middle finger grazed the hilt of a machete, his body was pulled away and the creature swung him in the air by the ankle as if he were weightless. It spun Turk in helicopter fashion and Turk could feel all the bones in his leg crack and break as he spiraled through the air.

When the spinning abruptly stopped Turk felt a pain like none he had ever experienced. It was both sharp and dull at the same time. He felt his skin split and tear, and his lungs fill then flatten. When he opened his eyes, he was looking into the face of the creature, and for a brief second he was sure it had smiled at him—but as his vision faded all he could see was the blurry outline of his attacker.

Turk's neck went limp and his head fell to the side. The left incisor of the taxidermy hippopotamus was protruding from his chest. The yellowed tooth, almost two feet in length, suspended Turk above the ground, his feet dangling two feet from the floor. The creature looked at him inquisitively and reached out to touch the blood-slathered tip of the tooth.

Turk's head whipped up, and he gasped for air, adrenaline pulsing through his body. Startled, the creature grabbed the incisor and snapped it from the hippo's mouth, dropping Turk to the floor. The creature raised its foot and brought it down hard on Turk's head, crushing the safari man's skull with a wet crunch.

During the scuffle, the crimson box toppled off the mantel, and as it landed on the floor, it popped open and the domed scalp rolled out onto the carpet beneath the pool table. The creature crouched down and scooped it up in its callused palm. It raised it to his face and inspected it with flared nostrils that inhaled the scent of the dried, dead flesh. The creature's brow furrowed, and it tossed the scalp into the fire.

Turk's left leg was resting at the edge of the fireplace hearth, and a pair of embers landed on his pants just above his boot. They sizzled, and the material caught fire, and as the flames slowly moved across his body, the creature rumbled out of the game room, leaving what was left of Turk's corpse to burn in front of the animals he had mounted to the wall.

The wounded creature poked at the bullet hole in its shoulder as it stood in front of the elevator gate, blocking Everly from escaping.

"Jonathan!" she called out again, but the only thing that came out of the game room was the creature that had pulverized Turk's head. It walked over toward the bar where the third creature—the clean one—was waiting.

The wounded creature sniffed the air and its eyes locked onto the smoke as it billowed out of the game room. It turned and looked at Everly through the gate and calmly grabbed the metal with both hands. Everly backed up, expecting the creature to rip the gate from its hinges, but instead the long fingers tightened and with a delicate ease the creature twisted the gate in both directions, pinching it and locking it into place, trapping Everly behind a woven mess of metal.

The wounded creature turned and galloped over to the other two, its knuckles nearly dragging on the ground as it bound across the foyer floor. Then the three of them lumbered through the double doors and out of Everly's view.

With all of her might she attempted to pull the gate open, but it was no use, the metal was forged in place. As the smoke continued to pour out of the game room, Everly grew frantic, looking for an alternate escape.

Above her head was an exit hatch, a metal grate that could be pulled open to gain access to the top of the lift. She jumped and slid the slide lock free, then with her second jump she popped the hatch open. Her thin fingers gripped the edge of the opening and she hoisted herself up and out of the elevator. She stood on the roof of the lift and reached up to the second floor railing. She had to jump again—her hands locked tightly around the lower rung. She was still in great shape, even at her age, and she pulled herself up and over the railing and landed softly on the hallway carpet of the second floor. Running full bore to her room, she flung the door open.

Quivering in fear, Gregory was crouched down behind the bar top, clutching the bottle of thirty-year scotch. He could hear the heavy breathing of the creatures as they made their way into the room. He did his best to stay quiet, but he was hyperventilating, and his rapid breaths were anything but inaudible.

He had never seen one of the creatures alive before. He had observed the paintings that Charles Everly had done, and he'd admired the skins that Turk had brought back with him from his solo trips up the mountain, but he had never laid eyes on the creatures while there was still life inside them. He thought about all the times he had dined on their meat, which Igak had seasoned, tenderized and perfectly prepared, and he hoped that they would not be returning the favor.

A set of long fingers came into view and wrapped tightly around Gregory's head. The clean creature—the one that had grunted approval for Turk's execution—had reached over the bar top and palmed Gregory's skull like an apple. It lifted him up off the floor and Gregory's screams were muffled as he tried to call out for help from his friends.

The clean creature dropped Gregory down on the bar top, laying him out lengthwise across the wood. Gregory looked up at the three animals, the clean one, the wounded one and the one that had impaled Turk. He had not expected their eyes to look the way they did. He had not expected them to appear so human. The sketches and paintings that Charles had done years ago had depicted their eyes as glowing, demonic and otherworldly. There was nothing otherworldly about these animals though, for their features were a culmination of several animals familiar to him.

He tried to scoot away across the bar top, but the wounded creature grabbed his leg and held him in place. The clean creature rested his open hand across Gregory's chest and Gregory could feel the weight of it, around ten to fifteen pounds, like a baby or small dog lying atop him. The hand balled into a fist and raised into the air.

Gregory knew what was about to happen next, but all he could do was squeeze his eyes closed and pray that it wouldn't last long. As the creature's fist slammed down on Gregory's chest, he felt every one of his ribs shatter. The creature raised his other fist and slammed it down on Gregory's pelvis, and once again the butler felt his bones crack under the pressure.

The other two creatures hopped up and down in place, planting their knuckles on the floor and lifting their legs up and down joyously as the clean creature continued to alternate blows with its heavy fists like a gorilla. The creature didn't stop his beating until the grayish fur on its arms was stained red and Gregory's body was nothing more than a soupy mass of bone powder and organ bits. Then it leaned over the bar top and lapped up some remains before stepping back to let the other two have their turn.

Meanwhile, Everly had gone to her armoire and pulled out her Smith & Wesson Triple Lock, the big heavy handgun that she had carried on her during her time in Africa when she and Charles had gone to meet Turk for the first time. She didn't have to check that it was loaded, it always was.

With her second reach, she pulled out her gun belt and holster decorated with dozens of .44 shells overstuffed with powder. She cinched the belt around her waist and stepped back out into the hall just as the three creatures came out of the bar into the open foyer. The wounded one hurried back to the elevator, and when it saw that Everly had escaped out through the hatch, it howled to alert the others.

Everly didn't hesitate, she took aim and pulled the trigger, firing a bullet into the wounded creature's head. It dropped to the floor, and before she could realign her sights, the other two creatures were on the move. They leaped up into the air, grabbing the second floor railing and swinging themselves in a weightless fashion, like apes playing on a trapeze. Their long arms allowed them fluid movement, hoisting their heavy bodies up and over the banister.

Everly opened fire, shooting bullet after bullet at the creatures as they swung and dodged the gunfire. Her gun clicked as the chambers ran empty and she quickly began to reload. One of the creatures barreled down the hallway toward her, while the other leaped back down to the bottom level then jumped back up to the second floor a few yards away from Everly. They had her surrounded.

They howled as they charged at her. She worked furiously to slide the shells into the chamber of the revolver, but she wasn't quick enough. They were almost upon her and she had to make a split second decision.

Everly jumped over the railing and fell to the glossy floor below. As she landed, the impact sent a searing pain up her shin and her bone snapped and jutted out through the skin. Everly doubled over, but even as she cried out in agony, she continued to load the shells into her revolver.

As she slid the last bullet into the cylinder, she felt the floor rumble and quake. The two creatures had landed beside her, and the weight of their bodies as their feet planted caused the floor to crack and send a spiderweb of fractures snaking out in all directions.

Everly extended her arm and aimed the triple lock.

"Soulless beasts!"

Her finger squeezed the trigger, but before she could pull it all the way back, one of the creatures grabbed her by the wrist, and with brutal force, ripped her entire arm from its socket.

Everly wailed a horrific scream as blood pulsed from the gaping hole. She rolled to her side and tried to crawl away across the broken floor—the gore seeping into the cracks. The pain was unbearable—the bone jutting out from her leg, the ichor flowing from her shoulder. She began fading in and out of consciousness, no longer able to tell if she was screaming or if the shrieks were nothing more than the suffering exploding in her brain.

Flares of warm light caught her dulling eyes, and she saw that the fire from the game room had spread into the foyer. The flames ran up the walls, feeding off the oil and stain on the wood. The series of vases adorned with Neanderthal-inspired art had been knocked from their tree stump pillars and laid shattered on the floor. The fire reached the oil painting of the lodge that hung beside the door to the kitchen—the canvass had become charred and blackened from the heat.

Everly couldn't tell what hurt more, her disfigured body or the sight of her business burning around her. She reached out with her one remaining hand and swatted helplessly at the fire as if she could douse the overwhelming blaze with a wave of her palm.

The last bit of energy that she had evaporated. Everly's arm dropped and her cheek rested on the floor. The smoke obscured her vision and soon all she saw was the black of the ash that fell upon her face.

The creatures watched a moment longer as the life escaped her body. She was left in the middle of the room, surrounded on all sides by the inferno that had engulfed her precious Caliber Lodge.

Chapter Seventeen
THE RENDEZVOUS POINT

The back door of the lodge was open when Jimmy approached it. The blistering cold had nearly defeated him, and he collapsed to his knees as he stumbled inside. His fingers had frozen to the collar of Kristian's coat and when he tore them free, pieces of his skin were left attached to the fabric. He pulled the German the rest of the way in through the doorway, then shoved the door closed to cut off the piercing wind.

The chill had damaged his eyes, and it took several minutes for them to warm back to life enough for him to see anything. He was kneeling beside the unconscious Nazi in the mudroom where all of their expedition gear had been left and stored—the heavy coats, the layered pants and climbing boots—all neatly arranged on hooks and shelving, dry and warm. Jimmy pulled himself back up and stripped off the frozen clothing from his dying body. He pulled his Ballester-Molina out from his waistband, where he had tucked it for his journey back through the snow, and set it on one of the shelves. He wasted no time in gathering a fresh outfit from the rack and pulling it on to help bring his core temperature back up.

He sat back down beside Kristian and pressed his fingers against the German's neck, checking for a pulse. He felt the Nazi's chest rise and fall beneath his other thawing hand. It was a small victory and though breathing was still painful as his lungs continued to defrost, Jimmy grinned as he exhaled a sigh of relief. He wasn't at the finish line yet, but surviving his trek back to the lodge interior was the first step.

He reached up and pulled the pistol off the shelf, wondering if it would still fire after being exposed to the extreme temperature for so long. His heart was able to continue to beat, so hopefully the gun would still function. At the very least, it still looked operational and the presence of it would be enough to keep Kristian at bay whenever he woke back up.

Jimmy's senses had numbed and as they slowly kicked back into gear, he sniffed the air and caught a whiff of the smoke that began billowing in from the gap between the interior door and the floor. He stood and reached for the handle, and as he opened the door, he thought he was standing at the mouth of hell. A ghastly inferno loomed before him, engulfing the whole of the foyer. The great hall was ablaze. The walls were crumbling and pieces of the ceiling were crashing down from above. The once rustically lavish decor was melting and warping into cindery ash.

The heat came into the mud room like a blast furnace and the drastic change in temperature was enough to stir Kristian awake. His eyes peeled open, and he reached to cradle his bleeding scalp, but immediately stopped when he felt a surge of pain from his broken wrist.

"Fuck!" Kristian yelled as his healthy hand clasped his wounded wrist.

Jimmy spun around, pointing his pistol. Kristian clocked the fiery hellscape behind the Nazi hunter and his mind reeled as Amelia's screams in his memory once more erupted and rose to deafening volume. His good hand pressed firmly against his temple and he cried out.

"Enough! Give me silence!"

Jimmy stared at him in confusion. The only thing he could hear was the roar of the fire and the crashes from the deteriorating foyer. The Nazi sat up and crunched himself into a ball. He swayed from side to side, slapping the side of his head repeatedly.

"Enough! Enough of your screams!"

"Pull yourself together, dammit!" Jimmy shouted at him.

He looked into the foyer and saw Everly lying in the center of the floor, and for a moment he contemplated running in to see if she was alive or not. His heroic thought was dashed away when a hunk of the ceiling the size of a Volkswagen smashed down over her body.

"Jesus!" Jimmy yelled, jumping back.

He leaned down over Kristian and grabbed him by the lapels. "Where is the book?" Jimmy shouted in a tone so intense that Kristian lost focus on everything else around them.

"The book?" Kristian asked weakly.

"Your notebook. The one you kept during the war," Jimmy yelled over the sound of the crackling beams. Kristian's face contorted into a horrible grin. "Do you have it with you? Tell me!" Jimmy roared, violently shaking him.

"You'll never find that book, Knotts. Not ever," Kristian hissed.

The two men looked one another in the eye and Kristian could see the hatred swirling in Jimmy's pupils.

Jimmy turned away and looked back through the doorway into the fiery abyss. Something amongst the chaos had stirred at the sound of Jimmy's voice, and a shadowy figure rustled and came into view. It was one of the two surviving creatures—the one that had beat Gregory to death. It stood on the other side of the foyer, its back hunched, its bloody arms swaying calmly.

Jimmy quickly pulled the door closed, securing him and Kristian inside the mudroom. He wasn't sure if the creature had seen him or not—the visibility in the smokey foyer was limited. It was possible that it hadn't detected them, but Jimmy couldn't gamble. With the lodge burning to the ground, it was only a matter of time before the roof could crash down upon them. He had to get Kristian back outside and down to the rendezvous point.

Kristian could see that the anger in Jimmy's face had devolved into fear. "What did you see?" Kristian asked.

"Just stay quiet," Jimmy said as he lifted Kristian to his feet and shoved him to the exterior door.

"We can't go back out there. We'll freeze to death."

Jimmy knew Kristian may be right, but he'd survived out there with no protective clothing earlier, so with his fresh gear he felt confident in their chances. He checked to be sure Kristian was properly outfitted, secured a pair of goggles over his eyes, then pushed him out the door, back into the cold.

He kept his grip tight on the Ballester-Molina as he directed Kristian around the side of the lodge. The smell of smoke had filled the air and they could see the flames that had crawled out of the broken windows and up the thatched roof. The impressive architecture was crumbling before their eyes. The ominous beauty of the Caliber Lodge was now blackened, charred in sections, ablaze in others.

Jimmy wondered what had started the fire, imagining that any of the six fireplaces could have been the origin.

Did Turk or Mrs. Everly start the fire to defend themselves against the creatures lurking in the foyer? Or did the creatures themselves initiate the inferno?

Either way, Jimmy knew the lodge was lost. The fire was out of control, raging, still growing.

"Where are you taking me?" Kristian demanded.

"No more talk, Stengl."

Just over thirty-six hours earlier, Jimmy had left the base of the mountain where the private road began, and where the rendezvous point was designated. He had sat down inside the oil black Bentley and the driver had taken him up the winding road, the wheels barely able to grip in the snow. That road ended at the driveway of the Caliber Lodge. Now Jimmy was to make the reverse trip, albeit on foot and with his pistol pointed at the back of his captured target.

Jimmy and Kristian pulled the collars of their coats up and their wool hats down low, leaving only their goggle-covered eyes visible beneath the fabrics. They marched down the winding road.

While it was Jimmy's path to salvation, Kristian saw it to be his path toward reckoning. He knew there wasn't much he could do at that point.

If I were to escape Jimmy's sights, where would I go, he wondered. *Off the road? Deeper into the frozen mountain? Back to the burning lodge?*

He was out of options and settled with his best bet being to see where Jimmy's escape vehicle was and then try to commandeer it.

They turned down a bend in the road and the Caliber Lodge disappeared from their view. The only sign of its existence became the plume of smoke that curled into the night sky above the timberline. Onward they went, trudging through the snow that seemed to grow deeper as they progressed.

A drift had accumulated upon the road and soon they were up to their knees, and then their waists, pushing through the heavy snow. They had to kick and dig to make it through, shoving heaps of white up and out of their path.

As they turned around another bend, they made it through the bulk of the accumulation and the depth of the snow had returned to what it was when they began their journey.

Further down they went, Jimmy with his pistol at the ready, and Kristian still pondering his escape, when a crunching sound behind them made Jimmy turn to look over his shoulder.

Coming around the bend a hundred or so feet behind them, Jimmy saw a puff of hot air—the clear and recognizable breath of a living creature. He stopped and waited to see what animal had produced the breath, though deep down he already knew what it was.

The creature came into view, the deep snow drift only rising to its mid-shins. Its back was curved, head hanging low, but eyes looking up—looking at Jimmy. It was hard to tell in the moonlight, but Jimmy thought the fur on its arms looked darker than the rest of its body. It had a sort of two-tone look to it, and Jimmy had to shake himself out of the trance-like fear the creature's presence had sent him into.

"Run," Jimmy said in a voice just above a whisper.

Kristian turned and saw the massive creature up the road. He didn't wait for Jimmy to tell him again. He sprinted down the slick trail and Jimmy spun and followed behind. A bellowing howl reverberated through the air, and the creature launched itself through the snowdrift and gave chase.

Jimmy's goggles fogged up, and he ripped them from his face, then tossed them aside as he caught up to Kristian on the road. They ran, side by side, the treads of their boots keeping them steady on the icy road.

"Shoot it!" Kristian yelled. "Shoot the fucking beast!"

Jimmy knew the pistol didn't have the stopping power to even slow the creature down. He shoved the gun into his coat and kept running, hoping they would catch a spell of good luck. Maybe the U.S. Army would appear or the creature would just suddenly lose interest in them. Neither of those events came to pass, however, and the creature, with its long legs and enormous feet, began to gain on them.

Kristian saw his chance, a steep drop off from the road. He leaped off the path and Jimmy, hoping the Nazi knew something he didn't, followed. They slid down the hill, tumbling through the trees and brush, bouncing off small rocks and large protruding roots. As they slid, Jimmy looked behind them and saw the creature up above on the road. It watched as they continued to slide downward at an increasingly high speed.

Kristian grabbed hold of the trunk of a pine and jerked to a halt. Jimmy tried to do the same, but his gloved hands couldn't get a good grip and he continued to slide. If only he had grabbed one of the ice axes, he could have used it to stab into the earth and stop his descent.

He was on his stomach, sliding feet first down the hill and before he knew what was happening, he reached the edge of a small cliff and his speed and weight launched him over the side.

The few quick seconds he fell seemed like an eternity, and when he landed on the ground twenty feet below, Jimmy's left leg hit a skull-sized rock and he felt a striking pain course through his entire body.

He rolled to his side to examine his leg, expecting a shattered shin bone to be jutting out through his pants. There was a tear in the material, and blood was flowing, but luckily there was no protruding bone. He pressed his gloved hand over the wound and looked up at the cliff he had toppled from. He unclipped his pack and shrugged it off his shoulders, then pulled it into his lap and scrambled to find the first-aid kit inside.

The medical wrap wouldn't do much good over his pant leg, but the blistering cold would surely be devastating were he to tear the material apart further to get better access to the wound. He debated through the throbbing pain.

Bandage the wound and let the frost in? Or let the leg bleed and stay warm?

Jimmy didn't have the luxury of time to decide. The creature was still out there and was undoubtedly closing in on his scent. He tore the hole in his pant leg wide enough to see the source of the blood. He sighed in relief when he realized it wasn't as gruesome or severe as he expected it to be. He fumbled to unspool the gauze, his gloved hands making it difficult to get a good grip. It took him all of ninety seconds to bandage himself up, then he used the rest of the gauze to wrap around the hole in the pant leg to seal up the tear in an attempt to keep the chill out.

He stood and felt the striking pain once again as he took his first step. He shook it off and reached for the pistol he had tucked into his coat.

It was gone.

Jimmy panicked, searching all the inner pockets, then looking around the ground where he had landed. He crouched down on his hands and knees, dusting through the snow.

Fuck, fuck, fuck.

Jimmy looked up at the small cliff he'd fallen from, knowing he must have lost the pistol during his slide. He pulled himself back to his feet and fought through the pain as he marched toward the sloping hillside.

Above him, Kristian was still holding onto the tree trunk. The creature had vanished. This was his opportunity. Jimmy was gone, and he had evaded the animal that was pursuing them. He got to his feet and began running along the hillside parallel to the road above. He knew that wherever Jimmy had been leading him, it was surely at the base of the mountain. He imagined there might be a vehicle waiting down there that could get him to safety.

He kept a watchful eye behind him as he continued downward, and after a few more minutes of not seeing or hearing the creature, he grinned and sighed a deep breath of relief.

"Stupid fucking animal."

A mighty howl rang out, bouncing off the pines, cascading down the snowy hills. Kristian instinctually covered his ears for a moment and when he lowered his hands, they were both gripped by a pair of much larger, more powerful mitts.

The creature stood before him, lifting him up by both arms so they were face to face, eye to eye. Kristian tried to fight through the overwhelming sense of fear by belting out a battle-cry in the creature's face. He screamed, and he growled, doing his best to mimic the boisterous howl.

The creature's palms and fingers tightened around Kristian's fists and the rippling cracking of every bone in the Nazi's hands sounded rhythmic, almost musical.

Kristian screamed again, but this time it wasn't out of fear or attempted intimidation, it was pure, raw agony. The creature dropped Kristian to his knees in the snow, then kicked him in the chest with its colossal foot. The impact sent Kristian tumbling backward, rolling and somersaulting through the drift. His back smashed against the trunk of a pine tree, bringing him to an immediate stop.

He tried to sit up, but he was unable to move. His limbs were no longer following his brain's commands. He could lift his head—but nothing else. Only his neck seemed to work. The loss of bodily control had ceased the pain in his hands—he could no longer feel the torment of the pulverized carpals, metacarpals and finger bones inside the floppy bags of skin that his hands had been reduced to. The other parts of his body felt completely numb, as though they were no longer attached.

He bent his neck, pulling his cheek out of the snow, and looked over at the creature standing among the trees. It stared back at him, its heavy chest puffing hot breath that dissipated up toward the moonlight. Its orby eyes mirrored Kristian's vulnerability, and the pupils dilated as if focusing in on its prey like a camera lens. It took a step toward the Nazi, the snow compacting down beneath its weight. Kristian tried to move, but still he was paralyzed in place. Another step and the creature's wide stride brought it only a few yards away.

"Stay—stay back!" Kristian moaned.

The creature took another two steps and stopped directly in front of him. The snow collapsed around him and he rolled helplessly against the creature's furry legs. It slowly bent down and its clawed hand grabbed Kristian by the back of coat and lifted him up into the air like a feline hoisting her cub by the scruff.

Kristian dangled, his limbs sagging lifelessly. The creature rotated him so that he spun slowly and ended up face to face with the creature once again. This time, Kristian could not scream out any sort of ferocious growl. He simply hung there, looking at the thick saliva streaming from the crooked, sagging, lower jaw of the creature. He could smell its breath, the rancid, putrid aroma of death.

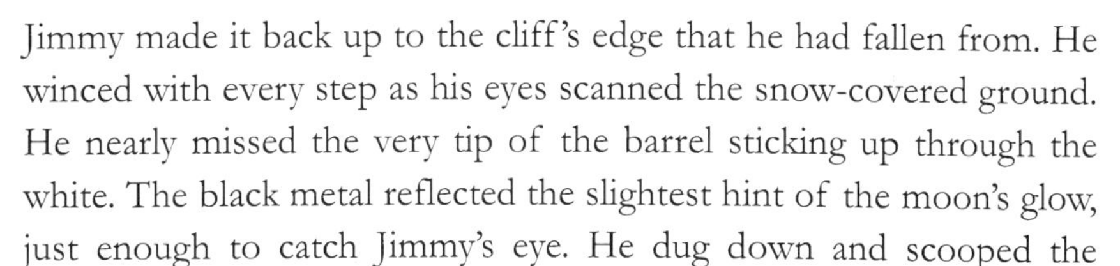

Jimmy made it back up to the cliff's edge that he had fallen from. He winced with every step as his eyes scanned the snow-covered ground. He nearly missed the very tip of the barrel sticking up through the white. The black metal reflected the slightest hint of the moon's glow, just enough to catch Jimmy's eye. He dug down and scooped the Ballester-Molina out and checked it for damage. It seemed all right, and he kept it in hand for the time being.

Fighting through the pain, Jimmy continued climbing back up, one movement at a time. As he ascended the hill he tried to ignore the fact that the sound of Kristian's screams had long since faded away. It had been at least ten minutes since he last heard any wails. Either the creature had caught him, or Kristian had escaped down the mountain. Neither thought pleased him as he pressed on, back up to where he had last seen Kristian, near the pine tree that he had snagged hold of during their slide.

Jimmy followed the trail of Kristian's footprints, limping along until he saw them converge with the trail of a much larger animal. The creature's prints looked just like the very first ones he had seen in the valley bowl early that morning. That's where Kristian's footprints stopped. It was only the creature's prints that trailed away from the scene, as if the animal had carried Kristian away over its shoulder.

Jimmy followed the tracks, albeit slowly, half out of exhaustion, half out of the understanding that there was nothing he could do to save Kristian should he catch up to him. Regardless of the futility, Jimmy pursued them back up the road, through the snowdrift, around each bend until the Caliber Lodge came back into view.

It looked like a flaming skeleton. The bare bones of the building were all that remained of the once luxurious structure. Where the walls once stood, protecting the interior from the harsh forces of nature, were only cavities, dark empty holes between the support beams.

He could see that the creature's tracks led out past the remains of the lodge and up into the mountain, far beyond the point that Jimmy dared to venture. The warmth of the burning building kissed his face, and he closed his eyes, basking in the macabre comfort.

Knowing full well that death from exposure was a genuine threat, he moved in near enough to the inferno to stay warm, yet far enough to avoid being crushed by the crumbling architecture. His energy had completely faded, and he sat down in the snow and pulled his extremities in tight. He hoped that someone would see the fire and come to his aid. Maybe Levi would arrive earlier than planned with a thermos of coffee to warm his stomach. He thought if the creatures didn't come for him, he just might survive till then.

Silent cushioned toes made their way across the snow. The arctic fox was light enough to scamper across the frozen crust without making an impression. It stopped six feet from Jimmy and rested upon its haunches. Jimmy gazed at it curiously as the furry visitor stared back at him with its onyx eyes. Unafraid, the animal lowered down and laid flat, its head between its paws, tail curled.

Though the tiny animal provided neither warmth, nor protection for him, Jimmy appreciated the company.

The crunch of approaching tires flattening the snow triggered his eyes to spring open. Jimmy had fallen asleep. He was unsure for how long, and when he realized he was lying in the fetal position near the glowing black embers of the Caliber's corpse, he couldn't believe he'd avoided being eaten alive.

The fox was gone.

The approaching vehicle, a cherry red Jeep Tuxedo Park, pulled up alongside him. The driver's door creaked open and Jimmy saw a pair of designer loafers step down into the snowpack.

"Talk about leaving your mark," a cockney voice cut through the wind.

Jimmy looked up to see Walt standing over him, a mouthful of aniseed twists gobbing up his speech. Jimmy chuckled weakly. The British Nazi hunter helped Jimmy to his feet, and when he realized his leg was injured, he all but carried Jimmy and set him down in the passenger seat of the Jeep.

"Aniseed twist?" Walt offered, extending the bag in front of Jimmy's face. He smiled and reached in for one of the red gummy candies.

"Thank you, Walter."

"Walt," Walt corrected him.

Jimmy echoed with respect, "Walt."

"Not too bad, eh, mate?" Walt said as Jimmy chewed the twist.

"Actually, it's fucking terrible."

Walt smirked, closed the passenger door, and walked around the front of the Jeep to the driver's side. They drove away down to the base of the mountain, leaving the ruins to smolder behind them.

Morning came quickly. Up the mountain, over the ridge, past the towering rock face and the valley bowl, inside the densely wooded forest—the creatures had covered the body of the pregnant female with branches and underbrush to create a sort of organic tomb. They sat together in a broken circle, eating fresh meat, slowly and solemnly. Every few minutes one of them would look to her resting place and snort in sadness.

A few yards away, mounted atop a pike made from a dislodged pine branch, was the severed head of Wilhelm Stengl.

EPILOGUE

Brownville, Nebraska. Six Months Later.

It was 102 degrees and the gentleness of the wind was no comfort as it swung the heat through the air, sopping the faces of Jimmy Knotts and Levi Aarons while they made their way up the concrete steps to the front door of the old house. Jimmy had recovered as much as could be expected from his time in Alaska, but he was unable to fully hide the limp that had permanently attached itself to his left leg.

Beneath their suit jackets, tucked into their waistbands, each of the men had their pistols loaded and ready. They hoped they would not need them, that this would be a relatively tame outing, but they always prepared for the worst.

The records department showed that the house was owned by a man named Kristian Beckett, who had purchased the property in 1962, just two short years after Jimmy and Levi had discovered the bloody aftermath at the Residencia Inalco down in Argentina.

The word "Nebraska" had been burned into Jimmy's mind since he heard the Nazi utter it in the lounge of the Caliber Lodge, and it didn't take him long to narrow down the exact address once he and Levi began digging.

Jimmy knocked on the door and the two of them stood alert, waiting, and hoping no one would answer. Jimmy knocked again and after another moment Levi pulled out a lock picking tool and rustled the door handle until it turned.

The air inside was musty. The windows had been closed for at least half a year, and all the staleness had been imprisoned within. Levi drew the curtains, and the sunshine poured in, bathing the tidy living area in its glow.

They wasted no time. Room by room the two men tore the house apart, pulling out every drawer, turning over every chair and table. They searched the cabinets and inside the oven. They searched beneath the mattress and inside the closets. They searched the attic, and when all else had failed they went to the corner of the living room and began pulling up the carpeting. They cut and rolled it and stacked the bundles against the wall, revealing a wood floor beneath. Plank by plank, they pried it up and looked below.

For hours, as they searched, neither spoke. They dismantled the entire house until every nook and cranny had been examined and checked off the list. When there was nowhere else to look, Jimmy turned to Levi, a defeated expression across his face.

"It's not here. He must have brought it with him to the Lodge. It's nothing but ash now."

His own words made him stop in place.

Of course, he thought.

He turned to the small fireplace where the remains of an old charred log sat dormant upon the hearth. He crouched down and brushed the soot away, feverishly dusting off the grate to get to the ash basket. He lifted the metal away and dug down inside with a hopeful gleam in his eyes. His fingers sifted through the blackness, searching, fondling—but there was nothing hidden below, and the hope in Jimmy's eyes vanished as quickly as it had appeared.

Levi put his hand on Jimmy's shoulder. "It's all right, son."

Jimmy rose and turned to his mentor. He had failed. After everything he had gone through at the Caliber Lodge, after the years of searching they had done prior, across numerous countries, it was all over, and they had failed.

Wilhelm Stengl's notebook, and the information it contained inside its binding, was lost forever.

Jimmy gently pulled the Ballester-Molina pistol from his waistband, the gun that had belonged to the informant Mauro whose death Jimmy now considered having been in vain.

"Time to move on. There's always another target," Levi said, attempting to pump any amount of positivity into the dour scene.

Jimmy hung his head. He looked at the gun in his hand and knew he no longer needed it. He no longer deserved it.

He set the pistol down on the corner of the fireplace mantel, and as the weight of the metal hit the stone, he heard a hollow thud. A false bottom dropped out of the mantel ledge, and with it a black notebook bound in leather.

Jimmy and Levi stared at the book on the floor. It was lying face down, a wispy, gold cord wrapped around the middle. Jimmy slowly crouched, reaching his hand out cautiously as if he were about to pet a strange dog that he feared might bite him. He scooped the book up and turned it over in his hands.

On the front of the notebook, embossed in the leather, was a swastika and the initials "W.S."

Jimmy looked up at Levi, and the two men shared a fortuitous smile.

THE END

COCKTAIL RECIPES

HEMINGWAY CLASSIC

-2 oz White Rum
-1/2 oz Luxardo Maraschino Cherry Liqueur
-3/4 oz pink grapefruit juice
-1/2 oz fresh lime juice
-Shake all ingredients together over cracked ice
-Stain into cocktail glass
-Garnish with a freshly cut lime wheel

VERY OLD FASHIONED

-Muddle 1 maraschino cherry and 1 sugar cube in a rocks glass
-Add and Muddle an orange slice
-Drop in a large cube or sphere of ice
-Pour in 2 oz of your favorite Bourbon
-Three dashes of Angostura bitters
-Stir lightly
-Garnish with an orange slice

PANAMA PREMIER

-1 oz White Creme de Cacao
-1 oz Brandy of your preference
-1 oz light cream or Oat milk
-Shake all ingredients together over cracked ice
-Strain into a cocktail glass
-No garnish

SAN MARTIN

-1 1/2 oz Tanqueray Gin

-1 1/2 oz Carpano Antica Sweet Vermouth (don't substitute)

-1 Teaspoon Green Chartreuse

-Shake all ingredients over ice

-Stain into cocktail glass

-No Garnish

SMOKED MARTINI

-Pour 1/4 oz of Ardbeg 10 Year scotch into martini glass

-Lightly swirl scotch to coat the inside of the glass

-Sip excess scotch out

-In a shaker of cracked ice, 2 oz of Stolichnaya or preferred Russian vodka

-Shake and strain into the scotch coated martini glass

-Garnish with a smile

One might also invest their time enjoying the signature drink of Ian Fleming's 1953 novel *Casino Royale,* which is mentioned in this book.

-3oz of Gin (Originally calls for Gordon's, however the potency has changed since the 60s so one might instead choose another Gin- preferably Tanqueray or Hendrick's)

-1oz vodka - this author recommends Zyr vodka if available- but certainly Russian.

-1/2 oz of Lillet Blanc (Kina Lillet is no longer produced)

-Shake over cracked ice & strain into martini glass

-Garnish with a long, thin slice of lemon peel

ABOUT THE AUTHOR

L.J. Dougherty has been both an animal lover and writer since he was a young lad, his goals always supported and encouraged by his loving family. He is a restaurateur by trade and holds a passion for perfectly prepared cocktails of all varieties. He has written and directed one feature film, *The Cylinder*, and intends to continue extending his filmography.

Beasts of the Caliber Lodge is his first novel. It was initially written as a screenplay, but due to the expansiveness and grandeur of the story, L.J. knew that he was unlikely to get a budget to produce a film of such magnitude anytime soon, so decided to put it down in novel form, allowing him to let his imagination run wild, and appropriately explore the characters and the world they reside in.

He lives with his amazing wife, talented son, goofy dog and moody cat.

You can find L.J. on social media.

On Twitter @LJ_Dougherty
On Instagram @l.j.dougherty

Or via email at LJDoughertyAuthor@gmail.com

VERY SPECIAL THANKS

To my incredible wife Tia, who supports my creativity even through life's changes and challenges. "Life, uh... finds a way."

To my oldest friends, Cameron & Tim, for beta reading every single thing I've written for the past 18ish years. God knows it hasn't all been good.

To my comrade Luke Newman, the artist behind the cover, for not just creating the artwork but beta reading the novel first to ingest the aura.

To my sister Molly—simply because.

MMXXI

The Hunt Continues in

PRIMAL RESERVE

BEASTS
of the
CALIBER LODGE

Printed in Great Britain
by Amazon

16923175R00146